I0649324

Alexander Winchell

Geological Excursions

The rudiments of geology for young learners

Alexander Winchell

Geological Excursions
The rudiments of geology for young learners

ISBN/EAN: 9783337387273

Printed in Europe, USA, Canada, Australia, Japan

Cover: Foto ©Andreas Hilbeck / pixelio.de

More available books at **www.hansebooks.com**

GEOLOGICAL EXCURSIONS;

OR,

THE RUDIMENTS OF GEOLOGY

FOR YOUNG LEARNERS.

By ALEXANDER WINCHELL, LL.D.,

PROFESSOR OF GEOLOGY AND PALÆONTOLOGY IN THE UNIVERSITY OF MICHIGAN.
FORMERLY DIRECTOR OF THE GEOLOGICAL SURVEY OF MICHIGAN.
AUTHOR OF "SKETCHES OF CREATION," "WORLD LIFE,"
ETC., ETC.

Science-teaching should begin early in the school-course.—
PRESIDENT ELIOT, Harvard University.

———————

CHICAGO:
S. C. GRIGGS AND COMPANY.
1884.

COPYRIGHT, 1884,

BY S. C. GRIGGS AND COMPANY.

CONTENTS.

PREFATORY NOTE.

THAT the elements of geology are so seldom taught either in our primary or secondary schools is a circumstance to be regretted. No tendency seems manifest toward any improvement in this particular. In Michigan, which enjoys a justly high reputation for the excellence of its schools and teaching, even less geology is studied in school than was customary a dozen years ago. No knowledge whatever of this subject is required for entrance into the University of Michigan in the "Classical Course," nor in the "Scientific Course," nor in the so-called "English Course"—though in the last two courses the candidate is given his option between preparation in Chemistry, Geology, Zoölogy and Physiology. Of necessity, Physiology, which is generally taught in the schools, is almost always the chosen subject, though next to this stands Chemistry. Practically, therefore, the study of geology in the University begins with the elements in every course. A similar state of things exists in most of our colleges. There is no course where geology is a prerequisite, so that the student on entering may find himself in position to push on to some advanced knowledge of the subject. One would anticipate that a course specifically denominated "Scientific," would demand a more extended scientific preparation than the old "Classical" course, and that a science which has done as much for industry, civilization and culture as geology has, would not fail to be enumerated among the requirements.

Since geology is not so required for entrance into college, it has ceased to be taught in the schools — as if geology had no

1

uses if not demanded as a preparation for college. This seems to the present writer a greater mistake than the other. For assuredly, the large majority of pupils, not expecting the opportunity for collegiate study of the science, have reason to complain that they must be deprived altogether of the opportunity to learn even the nature of the subject. When they enter upon the affairs of adult life, and especially, if they mingle in the intellectual life of the age, they find living questions agitating the world, before which they must remain dumb and uninformed, because their merits are rooted in the great facts of the earth's history and the history of life.

Such life-long ignorance of geology is quite as unnecessary as deplorable. The elements of the science are not a body of principles difficult to master, nor encumbered with a greater number of scientific terms than the sciences of physiology, chemistry and botany. The data of geology, moreover, lie all about us, and are the most obtrusive and noticeable of all the objects which we daily encounter. Stones and rocks never fail to awaken the curiosity of the boy or girl; and there are few children who have not made collections of stones, distinguishing their varieties by precisely the same characters as the most expert student. Assuredly, it seems a dictate of educational philosophy to take a hint from these childish predispositions and aptitudes, and shape the child's education with some regard to what he seems peculiarly fitted to study.

But, however appropriate and useful this study, where are the teachers who will properly lead the pupil? They are exceedingly few in number. As geology is not taught in the schools, and as nineteen-twentieths of our teachers have not studied it in college, there is almost no preparation among the teachers of primary and secondary grades to induct a pupil into an elementary knowledge of the subject. In this state of the case, it would seem very difficult to begin the desired improvement.

To the writer, the only hope of early reform seems to lie in furnishing teachers with a text book so framed as to be capable of successful use by a teacher without previous acquaintance with the subject. Certainly, no such text books exist; for, though there are several which might be employed by teachers thoroughly disciplined by previous study, the large majority of our teachers are not so disciplined, and it may not be necessary; and these text books, moreover, are too much conformed to the dogmatic or didactic method — telling about things which are far away, or, if near at hand, are not identifiable by the aid of the book. Due discrimination is not observed between those conceptions of the subject which are abstract and beyond the reach of the young pupil, or older novice, and those which can be attained through accessible concrete illustrations. Many of them are good systematic presentations of the subject, but they are pronounced "dry" and unintelligible. They are, in truth, *too* systematic and *too* complete.

The present author has pursued a fundamentally different plan, and hopes he has prepared a primer of geology so simple and so intelligible that no previous preparation of the teacher will be needed. Hence *any* teacher who will pursue the method will obtain an insight into the subject, and will be able, also, to lead pupils of very tender years. One lesson which the author has learned from much experience is here applied. The beginner, especially if young, retains, as the result of his first course of study in any subject, a surprisingly small amount of tangible and available information. This is the author's first principle of procedure. His second is, to enlist the *senses* and the *sentiments*. Hence the method is essentially inductive; the book speaks to the pupil in the second person; it leads to the application of each item of knowledge in some useful or interesting relation, and seeks to awaken the thought of the learner.

More specifically, it directs a large amount of attention to the pebbles and stones so abundant everywhere in the drift of the northern states; and to the phenomena of sedimentation and erosion everywhere accessible. From these most familiar illustrations, it passes to the phenomena of stratified rocks and the

way they are arranged upon the earth. Here much use is made
of maps and sections, as these train the learner to the indispensable conceptions of superposition, succession, continuity and
discontinuity. Not much is said about purely systematic geology,
and still less about palæontology and geological theory. These
divisions of the subject are more abstract and complicated, and
ought to be deferred till some familiarity is acquired with the
conceptions capable of illustration from familiar facts and
phenomena. Then much stress is laid upon the "Exercises."
These are not mere questions on the text. The answers to many
of the questions are only *inferences* from statements in the text.
Some are practical *applications.* Frequently the question leads
to an extension of knowledge. Some questions are asked which
will require considerable reflection — some even, which cannot be
answered categorically. It is intended that the pupil shall keep
the question in mind, and search for the proper answer by asking
his elders, by consulting books or by exploring in collections of
specimens. It is profitable to have something to ponder over.

The very gist of the method is, that the pupil shall do all that
is indicated, and positively see every thing that is described, as
far as possible. Great efforts must be made to render this possible. Just so far as anything must be studied *about*, without
the opportunity to handle and examine it, and make drawings of
it, so far the pupil is unfortunate; so far the plan of the book is
not brought into practice.

There is not a great amount of science imparted. It is surprising — often discouraging, to observe how limited is the total
amount of exact knowledge acquired even by older students after
a more thorough course. It is also an interesting fact that a
very little knowledge, if it is fundamental, and fully mastered by
viewing it from all sides, will serve to answer a very large number
of common inquiries. It is also true that a good deal of verbiage
is employed. Many sentences add nothing to the statement of
facts. They are intended simply to control attention and keep
alive the pupil's interest.

The very gist of the method is, that the pupil shall do all that
is indicated, and positively see every thing that is described, as
far as possible. Great efforts must be made to render this possible. Just so far as anything must be studied *about*, without
the opportunity to handle and examine it, and make drawings of
it, so far the pupil is unfortunate; so far the plan of the book is
not brought into practice.

A large part of these "Excursions" has been used in actual trials by actual teachers, while yet in manuscript. The result encourages the hope that they may be found suited to the object set forth, and may thus become instrumental in diffusing knowledge and appreciation of a branch of science as accessible as any, and as fruitful as any in results of high value in the industries and culture of modern civilization.

This primer is, therefore, commended to the candid consideration of teachers and school officers, in the hope that they already feel the desirability of early instruction in geology, and may be disposed to join with the author in testing the value of the method which is here proposed.

A WORD WITH THE TEACHER.

Here, ladies, is a little book in which I hope you will be interested. I address *you*, because nearly all the teachers of those for whom the book is suitable are women; and also because I have found women especially interested and apt in the studies which are here introduced. The book is thought to be so simple that it will literally "teach of itself," if you let it have its way. So you need not be deterred from forming a little class in "geology" in consequence of having geology omitted from your own education. It is, I confess, too childish in style for your own use as a learner; but please consider that you are not the pupil — only so far as you may find it desirable to become a pupil.

Now, please permit me to note concisely what seem to me the points most essential in making this little book a success: ·

1. *Positively do and have done everything indicated in the text.* Do not say some of these things are so simple or so obvious that the doing would be a mere form. Probably something will turn up which you or your pupils could not anticipate.

Do not be afraid to take hammers and collecting bags or baskets into the garden or the field, and actually break the rocks and study them and bring them home. No matter about keeping quiet in this class. The very study requires talking and movement. The novelty of the method and its conformity with the impulses and instincts of the child's nature will assuredly make it the favorite class of the school.

2. Should you happen to be located in a large city or upon a prairie or other section of the country where boulders are not easily accessible, the best recourse will be to a wagon load or two of boulders brought from some boulder region and thrown down in the school yard. These may be broken into moderate-sized fragments by any man with a large-sized stone hammer. All teachers, as a provision against rainy days, might have a large lot of fragments placed under a shed. Even teachers in states south of the boulder-covered regions of our country might get a supply by the cheap help of a freight car from the North.

3. A day or two before the class is taken on an "Excursion," read it over yourself so as to know what to expect, and be prepared for its requirements. When the excursion is taken, you may let every pupil carry a book; or if you think better, only carry one yourself, and read aloud from it, giving the pupils time to *examine* and *think* and *respond.*

4. Make yourself sure that *every* pupil sees and does and understands everything which is required, and does the best he can in answering all questions. *Be deliberate enough to render this possible.* Sometimes the lesson will need to be divided. With some classes it will be best to devote an hour to the excursion proper, and then the "Exercises" may occupy the time on the next day. This may be the best method with all classes. Sometimes the whole must be twice gone over. In almost every lesson the positions of localities mentioned will have to be studied from the School Atlas.

5. *Accustom yourself and your pupils to copying the figures*

in the book; and practise still more in making drawings of other things not figured, such as gravel banks, boulders, cliffs, ravines, landscapes. Do not say, "I never took a lesson in drawing," for the most finished draughtsmen were once in the same situation. Try. Try again, and so continue. If you are already somewhat practised in drawing, you will find your skill extremely useful. The geological sections required, and the other exercises on the geological map may be troublesome at first, but no exercises can be more profitable.

6. *Lay much stress on the "Exercises,"* and invent additional ones. Some of them are merely intended to set pupil and teacher to thinking and investigating. Some of the questions cannot be definitely answered. When a question is proposed which you cannot answer at once, say so frankly. We all have to confess ignorance. I think the "Exercises" will awaken much interest. You will, of course, have to ask many questions on the text and its subject matter; but these you will frame for yourself or find at the end of the book.

7. *Adhere strictly to the method indicated in the book;* but vary the details according to the circumstances, and extend the instruction and the observations according to your own judgment.

8. *Have every pupil collect, preserve and label specimens.* A good plan to pursue is the following: To each specimen attach a little circular bit of white paper to receive the "school number." Let each different species or variety of minerals and rocks receive a separate number. Those which are the same species or variety will receive the same number. In a little book write the numbers, and the names of the specimens corresponding to them. Let each pupil also attach to each of his own specimens, a little *colored* paper—each pupil choosing some different bright color; or, if the same color as that of another pupil, let it be cut oval or square or diamond shaped; so that each pupil's specimens can be picked out when all are placed in a pile together. Have each pupil also keep a cata-

logue. Then the number on the white ticket stuck to each of his specimens will give the name of the specimen as soon as he refers to his list. You will find, a little beyond, some practical directions for this work.

9. *Use other specimens additional to those collected by the class if it is possible to do so.* By this means you will get for study more species and varieties. There may be some small, neglected collections or single specimens in your neighborhood, lying on dusty mantels, what-nots and étagères. Look them up and press them into service. I am sure you will find many sorts which are not mentioned in this little book, because the book mentions the most *common* things, which it is most important to know something about; while people generally seek to lay up *rare* things from distant regions. But use all that you can. Besides this, there ought to be a small labelled collection obtained from some reliable dealer, furnishing true examples of the more common minerals and rocks. Such a collection can be purchased for two or three dollars, or a better one for five dollars.

All that may be learned by the aid of this little book will only conduct the pupil over the threshold of the subject. But even so much may be made highly interesting and indeed very useful. Beyond this threshold are departments of the subject not mentioned here, and a whole range of ideas and conclusions about the history of the world, and of other worlds, which would not be appropriate here, but which, nevertheless, are extremely fascinating to the student, and tend greatly to enlarge and ennoble his intelligence.

Now, I wish to feel in communication with all the teachers who try to use this primer. Please exercise the freedom to write on any point which you think may require further elucidation from the author.

ALEXANDER WINCHELL.

UNIVERSITY OF MICHIGAN,
ANN ARBOR.

SOME PRACTICAL SUGGESTIONS.

1. Hammers and some other instruments best suited for breaking and studying rocks are described in Excursions VI and VII.

2. For making the little circular or oval tickets, white or colored, a saddler's or tinner's "punch" is suitable. One which will cut tickets three-sixteenths of an inch in diameter is large enough for small specimens. If many tickets stick together as they come from the punch, place a lot in one hand and rub them with the fingers of the other hand. Fold the paper so as to punch through several thicknesses at each blow. Use a thin quality of paper.

3. For attaching the tickets do not use common mucilage, but prepare a cement as follows:

Clear Gum Arabic, ...	2 oz.
Fine Starch, ...	1½ oz.
White Sugar, ...	¼ oz.

Rub them together in a mortar; add as much water as the laundress would use for that amount of starch, and wait till the gum arabic is well dissolved; then cook the solution in a vessel suspended in boiling water until the starch becomes clear. The cement must be nearly as thick as tar. Keep it in a wide-mouthed bottle stoppered by a cork having a small round bristle brush passing through it. Drop in a small lump of gum camphor to prevent souring and mouldiness. It will keep a year or more. When too much dried away add a little water. This cement is strong, and is good for repairing breakages of specimens, and also for attaching specimens to cards for exhibition.

4. When many specimens are to be ticketed at once, spread them on a table and touch each one in a proper place with the tip of the brush, leaving a little cement, but *not too much.* Spread a quantity of well separated tickets on the table; moisten the tip of your finger on the tongue or a damp towel, and pick up a ticket and press it *firmly* on one of the gummed spots; then, as some of the cement probably adheres to your finger, remove it on your tongue or the damp towel, and pick up another ticket and attach it in the same way. This method is rapid. After a half hour the tickets will be dry enough to receive the numbers. Use only the blackest and best ink in writing them, with a fine-pointed steel pen, and make the figures perfect as possible.

5. Good cabinet rock specimens are generally dressed to a rectangular shape if possible. For a school cabinet they may be about two and a quarter by three inches square, and one or two inches thick. But it is better to have a shapeless specimen than none at all. Most of the pupils will probably be suited with mere fragments. But in all cases, some approach may be made to the standard form. Mere minerals must be preserved as we can get them. When a specimen is reduced nearly to the requisite size, the trimming may be best done while holding the specimen in the left hand and striking a quick blow with a light hammer, so as to chip off small pieces. Remember, the sharper the blow, the less liable is the specimen to shatter. The last of the dressing may be done by striking the specimen square on the edge. This is especially practicable with quartzose and all crystalline rocks. Fossils should be worked out of the rock with hammer and chisels and other appropriate tools, or at least the adhering rock should be as much removed as possible.

6. When specimens are to be boxed for transportation, wrap each separately in paper, and use enough packing material of paper, hay or straw, to prevent rubbing against each other. *Always fill the box as full as possible.* If the specimens will not do it, use waste paper, sawdust or anything—even fine chips—to fill all the empty spaces.

STANDARD SAMPLES OF MINERALS AND ROCKS.

[To illustrate Winchell's "Geological Excursions."]

The whole list forms "Collection No. 1." The list omitting the starred names forms " Collection No. 2."

1. Quartz (at least one crystal with termination).
2. Chalcedony or Agate.
3. Red Jasper.
4. Hornstone or Chert.
5. Orthoclase, showing crystalline form.
6. Labradorite.
7. *Albite, or at least some third feldspar.
8. Muscovite (common mica), showing crystalline form.
9. Hornblende. Dark variety, showing crystalline form.
10. *Actinolite.
11. Augite, common variety, showing crystalline form.
12. Talc, foliated variety.
13. Calcite, rhombohedral and dogtooth varieties.
14. *Pyrites.
15. *Selenite.
16. *Hematite.
17. *Magnetite.
18. *Limonite.
19. Quartzite, vitreous.
20. Quartzite, granular.
21. Quartzose Conglomerate.
22. Sandstone, gray.
23. *Sandstone, red.
24. Granulite (Quartz and Feldspar).
25. Granite (Quartz, Feldspar and Mica), strictly unstratified.
26. Gneiss, distinctly stratified.
27. Mica Schist.
28. Hydromica Schist.
29. Hornblende Rock (Amphibolite).
30. Hornblende Schist.
31. Syenite (Quartz, Feldspar and Hornblende) strictly unstratified.
32. Syenitic Gneiss, distinctly stratified.
33. Hyposyenite (Orthoclase and Hornblende).
34. Diorite (Plagioclase and Hornblende).
35. Diabase (Plagioclase and Augite).
36. *Dolerite.
37. *Modern Lava.
38. *Epidote Rock (or Epidotic Rock).
39. *Talc Rock or Steatite.
40. Serpentine.
41. Argillite or Slate.
42. Shale, argillaceous.
43. *Kaolin.
44. *Petrosilex (Cryptocrystalline, Quartz and Orthoclase).
45. Felsite (Cryptocrystalline, Quartz and Plagioclase).
46. Porphyritic Rock.
47. *Marl.
48. Common Limestone, with Fossils.
49. Marble (Crystalline Limestone).
50. Dolomite.

1223 BELMONT AVENUE,
PHILADELPHIA, PA., January 8, 1884.

I agree to supply suitable standard specimens, according to the foregoing list, for schools using Winchell's "Geological Excursions"—the rock specimens to be dressed to cabinet shape, and all to be permanently labelled, and delivered in Philadelphia according to directions, for the following prices:

For "Collection No. 1," Students' size, $3.00; Teacher's size, $5.00.
For "Collection No. 2," Students' size, $2.00; Teacher's size, $3.50.
For Fragments, or undressed specimens, "Collection No. 1," $1.50; "No. 2," $1.00.

Extra for *compartment tray* (if ordered) with lid, as follows:

Pasteboard Tray, No. 1, Students' size, $1.00; Teacher's size, $1.50.
No. 2, Students' size, $0.75; Teacher's size, $1.15.
For Fragments, "No. 1," 75 cents; "No. 2," 50 cents.

With sides and top of black walnut, double the above prices.*

A. E. FOOTE.

* The "fragment" collections may be sent by mail—the "Collection No. 1" for about 35 cents, and "No. 2" for about 25 cents.

GEOLOGICAL EXCURSIONS.

EXCURSION I.—*In the Garden.*

Organic and Inorganic.

LET us step into the garden. Here is a gravel walk; its surface is covered with small rounded stones. If it is not a gravel walk we can at least find a few small stones in it. These stones do not grow, like asparagus and roses. They do not take food of any kind; they do not see or feel as we tread upon them. Here are some plants. Probably they do not see or feel; but they grow, and they take in nourishment through their roots and leaves to enable them to grow. Here is a toad, sheltering himself under the leaves of the plant. He is waiting till sunset, when he will hop out and search for insects to eat. The toad also feeds and grows; and in addition he sees and feels.

We say the plant and the toad and the insect are *organic;* because they have organs or parts which enable them to do all the various things which their lives require. State what some of those things are. The power to do one of these things we call a *function.* The heart is an *organ* whose *function* is to propel the blood through the blood vessels. What is the function of the teeth? Every organ has some function. But the stone has no organs, and it performs no

13

functions. It simply lies still, and permits the atmosphere, the rains and the frosts and the sun to do all they can to dissolve it, or crumble it to powder, and cause it to waste away. It is *inorganic*. It has neither mouth nor legs, nor liver, nor any other organs. If we should examine it with a microscope, we should not be able to find any cells, or fibres, or membranes, or vessels, as we would in a plant or an animal. The stone is very similar all through, from side to side. So we see a great difference between an inorganic body and an organic body. The substances of which an inorganic body is composed are called *mineral* substances. The chemist tells us that an organic body is also composed of mineral substances; but the difference is that in the organic body the substances are made first into compounds which do not exist in the inorganic body, and these are then made into organs, which are also wanting in the inorganic body.

All organic bodies have life, or have had life. An organic body when dead is still organic until it is decomposed. Its parts are then inorganic. Organic beings may produce substances which have no organic structure—such as sap, spider's web, perspiration and dandruff. These are organic *products*, and are therefore organic.

EXERCISES.

Name several organic bodies. Name several sorts of inorganic bodies. In what respect is a silver coin like a stone? Is a stone organic or inorganic? Is the head on the coin organic or inorganic? How is it with a board? a pen? the outer dead bark of a tree? a linen handkerchief? a silk dress?

a dinner plate? a potato? a dish of mashed potatoes? the breath from your nostrils? a dead leaf? an extracted tooth? milk? beer? molasses? clay? paper? a squash? the same squash mashed for dinner? the ashes from a coal fire? the ashes from a wood fire? lemonade? a pocket knife? an oyster shell? a peach stone? the sting of a bee? a loaf of bread? a loaf of bread burned to ashes? a dead bird? chewing gum? hair of a mouse? gelatine? stove-mica? lamp smoke? air? Which are more abundant, organic things or inorganic things? Which are more useful? Which decay more easily? Are you organic or inorganic? Is there any mineral matter in your composition? In what respects do you resemble a stone? In what do you differ from a stone?

EXCURSION II.—*In the Garden and Field.*

Boulders and Sand.

Let us go into the garden again. Look very carefully at the gravel on the walk. Here, where there is no gravel walk, we still see some little stones just like those which form gravel. The stones are of various sizes. Some are so small that we might call them grains of sand; and some are large enough to be called pebbles. Still others are so large as to be called cobble stones, and are sometimes used to pave streets, or at least, to pave the gutters along the sides of the streets. The little stones which the boys throw are rounded pebbles; the larger ones which they use to crack nuts are cobble stones.

But then, what is the difference between a cobble stone and one of those larger rounded stones in the field or by the roadside which a boy could scarcely lift?—or even those

still larger ones which a man could not lift? Is there any
difference except in size? Let us examine some of them.
We must go into the field. There is no difference. If we
inspect grains of sand, we see that most of them are light-
colored when washed clean. But many are stained, and
some are brown, and some are even black. Different grains
thus differ among themselves.

Now collect a lot of pebbles. You see that they differ in
the same way as the grains of sand. Only you see some
pebbles which seem to be made up of different sorts of
mineral matters. Some look as if a great many grains of
sand had been stuck together to form a cobble stone. Each
different kind is a separate *mineral*. Most of the large,
loose rocks in the field present the same appearance. Sometimes a larger stone seems to be made of several pebbles.

Well, if we turn now from the larger to the smaller again,
you will find some of these grains of sand, on close examination, to be composed of different mineral materials. Let
us select a number of such grains. You may know them by
the difference of color in different parts of the grain. How
many colors in this grain? How many in the next one?
What colors are they?

Of course, the stones larger than pebbles and cobble
stones generally contain various mineral substances also.
Let us examine some of these stones. Here is one in which
we can detect much white rock, together with some pink and
some smoky. Here is one with white and cream color and
black. Here is one with two kinds of white and also black.
Here is one full of red rounded spots or pebbles, with some

smaller dark-colored ones, and many white or glassy ones. Here is a large rounded rock with white grains of two kinds and black grains of two kinds.

Now, perhaps, where you are you will not find exactly such kinds and such mixtures of minerals as these, but you will find some kinds. You can also tell what colors they are and how they are mixed. Do not fail to tell all that you can. How many colors or kinds of minerals can you find all together? Are the separate minerals always rounded? Are the separate minerals ever angular like grains of coarse salt? See if you can find rocks with the same mineral colors as I have just mentioned.

Well, all these rounded stones are called boulders. Some stones are not boulders. All stones taken from quarries are not boulders. All stones which have been broken from a ledge of rock not far away are not boulders. You may know a boulder by its rounded and smoothed appearance, and by the fact that it is a different kind of rock from any ledges or quarry stones in the neighborhood. Would you call a boy's pocket marbles boulders?

In some regions there are no stones to be found except boulders. This is the case in some parts of the western states. In the Lower Peninsula of Michigan there are very few ledges of rocks; and the people sometimes break up boulders for building stones. Sometimes boulders are large enough to weigh fifteen, twenty or even hundreds of tons. In New Hampshire and Vermont are many enormous boulders. Here is a picture of one in New Hampshire, which is 46 feet long, 24 feet wide, and 26 feet high. You see a

FIG. 1.—GREAT BOULDER NEAR GILSUM, N. H.
(C. H. HITCHCOCK.)

school house in the shelter of the rock. A piece 33 feet long and 10 feet wide was split off by frost in 1817. The whole stone before splitting contained 32,000 cubic feet, and weighed 2,286 tons. Far away, a thousand miles from this, large boulders are equally abundant. Here in Figure 2,

FIG. 2.— GREAT BOULDER OF PORPHYRY AT ST. IGNACE, LAKE SUPERIOR,
(PHOTOGRAPH.)

is a view of one at St. Ignace, Lake Superior. It is composed
of porphyry, and is 25 feet high. Notice how it is rounded.
You can see also, that the region abounds in smaller boulders.
In most parts of New England large and small boulders are
everywhere to be found. Here in Figure 3 is a view near

FIG. 3.—A BOULDER-COVERED FIELD NEAR GLOUCESTER, MASS. (STEELE.)

Gloucester, Massachusetts. In Connecticut, in the neighborhood of Long Island Sound, some regions are so thickly
overspread that one can cross a field without touching the
ground. On the contrary, there are some regions where no
boulders are to be found. There are very few on the prairies
of Illinois. There are none south of Virginia, Kentucky
and Missouri. In some of the southern states also, there
are almost no ledges of rocks; and the people have no
building stones except such as are brought from a great distance. But almost everywhere some pebbles may be found.

Now, one thing more. Examine this soil. What does
it seem to be composed of? It is partly fine and partly

coarse. Let us try an experiment. Take a tall glass vessel,
or even a clear glass bottle or fruit jar, and stir
a handful of soil in the vessel full of water.
There, how muddy the water becomes!—but
most of the matter sinks quickly to the bottom.
Some, however, settles slowly. Watch it.
Now we have a handful of soil assorted. The
coarser parts are at the bottom; the coarse
sand is above these; the fine sand next, and
the particles of mud are floating in the water.
We will pour off the muddy water and fill the
vessel again with clear water. The water is
still stained; but most of the matter in the
vessel can now be seen to consist of sand, with

FIG. 4.
ASSORTMENT
OF MATERIALS
IN THE SOIL.

a few small pebbles. Is it possible? The soil itself is
almost wholly composed of mineral substances, which do
not differ from pebbles except in being finer. These finest
substances and the coarser all belong to one class. Whatever made the larger boulders and the pebbles, made also
the principal part of the whole soil.

EXERCISES.

What was the mud composed of which we poured off with the
water? Did it consist chiefly of still finer mineral substances?
Are there any organic substances in the soil? What is the
reason for your answer? What could be the origin of any
organic substances in the soil? Do the roots of plants use anything in the soil? What is the use of the soil to a tree except
to support it just like a fence post? If plants use anything in
the soil, do they use it in a solid state or in a state of solution?
What substances may serve as food for plants? Do any of these

come from the mineral matters in the soil? Would plants grow in a soil composed of clean sand? Why do you answer thus? Do you suppose the grains of sand were ever parts of larger mineral masses? Could you make sand out of a pebble? Could you make mud from a pebble? Are these pebbles undergoing any changes? Are there any causes which reduce them slowly to the condition of sand and mud? Take this pebble home and bring it back as mud. What is a brick made of? Is clay in any respect like mud? How was the brick made so hard? Is the brick a rock? Do you think any of the rocks may have been made of mud originally? Can you think of one way in which the mud and gravel could have been hardened into rocks? Are there any boulders about the place where you live? How many kinds of boulders can you bring from your garden? Try it; and if a boulder is too large, bring a piece of it.

EXCURSION III.— *To the Gravel Bank.*

The Drift.

Let us make an excursion to some gravel bank. We may find it alongside of the river or brook, where the stream flows close to the high land. Or we may find it on the railroad in the "deep cut." Or just in the border of the town, where the authorities obtain gravel to spread on the streets, or the masons dig for sand for making mortar. Somewhere is a gravel bank. Here it is. (See Fig. 5.)

This is a common gravel bank. Here is the soil at top, such as we found in the garden; but in this place we see what lies beneath the soil. First, we have the subsoil, which is very commonly of a yellowish or reddish color, and is apt to have many gravel stones and pebbles scattered

through it. The subsoil is indicated by *a a a a*. In one
place we see a deep funnel-shaped prolongation downward,
which is perhaps a place once filled by the tap root of some
tree which grew there. The subsoil shows very little *stratification.* That is, it is not arranged in layers. Beneath the
subsoil we find beds of gravel stones and fine sands arranged in irregular layers, which constitute a confused stratification. First, we see some gray gravel beds, *b b b*, which
incline in different directions. Then we come to a thick bed
of pale buff fine sand, *c c c c*, which is pretty evenly stratified, with the thin layers or *laminæ* nearly horizontal. Beneath this is a course of pebbles, *d d d*, and at *e e e* is
another course. Between them is a stratum of pebbly sand
which is obliquely *laminated.* Below *e e* is a bed of gravel,
f f f, quite distinctly laminated, but with the laminæ inclining toward the left instead of the right. At *g g* is a bed
of coarse sand, with laminæ inclining toward the right. It
reaches up and partially blends with the gravel stratum between *d* and *e*. At *h h* is another stratum of fine buffish
sand, with lamination inclined steeply to the right. All
these bands and strata are distinguished by differences in
coarseness and by differences in color. At the foot of the
bank is a sloping pile of sand, *i i i*, which has run down
from above. In one place, *j*, is a collection of lumps of
red subsoil fallen down from the top. A sloping bank of
rubbish at the foot of a bluff of gravel or rocks is called
a *talus.* Often we find cobble stones along the foot of the
bluff which have rolled out of the bank above. These are
sometimes iron-stained ; sometimes covered by a white crust,

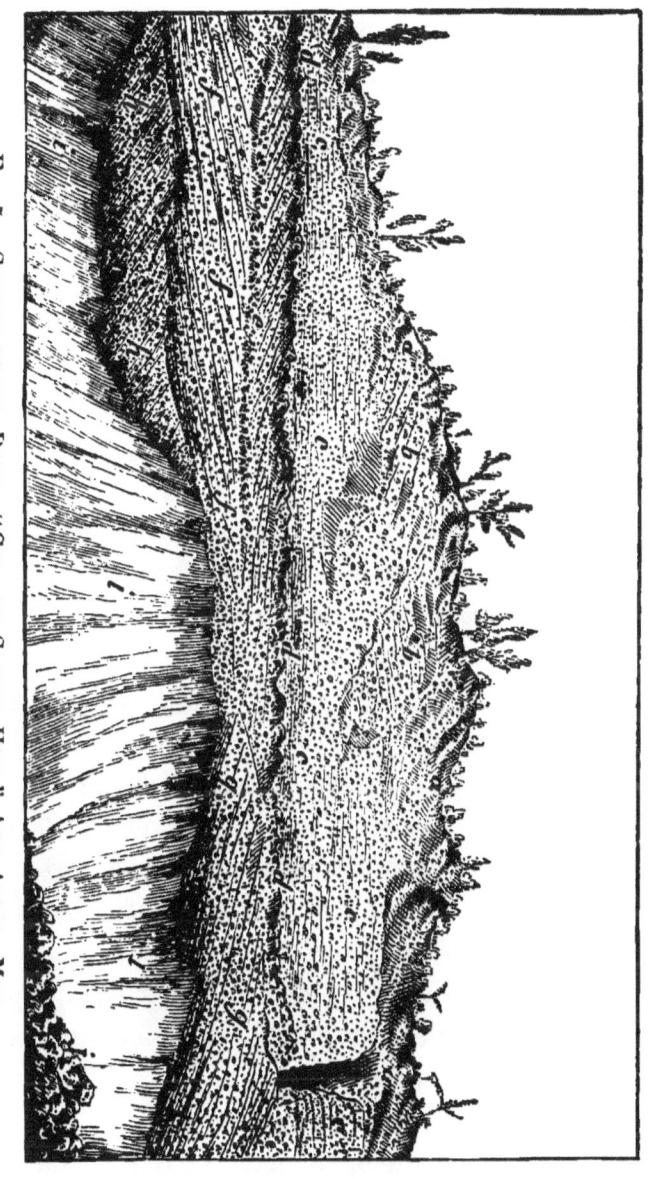

FIG. 5.—SECTION IN THE DRIFT, "CUP AND SAUCER HILL," ANN ARBOR, MICH.

which holds gravel stones cemented to the larger stones. This crust is a precipitate of calcium carbonate. This will be explained hereafter.

This fine example of a gravel bluff simply illustrates what may be found on almost every square mile of the northern states. This view is 129 feet above the bed of the Huron River, and 204 feet above the bed rock, which has only been found by boring. On the bed rock the drift is found to be a heavy mass of unstratified clay, with many large boulders dispersed through it. At other localities this bottom boulder clay is found exposed at the surface.

We may find these loose materials lying upon the surface in all parts of the northern states. The depth varies from nothing to one, two or three hundred feet. It is wonderful that by any means such an enormous amount of loose materials could have been spread over the country. The sands and clays are generally somewhat assorted, and arranged irregularly in separate layers. Can you not recall some railroad cut where this assortment is shown? Such arrangement is known as *stratification*, and the separate layers are *strata*. When we wish to speak of one layer it is a *stratum*. Sometimes the finer materials have been completely removed, and we find only a bed of pebbles and large boulders, as at many places in Massachusetts. Visitors to Martha's Vineyard may find such a coarse deposit at many points along the beach. All these loose materials scattered over the northern states are *Drift*. The whole extent of the deposit forms the *Drift* formation.

Along the shores of the ocean and the Great Lakes the

sands are washed out by the action of the waves in certain places, and transported and deposited again in more protected places. Sometimes two habitual movements conflicting with each other cause the drifting sands to be deposited in enormous banks and sandy sloping beaches. When dried, the winds sometimes lift the fine sands which have been left high along the beach, and drive them inland. Thus are formed piles of dry sand called *dunes* or *downs*. The wind continues to drive the sand forward, and so, fertile fields, gardens, houses and forests are sometimes buried beneath it. At the south end of Lake Michigan — especially about Michigan City — may be seen some enormous sand dunes. At Grand Haven the sand buried the railroad track, fences and buildings, and the station had to be removed to the opposite side of Grand River.

EXERCISES.

What is the nature of the surface of Cape Cod? Can you imagine how Cape Cod may have been formed? Is Cape Cod extending or diminishing? Can you think of any other sandy cape forming in a similar way? What is Sandy Hook? Are there any sand dunes on the coast of New England? What is the connection between dunes and the prevailing direction of the wind? Why are there so many dunes on the east shore of Lake Michigan and none on the west? What is the prevailing direction of the wind in the northern states? Should there be any sand dunes on the coast of California? What is the fact in the case? Should there be any on the east side of Chesapeake Bay? What is the source of the materials which so suddenly form bars and new islands in the Mississippi River? Do you know of any bed rocks which are not covered with Drift? Where are they? Why does the Drift not cover them? Are all bed rocks ledges? Are all ledges bed rocks? Why is there so little vegetation on sandy surfaces? What is the desert of Sahara? Is there any way to prevent the drifting of the sands from dunes? Now make a sketch of the sand bank or gravel bluff, and bring it to the next meeting of the class.

EXCURSION IV.—*To Another Gravel Bank.*

Springs and Wells.

Let us go to another bank. It may be very near the first. Here is a little difference. A spring of pure water issues from the bank and trickles down the slope. Just underneath the spring is a bed of clay, and all the bank above is composed of loose materials. The clay bed or stratum can be traced in both directions some rods, and it is seen to show a concave depression at the spring. The water issues from a small opening which has been worn by the flow. Now it is plain that when the rain falls on

FIG. 6.— GRAVEL BANK AND SPRING.

the surface of the ground, it soaks downward through the gravel as far as this dish of clay. Then it follows along the surface of the clay toward a lower level. In this case its course leads directly to the face of the bank, and when it reaches that, the water issues as a spring. Suppose we go to the top of the bank and dig a well at a point not too far back; when we reach the clay stratum we shall find the water resting on it, and the water will flow into the well. If the clay stratum were not there we should have no spring and no well. But there is probably another clay stratum at some greater depth, and undoubtedly water would be found resting on that. So a well might be obtained by digging deeper. There are many gravel banks where several clay beds may be seen, or found by digging. But they seldom continue uninterrupted for great distances. Nor are they parallel with each other. They overlap each other in every fashion and are inclined in various ways.

Suppose some stones or substances exist in the gravel bank which are capable of being dissolved in water — like salt or limestone or gypsum or iron oxide. Then the water which issues at the spring will be a *solution* of such substances. The water will be a mineral water more or less strong.

Many times the water dissolves some substance in one place and then deposits it in another. Some mineral is very frequently deposited by the water where it escapes at the spring. This is because water generally cannot hold so much mineral in solution when exposed to the air as

it can while confined deep in a gravel bed. In New York
and the Western States spring waters often deposit large
amounts of matter consisting chiefly of limestone that had
been dissolved in the earth. The matter is not all thrown
down or precipitated until the water has flowed several
rods. If the water flows over a hard sloping surface, it
deposits a hard crust which continues to grow until something similar to a bed of limestone is formed. We call it
travertin. In some countries it forms extensive beds

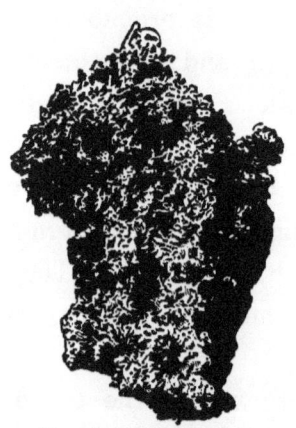

which are quarried for building
purposes. If the water flows over
flat ground and stands, the deposit
is spongy and irregular, and we call
it *calcareous tufa.* Often it is
mixed with earth and stones.
Sometimes the stems of mosses and
dry leaves and sticks and bones of
animals become incrusted with it.
Some very beautiful specimens of
so called "petrified moss" are produced. If the water is collected in
a pond or lake the deposit falls to the bottom and forms
a white powdery layer which we call *marl.* Here it
becomes mingled with dead shells of molluscs which
lived in the pond or lake, and thus forms *shell marl.*
These shells are real *fossils.* Sometimes shell marl becomes quite dry and hard. It is then extremely like a
common limestone with fossil shells in it. Water which
contains limestone in solution is called *hard.* In many

FIG. 7.—"PETRIFIED
· MOSS."

parts of New England there are no limestones in the
gravel deposits; and hence no "hard" water is produced.
The water of wells and springs is there *soft*.

Besides limestone there is often iron oxide in the earth
to be dissolved by the waters which circulate underground.
Such waters are called *chalybeate*. The iron is sometimes
deposited in marshy situations, and forms *bog iron ore*.
Frequently both lime and iron are deposited, and the mixture forms a sort of paint called *ochre*. The greater the
amount of iron the deeper the color. Also, when the iron
oxide is chemically combined with water, the ochre is
yellow, more or less pale; but if it is burned so as to
drive off the water, the ochre is of a red color. Before
the paint can be regarded of first quality it has to be
ground very fine. Iron deposits from springs are common
in most parts of the country. The pebbles and sand from
a bank of drift are often deeply incrusted and even cemented together by a deposit of iron. This is very strik-
ingly shown along the bluff shores of Martha's Vineyard.

EXERCISES.

Can you mention any chalybeate spring? Do you know any
spring whose waters stain the stones of a reddish color? Can
you point out any bed of bog iron ore? Are chalybeate springs
much resorted to for purposes of health? Have you ever seen
a bed of marl? Of what is marl chiefly composed? Where did
the material come from? Do the rains increase or diminish the
amount of soluble matter in the soil? Is lime in any form useful to vegetation? Is it ever used by farmers? Is it more used
in the eastern or the western states? What use may the farmer
make of the marl which accumulates in the ponds and low

grounds? A man dug a well and found water at the depth of twenty feet; his near neighbor had to dig sixty feet; why was that? On a gravel hill two hundred feet high the well is only fifteen feet, while at the foot of the hill water is found only by digging fifty feet; why is that? Can you make a diagram showing how the materials are arranged to produce such results? If I dig a well in sand near the sea shore and water enters below the sea-level, why is that water fresh? Why are some wells lower in a wet spell than in a dry one? Why do the rivers not cease to flow during a summer drouth? Why does the earth retain some moisture even in the dryest weather? Which is best to retain moisture in a dry spell, a very clayey soil, or one with a good proportion of fine sand? What is the cause of the crust which forms on the bottom of the tea-kettle?

EXCURSION V.—*To Our Laboratory.*

How Things are Put Together.

You know already that many different kinds of rocks exist. They are of different colors and different degrees of hardness, and they are also different mixtures of minerals. We are very anxious to know more about rocks, so as to be able to call each one by its name. Most rocks are mixtures of different minerals, and we must therefore learn a little about minerals. But minerals are mostly composed of two or more substances or chemical elements; and therefore we must learn something about chemical elements and the way they combine with each other.

Now let us perform a couple of little experiments. First, take a piece of chalk and drop a little strong acid upon it. Vinegar will answer if strong. Do you see the little bubbles rise as if the chalk were boiling? A drop of water or oil will not produce such a result. This is chemical action; we shall try to understand it.

Again, let us take a vial of lime-water. We can procure it of the druggist, or can prepare it ourselves by shaking up some quick-lime in water and pouring off the clear water into a glass bottle after the mixture settles. Now take a glass tube, which can also be had of the druggist; or otherwise take a simple oat straw and breathe through this into the clear lime-water. Do you see the white cloud which forms? Continue to do so for two or three minutes, and then let the lime-water stand for some time. There, do you see the fine powder settling on the bottom? It will all fall down and leave the liquid clear above. This is also a chemical operation. Now let us see how it can be explained.

You remember the stone which you took and pounded to a fine powder, and, by mixing a little water, made into mud. Well, however fine you made the powder, each particle might, by some means, be made even smaller. We can at least think smaller particles. But it is commonly believed that there are really particles so small that it would not be possible by any means to make them smaller. These are called *atoms*. They are really vastly finer than the finest particles of the finest dust which floats in the air. If we could take a drop of water and magnify it to the size of this earth, and magnify the atoms in it in the same proportion, the atoms would be about the size of small shot. All substances are made up of these minute atoms. Iron is made of atoms. Water is made of atoms. The air is made of atoms.

There are about sixty-four different kinds of atoms known. Iron contains one kind, sulphur another kind, silver another. The atoms of each kind have a strong attraction for certain other kinds of atoms. This is chemical *affinity*. The two kinds come together when they can, and remain close together. This is a chemical combination. So most substances are compounds of different kinds of atoms. Water is made of two kinds of atoms; that is, water is a *compound*. But iron is composed of only one kind of atom; that is, iron is an *element*. All the metals are elements. Now there are only sixty-four elements known in all the great mass of the earth. Not more than thirteen of these are very important in making all the rocks. I will give their names because they ought to be learned. If we should take 100 pounds of the average solid earth, there would be in the mass

Oxygen,	. .	45 pounds.	Potassium, . .	2 pounds.
Silicon,	. .	25 "	Carbon,	
Aluminum,	. .	10 "	Hydrogen,	
Iron,	. .	8 "	Sulphur,	All together nearly
Calcium,	. .	6 "	Nitrogen,	1½ pounds.
Sodium,	. .	2½ "	Chlorine,	
			Magnesium,	

In the atmosphere and in water there are larger proportions of Nitrogen, Oxygen and Hydrogen.

Oxygen has a strong affinity for most of the other elements, and the compounds which it forms with them are called *oxides*. So chlorine unites with other elements and forms *chlorides.* We are very familiar with many of the oxides. Water is hydrogen oxide. Lime is calcium oxide. Caustic soda is sodium oxide. Caustic potash is potassium oxide. Iron rust is iron oxide. So common salt is sodium chloride. Now state what these different oxides and chlorides are composed of. Some compounds contain two or three times as much oxygen or chlorine or other elements as other compounds contain; but we cannot go so far as to take any account of that at the present time.

The union of oxygen with certain elements results in *acid-forming oxides.* With other elements bases are formed. The addition of hydrogen to the acid-forming oxides makes *acids* of them. The names of the acids most important for us end in *ic.* Thus, sulphuric acid, or "oil of vitriol," is composed of sulphur, oxygen and hydrogen. Nitric acid is composed of nitrogen, oxygen and hydrogen. The basic oxides have names which end in *a.* Many of them have also old popular names. Thus the oxide of potassium or potassium oxide is *potassa* or potash; the oxide of sodium is *soda*; the oxide of calcium is *lime;* one oxide of iron is *iron rust.*

Now please have patience with a little further explanation. The acids generally have strong affinities for the bases, and the compounds which they form are called *salts.* When the name of the acid ends in *ic*, the name of the salt ends in *ate.* If sulphuric acid unites with potash the salt is sulphate of potash, or as it is now called, potassium sulphate. So sulphate of soda, or sodium sulphate, is formed from sulphuric acid and soda; silicate of lime, from silicic acid and lime; carbonate of lime (common chalk, marble, limestone or marl) is composed of carbonic acid and lime.

Some acids have stronger affinities than other acids have for certain bases. Sulphuric acid attracts lime more powerfully than carbonic acid does. So if we should mix sulphuric acid, carbonic acid and lime together, the lime would be taken by the sulphuric acid. Even strong vinegar, which is acetic acid, would do the same thing. More than this, suppose carbonic acid to be already combined with lime, forming chalk; then suppose a little strong vinegar or sulphuric acid to be brought into contact with the chalk, it seizes the lime and drives the carbonic acid off with much ado. Carbonic acid is a gas, and that is the reason why its escape produces effervescence. But if we introduce carbonic acid into water containing lime in solution, this acid unites with the lime, forming carbonate of lime in the water. As carbonate of lime is not much dissolved by water, the particles remain suspended in the water for a time. They finally settle down, however, as a white powder. This is of the same nature as chalk and marl. It is even called *precipitated chalk*. This is the explanation of the little experiments just made.

EXERCISES.

Cut about seventy-five small square pieces of white cardboard. On ten of these write a heavy capital O, which stands for oxygen. On six of them write H, which stands for hydrogen. Put also the symbol of each of the other principal elements on four others, thus: Si for silicon, Al for aluminum, Fe for iron, Ca for calcium, Na for sodium, K for potassium, C for carbon, S for sulphur, N for nitrogen, Cl for chlorine and Mg for magnesium. Then put S and O together, representing an acid-forming oxide, and to show that it is such add a card having on it a cross made with red ink. Add H, and you have an acid. What is, the name of it? Then put Ca and O together representing a basic oxide; and to show this put with them a card having on it a cross made with blue ink. What is the name of this base? Then put the acid and the base together, and tell what is the name of the salt. Examine the cards now and see what different elements enter into this salt. With these little cards illustrate the other combinations mentioned. Also those to be mentioned in these exercises.

Now, what caused the effervescence when we dropped a little acid on the chalk? What is the name of the acid which escaped. Represent it with the cards. What became of the lime? Represent it with the cards. What is the name of the salt formed? What became of the carbonic acid? When you breathed in the lime-water what caused the white cloudiness? What was the substance which fell to the bottom? Represent its composition by means of the cards. If oxygen unites with iron what is the name of the compound? Show me some oxide of iron. When chlorine unites with sodium what is the name of the compound? What is its common name? If oxygen unites with aluminum what results? Suppose silicic acid combines with alumina, what is the compound? When lime-water stands exposed to the air what causes the crust which forms on the top? Why does the druggist keep his lime-water close-stoppered? What complaint of the stomach is lime-water good for? Suppose you put a little strong acid in a bottle half filled with water, and then drop in some chalk and stop the bottle tightly, what would result? What, if you should drop in some bits of marble? Suppose pulverized chalk and flour are well mixed, and then the whole is kneaded with vinegar and water, what would result? Suppose carbonate of soda, tartaric acid and flour are mixed and kneaded with water, what results? Can we see the atoms of matter with a microscope? What are the components of sulphate of potassa?

EXCURSION VI.—*To the Field.*

Quartz.

Now we will walk into the field again, and will take some simple implements with us. We shall want first of all one

a

b

FIG. 8.—GEOLOGICAL HAM-
MER, PALÆONTOLOGIST'S
PATTERN.

or two hammers. If each person can have a hammer that will be better. A good form of geological hammer is here shown in Figure 8. The pene *a* is at right angles to the face *b* and the handle. The face is flat, and a little longer than broad. The hammer should be of fine steel, with the temper of a stone mason's hammer. The eye should be large, and the handle of hickory. For student's use a hammer weighing

FIG. 9.—GEOLOGICAL HAM-
MER, QUARRYMAN'S PAT-
TERN.

from half a pound to a pound will be most generally useful. But a hammer weighing two pounds or more will frequently be needed also. The form of the regular stone mason's hammer (Fig. 9) is quite as suitable for working among very hard rocks. It is better to use any hammer which can be had than not to break the rocks at all. We shall want, also, a pointed piece of hard tempered steel to test the hardness of minerals. A good strong knife blade

will answer well; but if you feel unwilling to subject a knife
blade to such use, you can employ a simple implement like
Figure 10. This is simply a piece of steel rod flattened and
pointed at one extremity, and rather high tempered. But

FIG. 10.—HARDNESS TESTER.
a. View of flattened side of point. *b.* View of taper toward the point.

whatever implement you become accustomed to should be
used every time. It will be well to have also a small vial
of acid—either very strong vinegar or diluted hydrochloric
acid.

Well, here we are amongst the rocks. Let us first give
attention to the boulders, for we can find more varieties of
rocks among them. We first pick out a rock showing a
mixture of light and dark colors. These are probably differently colored minerals. Now fix your attention upon one of
these minerals and see if you can scratch it with your steel.
Do you say yes? Well, look at it closely, so that when you
see another piece of the same kind you will know it. See
if you can find another just like it. Well, does your steel
scratch it just about as easily ? Try another light colored
mineral, does your steel scratch it? If not, this is a harder
mineral; it is a different mineral. Your steel leaves a dark
line on it. The mineral which you cannot scratch is *quartz*.
But see, there are several differently colored minerals which

the steel does not scratch. Do you find them? They may
not be all in one stone. Well, they are all quartz. They
are different *varieties* of quartz. You will find one variety
to be white and *opaque* like porcelain; another will be transparent; another slightly rosy; another smoky; another
almost black; another brick red. That is, you will be able
to find all these sorts if you examine different rocks. But
they all have a glassy appearance. Quartz is the hardest
mineral you will have to deal with. It is hard enough to
scratch glass. Besides its hardness, you may know it by its
glassy lustre. The freshly broken surfaces glisten like broken
glass. Further, it always breaks with an irregular fracture;
and this is also like glass. Sometimes you find a boulder
composed entirely of quartz. They are generally white or
very light colored. They are often called "flint rocks."
But *flint* proper has generally a little duller lustre, and is
apt to be dusky or dark colored. The red quartz is mostly
red jasper. Many gems are little else than quartz. This is
the case with agate, amethyst, carnelian, chalcedony, onyx
and some others. The colors are caused by the admixture
of impurities.

Well, what is quartz? It is only silicic acid ; or we commonly say when this oxide is not combined with the base, it
is *silica*. It is, therefore, composed of only two elements,
when pure. It forms also, beautiful crystals — beautiful in
form and beautiful in glassy transparency. Here are some
quartz crystals (Figure 11). You see each one has six
sides. It is a *hexagonal prism*. The sides may all be
equal; but generally they are not so, because more

crystalline matter has been deposited on one side than on others. See also, how the end of the crystal tapers off. The taper too is six-sided. Sometimes both ends have such a *termination*. Whenever, in studying minerals, you find a very hard glassy mineral which is not so broken but that you can detect a portion of such a form as this, that circumstance is probable proof that the mineral is quartz.

FIG. 11.—A GROUP OF CRYSTALS OF QUARTZ.

If, in addition, it has a glassy lustre and the hardness of quartz, the proof is conclusive.

Let us see now how many varieties of quartz we can collect. Break the boulders to pieces, and save the pieces which contain minerals too hard to scratch. It is very necessary to know quartz in all its conditions—whatever its color, however mixed with other substances. When you can identify quartz with certainty, and distinguish it from two other white minerals next to be considered, you have made excellent advancement.

EXERCISES.

Look over the small pebbles before collected, and see whether any quartz exists among them. Are any of them composed wholly of quartz? Examine this washed, clean sand and say whether the grains appear to be quartz. What proportion of all the grains may be considered quartz? Try some sand from another location, and ascertain whether as large a proportion is quartz. Is the fine sand which makes up the greater part of the garden soil quartz? Is it true then, that quartz forms the greater part of the drift? Are these grains, pebbles and other boulders angular or rounded? Were they always as they are now in this respect? Does it appear that they have been worn? Why are they not worn completely to powder? Why are there so few boulders of rocks less hard than quartz? Look at this boulder with a white streak through it; is that quartz? Is there any quartz in the rock besides this *vein?* What makes this white vein project above the general surface? Can you find a boulder with more than one quartz vein through it? Can you find a specimen with one quartz vein cutting another? How many varieties of quartz have you now?

EXCURSION VII.— *To the Field.*

The Feldspars.

Now we have made the acquaintance of one mineral which is almost always light-colored — sometimes looking almost exactly like glass. This quartz we find everywhere. It is in almost all rocks. If we should take one hundred pounds of the average rocks, about sixty pounds would be quartz. When we know quartz thoroughly we are acquainted with more than half of all the mass of the earth, so far as it is in sight.

But there are other white minerals which we found not to be quartz. We must study them further, because we see they are very abundant also. Now we try our steel on a number of them. Those which are not scratched when we press hard we know to be quartz, and take no further notice of them. But see, here is one which we can barely scratch.

A piece of quartz will also scratch it. Probably we shall find others which scratch quite easily; let us pass these by for the present.

Now look at this one, which we can barely scratch. Does it look altogether like quartz? Tell me how it differs from quartz. Has it a real glassy lustre like quartz? Yes, you say; but after all, it is not quite so glassy. Turn it until your eye catches the light reflected from one of its surfaces. It may be a very small surface; but if you can catch the reflection, you will perceive that it does not glisten quite so brightly as a quartz surface. If you cannot get this reflection from one surface, try another. You need not break them out of the rock to make these trials.

Next, tell me if the form is entirely like that of quartz. In the first place the real crystalline form of quartz can seldom be seen in a rock mass; there is no portion of a hexagonal prism. Very little of the quartz in an ordinary rock shows that it was broken from a hexagonal prism. But then, in the second place, you can find a form in many rocks which does *not* belong to quartz. Now look carefully among these whitish minerals which are *not* quartz, if we may judge by their hardness. You will see here and there some smooth, flat surfaces like *a* in Fig. 12. Well, quartz in the rocks seldom shows flat, smooth surfaces, as we just now said. But look once more, and you will see that some of these smooth, flat surfaces are bounded, on one side at least, by a straight line. It is *not* an irregular fracture, as if the surface had been simply broken off

FIG. 12.

FRAGMENT OF
FELDSPAR
CRYSTAL.

there. You will also perceive that this line is the border
of another surface which stands about at right angles with
the first surface, like two sides of a box. In the figure, *b* is
this other surface. You see it is long and narrow. Sometimes
you may find it wide. Now, have you seen anything in
quartz like these two surfaces? Not at all. This is quite
another mineral. We call this mineral *Feldspar*.

These are poor specimens of feldspar; but this is the
condition in which we generally find it, and we must learn
to know feldspar as it ordinarily occurs in the rocks. Very
often, however, we meet with good specimens, which show
the form quite completely. If we can find a *vein* of whitish
mineral in a rock of some other kind, we shall be likely to
get a better view of the *crystalline form*, as we call it.

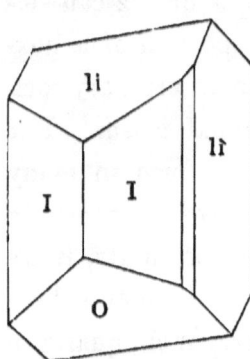

Here is a crystal which will enable
you to understand more clearly the
form and *lustre* of feldspar. The flat
surfaces are called *faces* or *planes*.
See, here, one plane, 1i, at right angles
with another, 1ì. Also O at right
angles with 1ì. Who among us has
the best crystal of feldspar? Every
person must keep the best he has
until he finds a better.

Fig. 13. — Large Crys-
tal of Orthoclase,
a Species of Feld-
spar.

Now, we have talked about feldspar
as if it were one kind of mineral, like
quartz; but, in truth, we have several
species of feldspar. Most commonly feldspar has a cream col-
or or pinkish color. Sometimes it is very white. Sometimes

it is somewhat transparent, like glass, and has a more glassy lustre than common feldspar; and, in this case, is apt to be composed of thin layers or *lamellæ*. These are likely to be different feldspars; but we must not try to name different species till we have made more advancement. There is another little peculiarity of certain feldspars. Often, when the light reflected from the surface strikes the eye, very fine parallel lines or *striæ* may be seen. These generally indicate a feldspar which is *not* the common species. Let us look carefully for a surface having these lines. Do not look too long in one rock. Try another. Sometimes all the feldspar in one rock will be of the common kind, while in another it will present the *striated* surfaces. In making the examinations you should have a cheap pocket magnifier. When you learn how to use it you will find it almost as indispensable as a pocket knife. (See Fig. 14.)

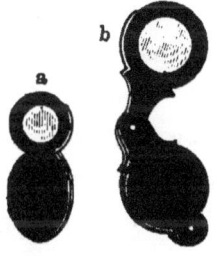

Fig. 14. — Magnify- ing Glasses. a, Oval. b, Bellows- Shaped.

If you are unable to collect these different species readily look in some collection of minerals, and pick out all the quartz and all the feldspar, and point out the different feldspars.

The most important difference between quartz and feldspar we have said nothing about, because it does not appear to the eye. Feldspar is made of different elements. Do you remember what is meant by elements? The chemist knows how to separate feldspar into all its different elements, and ascertain how much there is of each one. We are not prepared to do this for ourselves; but we *will* do it, if we stick to the study. Well, the chemist has ascertained that all feldspars contain *silicic acid, alumina* and some *alkali.* Now the acid unites with the base alumina, and if the alkali were not present, there would be formed simply *silicate* of *alumina,* which is also called *aluminum silicate.* The acid also unites with the alkali, and if the alumina were not present there would be formed simply a *silicate* of some *alkali.* But as all are present, there is formed *silicate of alumina and an alkali.* Now, there are several alkalies. Potash, soda and lime are alkalies. Either one of these may be the alkali in a feldspar; and that is the way we get different species of feldspars. So one is a potash feldspar—and that is the most common feldspar (*Orthoclase*). Another is a soda feldspar —and that is generally white (*Albite*). Another is a lime feldspar—and this is glassy and transparent (*Anorthite*). Others are soda lime feldspars; and one of these is gray, brown or greenish, and sometimes shows a beautiful play of colors in reflected light (*Labradorite*). Another (*Oligoclase*) is white, with a faint greenish tinge, and fine striæ on the principal surfaces. But you need not learn all these names at present. All the feldspars mentioned which are not orthoclase may be called *Plagioclase.*

Any feldspar is composed of silica, alumina and an alkali. The different colors are caused by minute quantities of iron and other substances. If we take one hundred pounds of common feldspar, about sixty-five pounds are silica, eighteen pounds alumina, fifteen pounds potash, about one pound iron; and the remaining pound is soda, magnesia and lime.

When feldspar decomposes it forms a pure white clay called *Kaolin*. Feldspar is used extensively in the manufacture of porcelain.

Feldspars are very common in crystalline rocks. Fine specimens occur in St. Lawrence and Orange counties, New York. Also in Haddam and Middletown, Connecticut; and at Royalston and Barre, Massachusetts. Fair specimens may be had in boulders all over the northern states.

EXERCISES.

Now, how many specimens of quartz and feldspar have you? Are all your specimens of quartz different varieties? Have you a specimen of pink feldspar? Have you a specimen of pink quartz? How does the pink quartz differ, to your eyes, from the pink feldspar? Have you a specimen of cream-colored feldspar? What other minerals, so far as you can answer, were in the same rock with it? Show me a feldspar with striations. Is it more or less glassy than one without striations? Is it orthoclase or a plagioclase? Can you see the striations with the naked eye? Here is a piece of common feldspar weighing one hundred grains; how many grains of silica in it? How many grains of potash? What constituents of feldspar contain oxygen? What are the different elements in common feldspar? Try and find a piece of dark feldspar. Do all your specimens of feldspar show some of the peculiar crystalline forms of the mineral? Take your chemical cards and arrange them so as to show the composition of common feldspar. Also the composition of other feldspars.

EXCURSION VIII.— *To the Field.*

Calcite.

I wish you next to make the acquaintance of another light-colored mineral. It is much softer than feldspar, and you will not be very likely to find it scattered through boulders containing feldspar and dark minerals. We had better look for veins or seams of white mineral matter cutting through other rocks. We shall probably find some among the boulders. Ah, here is a white vein. Try your steel on it. Is it hard? Can't you scratch it? Then you know it is a quartz vein. Besides, see how glassy it looks. We may find many quartz veins. Here is a soft vein — very much softer than feldspar. The steel scratches it very easily. Certainly, then, it is neither feldspar nor quartz. This is probably our *Calcite*. Now let us inspect it as we did feldspar. Can you find a smooth face anywhere? There may be plenty of them. Well, look at this face or flat surface; how smooth, shining and even it looks! It does not seem to be a common fracture. How much like feldspar it is! And yet it is not so pearly as feldspar. Do you see one straight edge to this face? Search till you find a face which shows a straight bounding edge. Here it is.

FIG. 15.
FRAGMENT
OF CRYSTAL
OF CALCITE.

The face *a* is bounded by the straight line *m n*. Now you can see that the line shows where the face *a* is cut by another plane, *b*. This is just like feldspar, you say. Not quite, for you perceive that these two faces do not make a right angle with each other. The angle is considerably more or less than a right angle. That makes the plane angle at *m* either acute or obtuse. How is it in your specimen?

You can even detect something further. A close examination of the face of your crystal probably shows fine lines like cracks running across or partly across. There are two sets of them. One set runs exactly parallel with the side *m n*, and the other parallel with another side. These are *cleavage* lines. The crystal breaks most easily along those lines. Very likely you might break out fragments which would show several faces — even six faces, somewhat perfect, all bounded by lines parallel on opposite sides. Here is a fine large specimen. We often find such. They are generally rather opaque; but sometimes they are clear as glass. You must remember seeing such crystals on some one's mantel or "what-not," or in some cabinet of specimens. You can generally detect cleavage lines on the surfaces of these specimens. This is calcite.

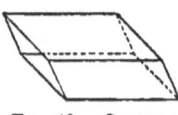

Fig. 16. — CRYSTAL OF CALCITE.

But this handsome mineral often presents itself under another form, called *dog-tooth spar*, because resembling somewhat the canine tooth of a dog. Here is a figure of a couple of such crystals grown together, as we generally find them.

This mineral is largely composed of lime. It is by far the most important lime-containing mineral. If we take one hundred grains of pure calcite it contains

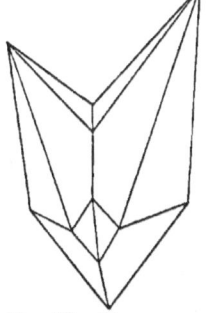

Fig. 17. — DOG-TOOTH SPAR.

forty-four grains of carbonic acid and fifty-six grains of lime. It is therefore *carbonate of lime* — also called *calcium carbonate*. This is the same composition as chalk. What will be the effect of a little dilute acid applied? It should effervesce like chalk. To make sure of a fair test, it is better to pulverize the calcite and drop a little acid on it in a test tube.

There are two other minerals quite similar to this, differing chiefly in having magnesia in place of all the lime (which makes *Magnesite*), or about half of it (which makes *Dolomite*). But it will not be best to attempt to study them at present. They do not effervesce so readily as calcite. The pulverized mineral in the test tube with dilute acid must be heated to produce active effervescence.

Now you have made the acquaintance of the three most important white or light-colored minerals. If you know them well, and can always distinguish each one from the others, you can make good headway in naming rocks as soon as you know two or three of the dark minerals. Calcite you can certainly distinguish by its comparative softness. Feldspar can generally be distinguished by its hardness and lustrous cleavage faces. Though generally somewhat glassy, they are seldom as glassy as quartz. After a good deal of practice you will be able to decide at a glance that the feldspar is generally more pearly than quartz. In any case, the cleavage planes, if you can detect any, will decide the case. Hold the specimen so that you get reflected light. Turn it in different positions, until the reflected light reveals a cleavage plane. The "glassy feldspars," it must be confessed, will sometimes trouble you. They look extremely like quartz in lustre, and the crystals are often so broken up that it is difficult to detect unmistakable cleavage planes. But we must keep trying and searching. Very seldom is it really impossible to distinguish feldspar from quartz, either by lustre, cleavage planes, lines, angles or inferior hardness.

EXERCISES.

Which of the three white minerals contain silica? What is in calcite and not in feldspar? What is in feldspar and not in calcite? What is in feldspar and not in quartz? Suppose you have a square box, and, placing your hand on one corner, crush it over by pressing toward the opposite corner at the bottom, which mineral does the box now resemble in form? How must you press the box to produce the form of one of the other minerals? Did you ever see a crystal of transparent calcite? Take one if you have it, and lay it on a printed line; what is peculiar in the appearance of the line? Have you found any brown crystals soft as calcite? Have you any brown crystals with curved surfaces? The brown crystals probably contain magnesia. Try and detect some intermediate forms between calcite and dogtooth spar. Inquire among your friends for specimens of crystals, and see what minerals they are. Of course you can't name them all yet. Please do not neglect this, for we shall get much help in this way. Some specimens worth nothing where they lie may be exactly the things which a student wants to see.

EXCURSION IX.—*To the Field*.

The Micas, Hornblende and Talc.

There are two or three dark minerals of first import-
ance. One of these is *Mica*, although it is not always
dark. Almost every one is familiar with transparent mica
as used in our stoves; but we will go among the boulders
again for the purpose of studying it as it enters into the
formation of rocks. We will seek a boulder with whitish
and dark varieties of minerals mixed together. We shall
soon find one in which the dark mineral exists in small
thin scales, or piles of thin scales. That is mica. Some
people ignorantly call it isinglass. Now select the largest
specimen at hand and try with a knife-blade to separate
the thin leaves. You see there is almost no limit to the
possible splitting of the mineral. If the mica is bright,
the leaves are elastic and tough. If it is dull, the mica is
softer and less elastic. In some rocks the mica is all dull.
In hardness mica is not far from calcite. Common mica is
transparent or translucent, and is generally brown, pale-
green or white. Deep-black mica is another species (*Bio-
tite*). In New Hampshire there are plates of mica over a
yard in diameter.

Now, as to substances in its constitution, we must say
that mica is the name of a family, as in the case of feldspars. But the micas all contain *silica, alumina* and *potash*, and almost always *iron*. The common mica (*Muscovite*) contains much iron, and that seems to give it its
dark color. It also contains *magnesia* and *soda*. `Water

is often present, and that causes the duller lustre, lighter color and less elastic leaves (*Hydromica* or *Margarodite*). Mica is a mineral which you can hardly mistake. Let us examine next another dark mineral called *Hornblende*. It is sometimes green or dark green, and frequently black. It is exceedingly common in the boulder rocks in all the northern states. It has about the hardness of feldspar, and if you scratch it the streak is white or whitish. You can generally detect a crystalline face, and sometimes you find a crystalline form like a four-sided rod. Sometimes the structure is lamellar—that is, in layers which are much thicker than the leaves of mica, and are not elastic, but are apt to break as you attempt to lift them up. Many times, however, you will not find any crystalline face. The hornblende is simply a shapeless fragment closely imbedded among other minerals.

FIG. 18. — CRYSTALS OF HORNBLENDE.

This is also a silicious mineral, and it generally contains much iron, magnesia, alumina, and lime. There are many varieties, some of which are white and fibrous (*Tremolite*, *Asbestus*). One variety (*Actinolite*) consists of bright-green, radiating fibres. There is also another mineral (*Augite*) very similar to hornblende, but more inclined to greenish and whitish colors, and less commonly to black—though it is sometimes black. It has cleavage surfaces nearly at right angles with each other. But it is difficult to distinguish augite from hornblende by any means which we can at present employ, though it is

very important for the geologist to do it. Augite is
quite common.

There is only one other mineral to be troubled with in
this course of study. That is *Talc*. It occurs often in
thin scales like mica, and glistens somewhat. You might
easily mistake it for mica. But let us take a specimen
and pick apart the thin scales. See how soft this mineral
is. It is the softest mineral in the world. When you lift
up a scale does it tend to spring back on removing your
knife? No, you say. Well, these scales are not elastic.
The scales of mica are elastic. These are two excellent
ways for separating mica and talc. Sometimes they may
be separated by the color, for talc is pale and silvery-
greenish, and never black. The chemist tells us, moreover, that talc is a magnesian mineral. It contains silica,
magnesia and water. It is a silicate of magnesia.

Talc always feels smooth and greasy. Remember this
when you find a specimen large enough to test by the feel.
Soapstone is nothing but talc all crushed and compacted
together. It is sometimes made into inkstands and grid-
dles and foot-warmers. What the well-borers call soapstone is only clay shale or indurated clay.

EXERCISES.

Now let us think over some of the things learned. What is
the name of the glassy mineral? What are the white minerals?
Are they always white? What are the two scaly minerals?
What minerals are sometimes black? Which is the softest of
the white minerals? Which is most glassy? Which is the softest
of the black minerals? Which mineral effervesces when acid is

applied? Why does not hornblende effervesce? Which ones
of all these minerals will scratch calcite? Which will calcite
scratch? Which cannot be scratched by any of the others?
Which minerals contain silica? Which contain iron? Which
calcium? Which magnesium? Which aluminum? What
other chemical elements exist in any of these minerals? Which
ones are most easily detected by their crystalline form? Which
by its hardness? Which by its softness? Have you ever seen
the crystalline form of mica in any rock? What minerals are
often green or greenish? Which minerals sometimes occur
black and sometimes white? Which one is sometimes shaped
like needles? Which like fine silk fibres? What minerals are
likely to be kinkish? What ones of a cream color? Which
ones will scratch glass? Which cleave most readily? Which
least readily?

Here is a table showing the composition of all these minerals.
Their names will be seen at the head of the columns, and the
names of the various substances which combine together to form
the minerals are at the left. In the case of feldspar we have
considered simply common feldspar (*Orthoclase*), with its most
common composition. The same is true of mica and hornblende.
The figures show how many pounds or grains of each element are
present in 100 pounds or grains of the mineral.

	Quartz.	Feldspar.	Mica.	Horn-blende.	Talc.	Calcite.
Silica,	100	65	45	47	62	..
Alumina,	..	18	32	12	..	..
Alkali,	..	15	10	..	..	..
Magnesia,	..	..	..	15	31	..
Lime,	..	..	1	11	..	56
Iron Oxide,	..	1	5	12	2	..
Carbonic Acid,	..	..	..	..	..	44
Water,	..	..	4	..	4	..
Other Substances,	..	1	3	3	1	..
	100	100	100	100	100	100

EXCURSION X.—*Among the Boulders.*

Quartzose Rocks.

Let us continue our wanderings among the boulders. We are ready now to learn the names of some of the commonest rocks. The rocks are composed of mixtures of minerals, or, in a few cases, of single minerals. The majority of all the rocks are formed from the six common minerals which we have studied. This seems surprising; but we must remember that each mineral may present many variations in color, and that feldspar and mica exist each in several species. Then, again, the same minerals may exist in different proportions in different rocks, and the minerals may be in different conditions as to fineness and as to crystallization. Also, rocks having the same mineral ingredients may differ in structure. All these things we will now proceed to see for ourselves.

One of the very commonest of rocks in all the northern states and among the pebbles of the southern states is composed of a single mineral, and that mineral is quartz. The name of the rock is *Quartzite;* but there are almost endless varieties of it. Let us find a white boulder nearly uniform in color. Here it is. Test it for hardness. Is it as hard as quartz? If not, we will pass it by. If this white rock is as hard as quartz, then it is one variety of quartzite. The farmers would say it is a "flint rock," or a "hard head." Now look closely at it. Very probably you will notice some variation in color in different parts. Probably, also, you can discover an obscure bounding line to the differently colored parts. If, however, the bounding lines are indistinct, and the whole rock breaks through like glass, this is a *vitreous quartzite*. Some vitreous quartzites show quite striking contrasts of color in different parts. These are apt to be coarse or *conglomeritic*. Let us find a vitreous quartzite which is *jaspery*.

In many quartzites the different parts, whether of different colors or not, are clearly so many different pebbles or cobble-stones. The rock seems to be a mass of rounded quartz stones cemented together. This is a quartzose *conglomerate*. There are also, sometimes, conglomerates composed of rounded stones which are not quartzose. Also, many conglomerates have the different stones feebly cemented together. But here we come on something different. It is a quartzite composed, evidently, of grains of sand, for we can see the outlines of separate grains throughout. Well, this is a *granular quartzite*.

Now suppose the granular quartzite to be a little less firmly cemented. It is simply a coarse *sandstone* or *grit*. When you break this sort of rock you do not notice the glassy lustre of the quartzites. The grindstone is a sandstone. The "Nova Scotia stone" so much admired for building purposes is a sandstone, and so is the "brown stone" used so extensively for fine buildings in New York and other eastern cities. It is found in great abundance along the valley of the Connecticut River and in northern New Jersey. Throughout the states of New York and Pennsylvania are many reddish, yellowish and grayish sandstones. In Ohio are many quarries of beautiful building stones known as Waverly sandstone. The sandstones and grindstones from Berea and Cleveland are mostly of a grayish and bluish color, and much admired for window sills and caps. In Michigan very similar stone is quarried at Point aux Barques on Lake Huron. In the southern part of the state the same stone is often quite reddish. In Ottawa county it is bluish. In Iowa, at Burlington and in that neighborhood, it is yellowish. Other kinds of sandstones are always likely to be found in the vicinity of beds of coal. Often they have black charcoal-like specks in them. Sandstones are liable to contain various impurities, consisting most frequently of lime or clayey matter or iron-oxide. Many sandstones have minute mica-scales scattered through them. These are micaceous sandstones.

EXERCISES.

It is time to get together all our specimens of *quartzose rocks*. There are endless varieties, although only one of our six common minerals has been employed in their formation. Please pick out the specimens which you think might be called quartzites. Are all the rest sandstones? What is the difference between a sandstone and a quartzite? Are both quartzose? Are both silicious? Have you any granular quartzites? Separate them from the others. What kind of quartzites are the others? What is the most compact variety of quartzose rocks? Show me a jaspery quartzite if you have it. Show me a quartzite with dark flints in it. Have you noticed any mica-scales in any quartzite? What other minerals have you seen in any of your quartzites? Is there any feldspar or hornblende? Have you seen any quartzite with black straight crystals running through it; and are they hornblende? Are the sides curved and unevenly striated? If so, they may be *Tourmaline*. Have you found any pure quartz running through a rock which was not all quartz? If so, there was a *vein* of quartz. Have you found any calcite in contact with quartz? Was it in a quartzite? Do you discover any talc scales in any quartzite? What is the difference between a granular quartzite and a gritty sandstone? What sort of rock is a whetstone? What is an oil stone? What is a ,hone? Is there anything peculiar about a scythe stone? Examine a piece of sandstone with your magnifier and see if you can clearly perceive the grains of quartz. Is the quartz clear or colored? Do you see anything except grains of quartz? What seems to hold the grains together? What is the color of the other material? Put a drop of your acid on the sandstone; does the rock effervesce? If not, what do you conclude the other material to be? If it does, what is indicated? Would carbonate of lime hold the quartz grains together? Now try and make a sandstone yourself. Put some loose, clean, fine sand in a small box and pour some lime water on it, allowing it to leach through slowly. Then, after an hour or two, pour on a little more. Repeat this a number of times, and then allow the sand to dry, and see if the grains are cemented together. Try this experiment at home and report success when we meet for next excursion. Bring your sandstones with you.

EXCURSION XI.—*Among the Boulders.*

Micaceous Rocks.

We stick to the boulders, and I will tell you why. It is because boulders are found almost everywhere, so that a person in any part of our northern states can easily find specimens of rocks. Another reason equally good is that these boulders are of so many different kinds that almost everywhere may be had all the principal sorts of rocks. In many places rocks which are not boulders may be found, and we will examine them by and by; but not at present, because most students do not live near quarries and ledges of rocks. Besides that, we can only find one sort of rock at a quarry or a ledge, generally speaking, while the boulders in one field will furnish ten or twenty sorts of rocks.

Well, how did you succeed with your experiment? Did you make any sandstone? Now, that is one way in which nature sticks together grains and crystals to make rocks. But take this rock with mica-scales in it and apply acid. It does not effervesce; so there is no calcium carbonate in it. But the parts are well stuck together; how is it done? Examine with the lens; do you see any kind of cement? There is nothing of this kind visible—and yet how firm the rock is. We must keep this question in mind, as we continue our studies.

You see mica in this rock; what other minerals do you find? You say quartz, certainly; that is right. Mica and quartz have great fondness for each other, and are very generally found in company. But they have a mutual friend, feldspar, which seems to be equally intimate with both mica and quartz. Ah, you say feldspar is here too? Very likely, as I said. Well, now tell all about the appearance of this feldspar. How do you know it is not calcite? How do you know it is not another variety of quartz? Are you quite sure we have in this rock the three minerals, quartz, feldspar and mica? Is there no other mineral present? Only a very little of something, you say, in one corner of the specimen. Well, no matter for that. But are these three minerals evenly distributed through the specimen, or is the mica more abundant in certain streaks across the rock? Oh, you say the mica is arranged in streaks. Yes, the quartz, too, is not quite evenly distributed. This, then, is a *stratified* rock. Let us lay it aside, and take another specimen *not stratified*. There, this is entirely unstratified. But look closely and be sure that it contains quartz, feldspar and mica. Does it? And is there no other mineral somewhat plentiful in it? Well, this rock is what we call *granite*. Now think this over and state what a granite is. Granite is a most important rock. You have accomplished much when you can be sure whether any rock is a granite or not. Many other rocks are called granite by quarrymen and stone cutters; but you must judge for yourself.

Take notice. It makes no difference whether the granite is coarse or fine; it is still granite. A fine granite may be better for building purposes than a very coarse one. Sometimes quartz, feldspar and mica are thrown together in so coarse a state that the granite is worth nothing as a building stone. A granite with large crystals of feldspar scattered through it, is called a *porphyritic granite*.

FIG. 10.—PORPHYRITIC ROCK. Granite from Land's End, England. (Lyell.)

Any rock with such feldspar crystals is called *porphyritic*.

Take notice again. It makes no difference what is the color of the quartz, or what is the color of the feldspar, or what is the color of the mica. Well, how many possible variations there must be in the appearance of granites! In

some, the reddish spots are quartz; in others, the reddish
spots are feldspar. Sometimes, also, there are two kinds of
quartz. Sometimes there are two kinds of feldspar. Sometimes there are two kinds of mica. A good way for us is to
go to a stone cutter's and examine different sorts of granites.

Take notice the third time. Some granites contain but
little mica, and then the rock may be very light-colored.
But, if either the quartz or feldspar is reddish, the rock will
be variegated whitish and reddish. In some granites, on
the contrary, the mica is exceedingly abundant. If the mica
is black it gives a dark complexion to the rock. So the
number of varieties of granite is almost endless. In some
cases there is almost no mica, and the rock is then a *Granulite.* If mica and quartz are both wanting, or nearly so,
the rock is a *Felsite.* In some felsites, quartz is intimately
combined with feldspar. This forms a *Petrosilex* if the
feldspar is orthoclase, and a proper Felsite if the feldspar
is a plagioclase. Granite blocks are often used for street
paving.

You remember that all the granites are unstratified. We
had at first a rock with the constituents of granite, but we
found it stratified, and laid it aside. Here it is. Such a
rock we call *Gneiss* (pronounced Gn-ice, not Gne-iss). Of
course now, there may be just as many varieties of gneiss as
of granite. Some varieties are so little stratified that one
would take them for granites unless we had large samples
to examine. Such gneisses always pass for granites among
stone-cutters. Many of them are quite as valuable as granites for building purposes.

But here is a micaceous rock which is very distinctly stratified. See how abundant is the mica. It is arranged in courses of varying thickness, and between the courses is — what? Well, it is mostly quartz in grains. In one specimen it is wholly quartz; in another we can detect a little feldspar. Now, such a rock we call *Mica Schist* (pronounced *Shist*). A *schist* is any rock composed of beds or layers of crystalline minerals. There are many sorts of schists, as we shall see. Perhaps if we look around, we shall discover a mica schist with *garnets* in it. Every one knows garnets. We will keep this question in mind. If the mica is soft and lustreless we have a *Hydromica Schist*. We shall certainly meet with such. Mica schists are much used for sidewalks.

Occasionally we find an unstratified, granite-like rock consisting of quartz and mica. This is called *Greisen* (pronounced *Gri-sen*). But a little mica in a common quartzite would make a micaceous quartzite.

We must not forget about these important rocks.

EXERCISES.

Give the names of the micaceous rocks. Which ones are stratified? Which ·is most distinctly stratified? Suppose a fragment of rock is handed you and you find it unstratified and containing quartz, feldspar and mica, what is its name? But then suppose another fragment from the same boulder or ledge is stratified; what is the name of that fragment? Then would you say one part of a boulder or ledge is granite and another part of the same is gneiss? Just exercise your best judgment in giving the answer, for many questions cannot be answered positively. Suppose the part of a ledge which seems to be gneiss ten rods away from the part which seems to be granite, must we call it all granite or all gneiss? Suppose you find a granite boulder or a ledge with a vein of quartz running through it, does that make the ledge or boulder gneiss? Suppose a vein of feldspar runs through it, what kind of rock forms the ledge? Suppose a vein is composed of quartz and feldspar intermixed, what kind of rock is the vein? Does that prevent the ledge from being granite? Well, suppose the vein is of quartz, feldspar and mica, what kind of rock is the vein? Does that make the ledge stratified? May we have two sorts of granite in one ledge or boulder? Please find a granite in which the feldspar is glassy. Can you find one with a dusky feldspar? Have you found a porphyritic granite? Suppose we could remove the mica from a granite, what would the rock become? Suppose we find a granulite stratified, what should we call it? Suppose we could remove the feldspar from a granite, what would the rock become? Did you ever see such a rock? Did you ever see a rock composed of mica alone? Did you ever see a rock composed of feldspar alone? Ask your father or some other person to tell you the composition of granite. Ask some one to tell you the difference between granite and gneiss. If any person asks you such questions, do not fail to answer them satisfactorily.

Now let us hear about your success in making a sandstone. Show the sandstones made. Is such a sandstone different from old mortar? Now explain how it is that mortar becomes so hard. What would be the effect if much dirt were mixed with the sand used?

EXCURSION XII.— *With the Stone Cutter.*

Hornblendic Rocks.

For the sake of varying our excursions a little we will visit the stone cutter's yard, where many varieties of rocks may be found, such as are used for building and for cemetery monuments. In some parts of the West, churches and residences are constructed of rough-dressed boulders. The boulders are hauled from the neighboring fields and ravines, and workmen, with heavy sledge hammers, break them into suitable shapes for putting into the walls of a building. Cart loads of freshly broken chips are made, and the varieties of rocks which may be picked up are almost endless in number. If all that carting and hammering had been done expressly for the geologist, it could not have been better done. Such a place is even better than a stone cutter's yard; and we will visit it afterward.

Here at the stone cutter's. You see rocks white, clouded, reddish, red-mottled and red-specked, gray, black and white variegated, black and red variegated, and other sorts. Now, to-day we wish to study *hornblendic rocks*. We must look for rocks containing hornblende. What is the prevailing color of hornblende? Well, pick out your hornblendic rock. Here it is; what other minerals do you find in it? Quartz and feldspar, you say. That is a very common sort of mixture. Here you have the same two minerals in company which you found in granite. But the mutual friend is not mica. It is hornblende in this case. Such a mixture is not granite, whatever the stone cutter may tell you. It is *Syenite*. Bear that name in mind. It is the same kind of rock as the ancient Egyptians quarried at Syene, in Egypt, and the geologists thought it would be pleasant to name the rock from the place. But it is wonderful that the Syene rock should be found in all parts of the world.

Notice how much syenite resembles granite. Even some scientific writers include it in granite. We may also have numerous varieties corresponding to the varieties of granite. Often the feldspar is reddish, and then we have the so-called "Scotch granite." Some of these syenites are fine, some are coarser. Some have a dark complexion and some a light one. Most of the so-called granites from Maine to Massachusetts are syenite. The Quincy granite, which is sent to New York and the southern states and the West Indies, is a syenite. The custom house and other buildings in Wall street, New York, are of syenite. The capitol at Albany is chiefly syenite. There is a large amount of syenite in the Upper Peninsula of Michigan ; also in northern Wisconsin and Minnesota. Syenite is even more durable than granite. Syenite and granite are both found in enormous ledges and mountain masses along the eastern flanks of the Alleghanies to North Carolina. In Ohio you will only find syenite and granite in the form of boulders. The same is true of the Lower Peninsula of Michigan, of Indiana and Illinois.

It often happens that some mica is present in syenite, and then we have a *micaceous syenite.* If the mica is nearly as abundant as the hornblende we have a syenitic granite. If the mica is much more abundant than the hornblende, the rock is a granite, but it is *hornblendic.* Let us look around and find some of these species of rocks in the stone yard.

We shall have to go back to our boulders, after all, to get all the sorts of hornblendic rocks. Now here is a syenite-looking rock, but it contains almost no quartz ; what shall we call it? Well, if the feldspar is common feldspar, the rock is *Hyposyenite*—which some say is the only proper syenite. Is the feldspar reddish or creamy? Then it is common feldspar or orthoclase. But is the feldspar pure white? Then it is probably albite. Now, hornblende and albite form a rock called *Diorite*. This is a handsome rock, with its white and black or greenish colors. Sometimes diorite is coarse enough to enable us to study the minerals ; but sometimes it is very fine. If any other light-colored feldspar not orthoclase is mixed with hornblende, we call the rock diorite also. Diorite is a very tough rock, and makes a building stone of the first class. Diorites are very common about Lake Superior. Also among the boulders of all the northern states.

If the dark mineral in a diorite-looking rock is not hornblende, but augite, then the rock is *Diabase*. So diabase is a rock composed of augite and a feldspar not of the orthoclase group — that is augite and a *plagioclase*. Some maintain recently that most of our northwestern rocks heretofore called diorites are in reality diabases. But this is not certain.

All these hornblendic rocks are unstratified ; but, as with the micaceous rocks, we have many gneissic forms. Syenite stratified is *syenitic gneiss*. Diorite stratified is *dioritic gneiss*. Diabase stratified is *diabasic gneiss*. If the feldspar in a syenite is supposed diminished and the hornblende increased, and the rock is distinctly stratified, we get a *hornblende schist*. This corresponds to mica schist. If the quartz is supposed removed from a hornblende schist, little besides hornblende remains, and we have *hornblende rock*. This is a black rock, and by no means uncommon. It is, however, schistose, and has some lustre. Many black and lustreless rocks, not showing distinct crystals, contain other minerals besides hornblende. They are then simply hornblendic. Sometimes a dark feldspar (Labradorite) is abundant in such rocks. But we must not undertake to study this group of rocks at present. We will confine ourselves to rocks in which the crystals are visible to the naked eye, or, at least, with a magnifier. Such rocks are called *phanerocrystalline;* and those in which you cannot distinguish separate crystals are called *cryptocrystalline.* These are pretty long words, but they are no stranger than you can find by the dozen in any fashion book.

Take notice. In both the micaceous and the hornblendic series of rocks, we have mixtures of minerals which may be unstratified, or may be obscurely stratified, or may be very distinctly stratified. Now let us call the first kind *massive,* the second *gneissoid,* and the third *schistose.*

Just as we have micaceous and hornblendic rocks, so we may have a series of *talcose* rocks. Quartz, feldspar and talc, when massive, give us *Protogine;* when gneissoid, *protogine gneiss;* when schistose, *talcose schist,* since, in the latter case, very little feldspar is ever found. When a schist consists almost wholly of talc, it is a *talc rock;* and if the talc is pulverized and closely packed, the rock is *steatite.*

EXERCISES.

Now let us review again. Sit down by your collection of rocks and pick out all the hornblendic specimens. Next sort out those which are true syenites. Lay aside the hyposyenite. Pick out the diorites. Arrange the syenites according to their coarseness. Now arrange all the massive hornblendic rocks according to the amount of quartz in them. Next arrange the gneissoid and schistose rocks of the hornblendic series according to the amount of quartz in them. Suppose the hornblende in all these schistose rocks should change to mica, what would their several names become? Suppose it should change to talc, what would the names become? Take a specimen of syenite in hand and suppose the hornblende to change to mica, what does the rock become? Suppose the hornblende to change to feldspar, what is the name of the rock? But if you hold syenite and the quartz changes to feldspar, what is the rock? If the quartz changes to hornblende, what is the rock? Now, if you take hyposyenite, what kind of feldspar is in it? If the orthoclase changes to albite, what does the rock become? What, if it changes to oligoclase? If you take hyposyenite and add mica, what might we call the rock? If we add talc instead, then what? What sort of rock is the glistening scythe stone? Which is the toughest rock, diorite or granulite? Look on the weathered surface of a granitic or a syenitic boulder, and state what mineral projects most. Which has changed its color most? Which weathers most rapidly, hornblende or feldspar? What change in lustre does feldspar undergo in weathering?

You must be very particular to see for yourselves all the things about which these questions are asked. When you go home tell your people what hyposyenite is, and ask them to explain diorite.

REVIEW.

Here is a table to assist the memory and to aid in review. The minerals studied are placed at the top of the columns. At the side also are placed the minerals, as well as the names of rocks formed of two minerals; as also syenite. Then the names of rocks formed by uniting minerals and rocks named at side and top are found in the spaces where the vertical and horizontal columns intersect. Rocks whose names are printed in small capitals are massive ; those whose names are in ordinary letters are gneiss-

TABLE SHOWING THE MINERAL COMPOSITION OF COMMON ROCKS.

	Quartz.	Orthoclase.	Albite.	Oligoclase.	Mica.	Hornblende.	Talc.
Quartz.	QUARTZITE. *Quartz Schist.* *Siliceous Schist.* *Sandstone.*	*	*	*	*	*	*
Orthoclase.	GRANULITE. Granulitic Gneiss. *Granulitic Schist.*						
Albite.	ALBITIC GRANULITE. *Granulitic Schist.*						
Oligoclase.	OLIGOCLASIC GRANULITE. *Granulitic Schist.*						
Mica.	GREISEN. [ite. Micaceous Quartz- *Mica Schist,* [stone. *Micaceous Sand-*						
Hornblende.	Hornblendic Quartzite. *Hornblende Schist.*	HYPOSYENITE. Hyposyenitic Gneiss.	DIORITE. Dioritic Gneiss. *Dioritic Schist.*	DIORITE. Dioritic Gneiss. *Dioritic Schist.*		AMPHIBOLITE. *Hornblende Rock.*	
Augite.	Augitic Schist.	AUGITE HYPOSY-NITE.	HYPOSY-DIABASE. *Diabase Schist.*	DIABASE. *Diabase Schist.*			
Talc.	Talcose Quartzite. *Talcose Schist.*						STEATITE. *Talc Schist.*
Granulite.		GRANITE. Gneiss. *Mica Schist.*			GRANITE. Gneiss. *Mica Schist.*		PROTOGINE. Protogine Gneiss. *Talcose Schist.*
Gneissen.		GRANITE. Gneiss. *Mica Schist.*	ALBITIC GRANITE. Albitic Gneiss. *Mica Schist.*	GRANITE. Gneiss. *Mica Schist.*		SYENITE. Syenitic Gneiss. *Hornblende Schist.*	
Hypostenite.					MICACEOUS HYPO-SYENITE.		TALCOSE HYPOSY-ENITE.
Diorite.		ALBITIC SYENITE. Syenitic Gneiss. *Dioritic Schist.*					
Syenite.			ALBITIC SYENITE. Syenitic Gneiss. *Hornblende Schist.*		MICACEOUS SYENITE. Hornblendic Gneiss *Micaceous Horn-blende Schist.*		TALCOSE SYENITE.

oid, and those whose names are in italics are schistose. Some of the unfilled spaces might receive the names of rocks not mentioned ; but it is best not to be troubled with rare rocks. Also the spaces at the upper right hand, containing stars, might be filled with the same names as are in other parts of the table. The pupil may exercise himself in doing it.

EXCURSION XIII.—*To the Marble Yard.*

Calcareous Rocks.

You must have noticed that none of the rocks which we have studied thus far contain any calcite. It might be that calcite crystals should occur sparingly in some of these rocks, but they are not essential. If they should so occur we might describe the rock as *calciferous*. But when a rock is composed chiefly of calcite we call it *calcareous*. There are many such rocks.

Here we are in the marble yard. Nearly all marbles are calcareous. The stone cutter has many varieties of marbles. Pick up some of these marble chips and test them for hardness. They are all rather soft. Test some of them with acid. They all effervesce. If you find a rock having the hardness of marble, which does not effervesce, it is probably formed of dolomite instead of calcite—or at least, in part of dolomite. Pulverize a bit, put the powder in a test tube, pour in a little dilute acid and heat the tube. Now you perceive effervescence. Yes, this is also a carbonate, and the acid with heat (if not without) drives off the gaseous carbonic acid.

You will notice that some of these marbles are coarse.

If you look closely you will perceive plenty of crystalline faces. It looks as if a quantity of calcite crystals had been broken and compacted together. The so-called Potomac marble is of this kind. It has been used in building the Washington monument. It is too coarse for fine work. Here is a granular marble, white like loaf sugar, and having the texture of loaf sugar. Such marbles are called *saccharoidal.* Here, next, is a finer marble. It only differs from the last in fineness. The finest marbles may be used for making statues. For this reason they are called *statuary marbles.*

Some marbles are colored in various ways, and thus we get almost countless varieties of them. Many Vermont marbles are clouded and veined with a darker color than the ground color. The ground color itself is sometimes far from white, inclining to a bluish or clay color. Some marbles are reddish. The red color is either uniform or distributed in blotches, clouds or veins. There are some varieties with much dark matter as a ground color, or forming veins. Egyptian marble, so called, is almost black, with occasional veins of a lighter color. All the colorings of marbles are produced by impurities. Reddish colors are often caused by iron oxide closely combined with the calcite. Blackish colors are commonly due to carbon or bitumen disseminated through the rock. Bluish veinings and ground colors seem to be caused by *argillaceous* (clayey) materials.

Some fine varieties of marble are produced by the combination of distinct bodies. One of the Tennessee marbles is a conglomerate or pudding stone. This is a favorite marble for pillars of public buildings. Sometimes a compact, calcareous rock has numerous forms of corals, shells and other things distributed through it, and if it takes a fine polish, it forms what is called shell marble.

Light-colored and clouded marbles of various kinds are quarried at various localities from northern New England to Maryland. Western Vermont, Massachusetts and Connecticut, and also eastern New York, abound in marble ledges. Black marble is quarried at Shoreham, Vt., and also near Lake Champlain. Verd-antique marble occurs at Milford, Ct., and also in Essex county, N. Y. This is common marble clouded green with serpentine. Shell marbles are found in Onondaga and Madison counties, N. Y. White saccharoidal marbles, sometimes fine enough for statuary, are found extensively in the regions south of Lake Superior. All over New England and the northwestern states may be found boulders of marble.

We are still in the marble yard. You notice that the fine cemetery marbles are supported by bases of some sort of rock not marble. This is probably a calcareous rock. Try your acid on it. Does it effervesce? Well, it is a limestone not crystalline enough to take a fine polish. Still, it is composed mostly of calcite. You see it is distinctly stratified; the marbles are not so. There are many varieties of limestone; but there are three characters by which you may distinguish them from most other rocks. 1. They effervesce with acids. 2. They are easily scratched. 3. They are not composed of worn or rounded grains. There is a variety made up largely of uniform spherical pellets stuck together by a fine cement, or sometimes imbedded in it, but these are not grains rounded by wearing. It is called *oölitic limestone.* Limestones may contain various impurities—silica, clay, sand, iron, coal, bitumen, petroleum and still other substances. So we describe the limestone as *silicious, argillaceous, arenaceous, ferruginous, carbonaceous, bituminous* or *petroliferous.*

What is chalk? That we found to be capable of effervescing. It is simply a soft limestone. There are all grades of limestones in point of hardness, between marbles and chalk. The carbonate of lime precipitated in the bottom of a little lake is *marl.* It is often mixed with clay or peat. We can frequently find marl beneath the peat of a common swamp. The carbonate of lime precipitated from flowing spring water is *travertin* and *calcareous tufa,* as before explained. That which forms in the shape of icicles hanging from the roofs of caves is *stalactite.* When the same water falls on the floor of a cave and makes a deposit, we call it *stalagmite.* This is exactly like travertin.

When limestone is burned, the carbonic-acid gas is driven off and only *lime* remains. If lime is left exposed to the air, especially if damp or wet, it takes carbonic acid again from the air and water, and is reconverted into carbonate of lime.

EXERCISES.

Did you ever notice the crust formed around stones in the bottom of a brook? What is it? Where does it come from? How may stones or grains of sand become cemented together? What is the stone base of your oil lamp? Why is marble used instead of quartzite? How many sorts of marbles have you collected? Arrange them in order according to their coarseness. How many sorts of limestones have you? Arrange them according to their hardness. How does chalk differ from marble? What is the difference between stalactite and stalagmite? Does a stalactite increase internally or externally? Does other limestone grow? Which is most compact, marble or quartzite? What causes the surfaces of marbles long exposed to the weather to turn black? Can limestone be dissolved in water? What other rocks or minerals thus far studied can also be dissolved? Do the rains dissolve limestones? What effect have limestones on the soil? Are limestone soils desirable for farming purposes? Are sandy soils equally desirable? Why not? Have you ever seen a black marble or limestone? What causes rusty stains on the surfaces of some white marbles? Which are best stratified, marbles or common limestones? Suppose you find a limestone with fine sand distributed through it, what is the name of the rock? What is the taste of lime? Is lime soluble or insoluble? When limewater is exposed to the air, what causes the film which forms on the surface? How does this differ from limestone? Were limestones formed in this way? Take an oyster shell and test it with acid; does it effervesce? Now burn the shell and see if it becomes lime. Of course you will postpone this until you have a convenient fire. But suppose the shell burned, you will see that it has the acrid taste of lime. Could mortar be made of it? Take any other shell and test it in the same way. Suppose a common river clam shell (properly called *Unio*) should lie in the water until the shell disintegrates, what would the powder be? Suppose thousands of shells should disintegrate in the same way, what would be found on the bottom of the pond? Is this the way marl is made? Suppose calcareous spring water should flow into the pond, would anything be precipitated? What? How would this differ from marl? Now which way does marl originate? Which would you think most durable for building purposes, marble or granite? What causes the parallel lines in a piece of polished stalagmite? **Have** you found any fragments of a brown or blackish limestone? If so, rub it smartly with another stone and see whether any odor is emitted? What variety of limestone is this? Have you found limestones with hard flinty patches forming what is called *cherty* limestone?

EXCURSION XIV.— *To the Clay Pit and the Field.*

Argillaceous Rocks.

Let us begin to-day with this broken slate. It has been used in school for writing on, and is called *graphic slate.* Do you see any indications of quartz or calcite in it? How many sorts of minerals does it seem to be composed of? All one kind, you say. Try it with your magnifier. Can you see any crystals or grains? Not at all. It is *very* different from the granites and schists. Try your acid on it. No effervescence; it is not a carbonate. Let us put a fragment in a mortar and reduce it to fine powder. There, that is done. Now moisten the powder a little, and what does your slate look like? Like mud, you say. So it is mud.

Were you ever in a brick yard, or in a clay pit where material is obtained and ground up for bricks? Well, does the clay make you think of your pulverized slate? They are in fact both the same. The brick clay probably has some very fine silicious sand disseminated through it. You might dissolve the clay in water and allow the fine sand to settle to the bottom, as it did in the case of the garden soil. The remainder would be almost exactly like this pulverized slate. I must tell you what is the mineral in these sub-

stances which gives them their character; it is *alumina*.
But this is rather a chemical substance than a mineral. But
the *aluminous* substances are not formed of any distinct
minerals, as quartzite and marble are. The alumina enters
directly into the formation of rocks.

Did you ever notice in the coal bin an occasional flat
piece of stone called "slate"? You can almost always find
some "slate" among the coal. Here is a piece; try it with
your steel. Do you find it as hard as the graphic slate? It
is softer, you say. Well, pulverize a piece, and see whether
it makes a similar kind of mud. It does. Now, is there
no way to distinguish this from the graphic slate? It is
rough, but that is only because it is in a state of nature. It
is softer, you say. But there is no other difference. It is
an aluminous rock, but is softer than real slate. We call
such a rock *shale*.

If we stroll among the boulders again, we shall see some
blackish, fine-grained rocks which we never yet ventured to
take in hand. Do they seem to be hornblende rocks? No,
they have not sufficient lustre. Are they black marble?
No, they are too hard. It is difficult to scratch them.
Notice the fine, even lines of stratification; do they resemble a hornblende rock or hornblende schist? Not at all;
this is a kind of rock not yet studied by us. I must tell you
the name. It is *argillite*. It is composed of alumina and
silica closely mixed. It is true that hornblende is also
present with some argillites, and so are minute scales of
mica. It is also true that some very fine hornblendic rocks
resemble this. But the argillite is the rock with which we

are concerned. Examine it carefully. This is also an aluminous rock.

Thus we have a series of aluminous rocks ranging from argillite, which is almost flinty, to clay, which can be moulded in the hand. The purest sort of clay is *Kaolin*. It is nearly white, and we often find it in association with quartz and mica, in such a situation as to show that Kaolin is simply decomposed feldspar. The alkali has been dissolved out of the feldspar, and some of the silica has disappeared. What remains is nearly pure alumina and water. So we see how the decomposition of granite or other rocks containing feldspar has given origin to the vast beds of impure blue clay used for bricks, pottery, tiles and other purposes. The pure Kaolin is used for porcelain. Even feldspar is often ground up for the same purposes. The alkali in it gives the ware a translucent, glassy character.

EXERCISES.

Suppose, in the decomposition of feldspar, the alkali is not all removed, and the clay resulting is burned, what will be the appearance of the bricks? What causes the red color of common bricks? Why are some bricks *not* red? What is the peculiarity of Milwaukee bricks? Can you name another locality which affords light-colored bricks? Why is porcelain whiter than common bricks? What is the cause of the translucency of China ware? Did you ever observe statuettes of *biscuit*, or unglazed porcelain, to be called "Parian marble"? Are they of any kind of marble? Do the sellers seem to think they are real marble? How do they differ from marble? What is the difference between graphic slate and roofing slate? What are slate pencils made of? Are slates and pencils ever made of any other than an aluminous rock? What sort of slate pencils could be made of steatite? What is the "French chalk" used by tailors? Do all clays belong to the Drift? What are the colors of the slates which you have seen? How are letters and designs sometimes represented upon slated roofs? Of what are the tiles made which are used on floors and about fireplaces? What use do sculptors and modellers make of clay? When did mankind begin to use clay for pottery? Why are not silicious argillites employed for roofing? How does argillite differ from Egyptian marble?

REVIEW.

Now let us recall some of our lessons. We have had a series of silicious rocks and a series of calcareous rocks, and here is a series of aluminous rocks. Each series begins with rocks which are hard and not well stratified, and ends with rocks which are incoherent or soft. It will aid our memory to get these arranged in order in a table. Here is such a table:

TABLE OF ARRANGEMENT OF FRAGMENTAL ROCKS.

Groups of Rocks.	Crystalline.	Indurated.	Semi-Indurated.	Incoherent.
Silicious Rocks.	Quartzite — Vitreous. Granular. Conglomeritic.	Sandstone — Compact. Conglomerate.	Sandstone — Friable.	Sand.
Aluminous Rocks.	Argillite.	Slate.	Shale.	Kaolin. Clay.
Calcareous Rocks.	Marble — Conglomeritic. Saccharoidal. Statuary.	Limestone — Compact. Travertin. Calcareous Tufa.	Limestone — Soft. Chalk.	Marl.

This is a table of rocks which do not occur very extensively as boulders. Leaving out the "crystalline" "silicious rocks," those which remain are not sufficiently hard to endure the usage to which boulders have been subjected. Yet, leaving boulders out of the account, the most abundant bed rocks throughout the country are those designated above as "indurated" and "semi-indurated." That is, outside of New England and a region

along the eastern flanks of the Alleghanies, the common bed
rocks of the country are of the indurated and semi-indurated
sorts, until we are north of Albany, Lake Huron and Minneapolis.   But the boulder-forming rocks furnish us with a much
greater number of varieties than these fragmental rocks.   It is
in the fragmental rocks that we find fossil shells and corals.
These things are of intense interest for study, but we cannot take
them up until we reach a more advanced course.

Very often we find silicious matter mixed with aluminous and
calcareous rocks; also aluminous matter mixed with silicious and
calcareous rocks; also calcareous matter mixed with silicious and
aluminous rocks.   Then we have to prefix the qualifying word
"silicious," "aluminous" or "calcareous" to the proper name of
the rock.   So we may have *silicious* slates or limestones; *aluminous* sandstones or limestones, and *calcareous* sandstones or
shales.   Further, if iron oxide imparts its reddish or yellowish
color to any of these rocks they are also *ferruginous*.   In the
same way any of these rocks may be *bituminous, carbonaceous,
micaceous* or *petroliferous*.

EXCURSION XV.—*To the Specimen Drawers.*

Exercises in Identifications.

We may arrange an analytical table to enable us to
determine the commoner rocks.   This will also present the
subject in another light.   There is nothing in the table
which has not been included in the previous lessons.   It is
only requisite that the pupil should be able to identify the
principal minerals, and understand the terms which have
been already explained.

Now, let us take any specimen at random, and see if we
can ascertain its name by the use of this table.   Then we
will try other specimens.

ANALYTICAL TABLE FOR THE DETERMINATION OF THE COMMONEST ROCKS.

A. Crystalline, some of the constituent minerals having shining, lustrous surfaces, or fine, compact, and hard.

   I. Phanerocrystalline, consisting of minerals distinguishable with naked eye or pocket lens.

      1. No effervescence with acids.

        (1) Quartz present and no other mineral,   *Quartzite.*

        (2) Feldspar alone with quartz.

           (a) Structure massive,   *Granulite.*

           (b) Structure schistose,   *Granulitic Schist.*

        (3) Mica present in thin, glistening, elastic scales.

           (a) Quartz present, and no third mineral.

               (aa) Structure thick-bedded,   *Micaceous Quartzite.*

               (bb) Structure thin-bedded,   *Mica Schist.*

           (b) Quartz and feldspar present with the mica.

               (aa) Structure massive,   *Granite.*

               (bb) Structure thick-bedded   *Gneiss.*

               (cc) Structure thin-bedded, little feldspar,   *Mica Schist.*

        (4) Hydromica present in thin, lustreless, inelastic scales.

           (a) Quartz present, and no third mineral.

               (aa) Structure thick-bedded,   *Hydromica Quartzite.*

               (bb) Structure thin-bedded,   *Hydromica Schist.*

           (b) Quartz and feldspar present with the hydromica.

               (aa) Structure massive,   *Hydromica Granite.*

               (bb) Structure thick-bedded,   *Hydromica Gneiss.*

               (cc) Structure thin-bedded,   *Hydromica Schist.*

        (5) Hornblende-present.

           (a) No mineral but hornblende,   *Hornblende Rock.*

           (b) Quartz present and no third mineral.

               (aa) Structure thick-bedded,   *Hornblendic Quartzite.*

               (bb) Structure thin-bedded,   *Hornblende Schist.*

           (c) Quartz and feldspar, with hornblende.

               (aa) Structure massive,   *Syenite.*

               (bb) Structure thick-bedded,   *Syenitic Gneiss.*

               (cc) Structure thin-bedded, little feldspar,

                      Hornblende Schist.

           (d) Orthoclase only with the hornblende, structure massive,

                      Hyposyenite.

(e) Plagioclase only with the hornblende.

    (aa) Structure massive,   *Diorite.*

    (bb) Structure schistose,   *Diorite Schist.*

(6) Augite present.

    (a) No mineral but augite,   *Augite Rock.*

    (b) Quartz only, or chiefly, with augite,   *Augite Schist.*

    (c) Plagioclase only with augite.

        (aa) Structure massive,   *Diabase.*

        (bb) Structure schistose,   *Diabase Schist.*

    (d) Orthoclase only with augite,   *Augite Hyposyenite.*

(7) Talc present.

    (a) No mineral but talc,   { *Talc Rock.* / *Steatite.*

    (b) Talc alone with quartz.

        (aa) Structure thick-bedded,   *Talcose Quartzite.*

        (bb) Structure thin-bedded,   *Talcose Schist.*

    (c) Talc and orthoclase with quartz.

        (aa) Structure massive,   *Protogine.*

        (bb) Structure thick-bedded,   *Protogine Gneiss.*

        (cc) Structure thin-bedded,   *Protogine Schist.*

  2. Effervescence with acids,   *Marble.*

II. Cryptocrystalline, constituent minerals undistinguishable.

(Determinations uncertain by simple inspection.)

  1. Hardness equal to quartz, lustre glassy,   *Vitreous Quartzite.*

  2. Hardness a little less than quartz, lustre dull.

    (1) Color black [sometimes *Diorite* or *Diabase*, but frequently],   *Aphanite.*

    (2) Color very dark, structure generally banded, *Silicious Argillite.*

    (3) Color reddish, whitish, greenish, smoky, lustre horny, *Felsite.*

B. Uncrystalline (fragmental), distinctly stratified.

  I. Effervescence with acids, at least when heated.

    1. Rock hard, often containing fossils,   *Limestone.*

    2. Rock easily cut with a knife,   *Chalk.*

    3. Rock without much coherence,   *Marl.*

  II. No effervescence with acids, or only very little.

    1. No quartzose grains.

      (1) Rock can be cut with a knife,   *Slate.*

      (2) Rock very easily cut,   *Shale.*

    2. Quartzose grains present.

      (1) Grains cohering together,   *Sandstone.*

      (2) Materials uncemented,   *Sand.*

Do not think *all* rocks can be determined by this little table. If you try a specimen which can *not* be so determined, lay it aside until you have opportunity to take a more thorough course.

If you can use this table, and determine the more common rocks, you certainly have made an excellent start. You already know something about geology. Should you go no farther, you will have much satisfaction in understanding something about the most common rocks all over the northern United States.

EXCURSION XVI.—*By the Waterside.*
Sediments.

How often we have noticed a sediment in some standing liquid. This little observation is the key to the geological work which has made nearly all the rocks known to us. Let us go out and study some sediments recently made by geological action. We hardly step into the street without noticing some deposits left by the last shower. We walk along a country road and soon find a spot where the torrent of water has reached the level ground and laid down its load of sand and stones brought from the hill slope. See the method of assortment. First, the coarse stones were dropped as soon as the force of the water was slackened too much to bear them along. Then, after a little further slackening, smaller stones were dropped. Just beyond these we find small pebbles and sand; and the fine mud has accumulated in the hollow where the water stood. Why are there no pebbles at the bottom of the roadside puddle?

6

And why is there no mud at the foot of the hill where the cobble stones lie?

If we go down to the brook side in the meadow, we shall find a low, flat place which the stream overflows occasionally. A little examination will show that the soil here is simply a brook or river sediment. It is *alluvium*, formed from the deposit of the stream. There is drift material in it, composed of stems and chips and bits of lumber, besides leaves and grasses. There are also some whitened shells which once lived in the stream.

Let us go down by the pond. Do you notice the steep banks around one or two sides and the low, marshy margin on another side? See how the rushes and the cat tails rise from the shallow, stagnant water near the shore. See the sedges and grasses growing in the bog nearer the shore. These plants are killed by every winter's frosts, and the old stems fall down and go to decay almost exactly in the places where they grew. They decompose into a blackish sort of soil called *peat*. How thick a deposit of peat do you suppose might be accumulated in a man's lifetime? Would it not pretty nearly fill the pond, especially on the side where the vegetation grows so rankly? Now this query leads us to look a little farther back from the shore. Here is quite a broad, marshy belt (see Figure 20), and beyond is some meadow land. All this marsh and meadow land is as level as the pond or lake. Still beyond, the dry upland begins. Now it looks exactly as if the lakelet had once extended to the upland, and had become filled with peat as far as the level surface extends. Let us go and dig in the meadow

FIG. 20.— THE LAKELET SLOWLY FILLING.
FORMATION OF MARL AND PEAT.

and see if it is peat. Certainly it is. It is true, then, that
the lakelet is filling, and is made shorter every year on the
side where the vegetation grows so luxuriantly. But does
the filling and shortening take place only on one side? Let
us think a minute. Which way do the winds blow mostly?
Why, they blow from the side opposite the marsh. Then
all the leaves and twigs and grasses which get into the
water are blown over toward the marshy side. Certainly;
and when the lakelet first existed these drifted materials
were lodged at the foot of the slope on that side, and went
to decay and formed a sort of peaty material in the bottom
of the water. After some years the deposit became considerably extended. Meantime the plants which like to
grow in stagnant, shallow water made their appearance
there; and nothing else has been necessary but to let these
operations have time enough, and the whole breadth of the
peaty marsh would grow into existence just as we see it.
That is the explanation of the marsh and meadow on one
side of the lakelet. Of course, much dirt has washed down
the hill slopes on the other sides and has gone into the

lakelet. The coarser material has been left near the shore, and the finer has been floated into the deeper water. Some has floated over to the marsh side, and the fine aluminous mud has settled down and mingled with the growing peat.

Now, you ask if this pond or lakelet will not become completely filled by and by. Of course it will. There are plenty of lakelets which have been filled already. How do you suppose the place would look if the pond had been quite filled already? Why, that level meadow would extend all over it. There would be no more lakelet. There would be a level marsh. Well, don't you know any level marsh exactly such as you think this pond will become by and by? Of course, you know a good many of them. One is all overgrown with flags and rushes, and one is full of tamarac trees, and another has alder bushes growing all over it. If you ask your father or your uncle, or some other man who has lived here a good many years, he will tell you he remembers when the water stood in the place where that bog is. He may remember when the dam was built, and the mill pond formed — when the water first overflowed some of the land. He will tell you that the water at first was clear, but now you can see that the mill pond is half grown up with rushes, and is filling every year.

Now you are asking about that white substance which was dug from under the peat in a certain place. I will tell you about it. Come with me to the water. In most ponds and lakelets you may find some little shells — some *univalves* like snails, and some *bivalves* like clams. They form their shells from the calcium carbonate in the water; and the calcium carbonate comes from the limestone in the soil or rocks through which the water flows which fills the lakelet. This is not abundant in New England, but it is throughout the West. When the animal in the shell dies, the shell rests on the bottom and slowly decomposes. In time it forms over the bottom a bed of white, soft, calcareous matter called marl. So, as the peat bed extends, it forms above the bed of marl; and after the water is quite displaced by these accumulations, we find a bed of peat underlaid by a bed of marl. These marl beds are most abundant in the western states; but peat beds form wherever there are lakelets and vegetation. The bed of peat may be called a *stratum* of peat; and the bed of marl a stratum of marl. So you see what is the origin of these two *strata*.

In spring, after the heavy rains, the streams are full of sediment. Even a summer shower will muddy all the small streams. Where do these sediments go? The stream empties into another stream or into a lake, or into the ocean. But wherever the stream empties, the water gets finally into the sea, and some of the sediment is compelled to go with it. When the sediments reach the sea they may be tossed about for a time by the waves, but they must finally settle to the bottom. The water of the Mississippi River is full of mud at all times of the year. Immense quantities are brought down by the Missouri River. When you travel on a Mississippi River steamboat, they will fill your drinking glass with water from the muddy river. One accustomed to the clear water of the eastern and northern states can hardly endure such drinking water. Let a glass of it stand for thirty minutes and a frightful amount of mud settles to the bottom. Well, where does all this mud in the Mississippi go? Into the gulf of Mexico necessarily — except what settles upon the land at times of overflow. The sediment carried into the gulf is literally filling it up. Some of the finest floats a long time and settles to the bottom hundreds of miles from the mouth of the river. A larger amount is deposited at the mouth, where the current is neutralized by the gulf water. This deposit forms what is called the bar of the Mississippi, which so much obstructs navigation. It increases at such a rate that it advances 336 feet every year, The whole amount of sediment carried down by the Mississippi, if dried, would make every year a pile a mile square and 268 feet high. Much of the Mississippi sediment is spread over the region of the overflow, and is many feet deep. This deposit forms the *delta* of the Mississippi.

All streams emptying into the sea carry more or less sediment. So the sea bottom is becoming covered with layers of mud; and with the mud must be mingled the remains of all the animals which perish in the sea.

EXERCISES.

Mention some marsh with which you are acquainted. Is it quite level? What once existed in its place? Why is the lakelet not there still? What is the upper stratum of the marsh composed of? If you should find much earth or sand mixed with the peat, how would you explain that? If you should find white shells in the peat, how could that be explained? Is the peat chiefly organic or inorganic? Is peat of any use to the farmer? What is the use of marl? What is the composition of marl? Is the bar of a river composed chiefly of

fine or of coarse matter? How does the sediment far from a
river's mouth compare with that near the mouth? Can any
sediment get into the sea except that brought down by rivers?
Why is the border of the lake or the sea lined with pebbles and
cobble stones? When the waves wear away a gravel bank, what
becomes of the sand and clay? If you could dig through the
layers of sediment in the bottom of the pond, or in the bottom
of the Gulf of Mexico, would you find all exactly alike? Why
are some coarser than others? Why are they of different colors?
Has the Hudson River any delta? What might prevent a river
from having a delta? Mention some rivers having extensive
deltas. Why are some rivers clear and others turbid?

EXCURSION XVII.— *In the Gorge.*

Decay and Erosion of Rocks.

You saw how large an amount of sediment accumulates
in ponds and lakelets ; how much is carried down by rivers,
and how the sea is actually filling up through the processes
of sedimentation. Now, all this sediment comes from somewhere. Let us see if we can find the sources of it.

The muddy stream by the roadside — well, you are ready
to say at once that the mud comes from the street. Yes,
that accumulation of stones and sand which we examined at
the foot of, the slope is nothing but stuff washed down from
the roads. Just above is a deep, rugged gully washed out
by the rain. Look at it. Where has the stuff gone which
came out of that hole? Is it all at the foot of the hill? Is
there no more deposited there than was washed out here?
The wearing away of the ground we call *erosion.*

Now we have reached the ravine. This is on a hillside.

The hill may not be very steep, but it causes water to flow down. There is a little brook here which is always running. Look in the bed of the brook; why is it so stony? Has there been no soil there, nor sand? Here in the bank are sand and loam, and the only reason why such fine materials are not in the bed of the stream is that the water has washed them away. The sand and loam have gone down to the flat, and very likely we might find them there spread out just like the stuff brought down by the roadside torrent, which only worked one afternoon. But sometimes this stream is vastly larger than at present; then it moves the larger stones; and as these are taken away, others come from higher up. And when the water is high it washes these banks, and removes sand and stones, and in this way makes the ravine wider. Think of that; the stream widens this ravine every year. We can think of a time when the ravine was much narrower, and also shallower. We can think back to the time when the ravine first began to be formed. At present it is broad and deep; but it appears that it has all has been dug out by the water which has flowed down the

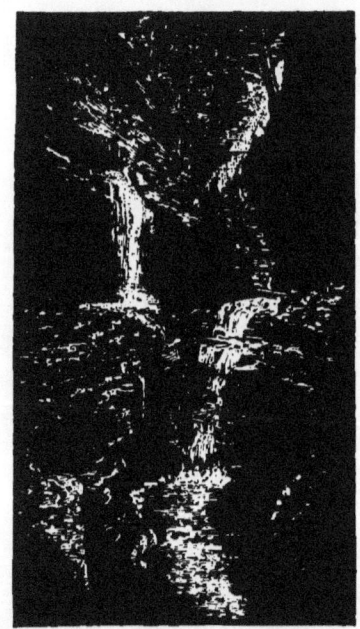

Fig. 21.—View in the Gorge at Watkins' Glen, N. Y. ("Rainbow Falls"), Illustrating Erosion by Water. (Photograph.)

hillside. If this hill had not so many stones and rocks in it, the ravine would have become much deeper than it is. In Alabama, where stones are fewer, or at least smaller, you can see deeper ravines excavated during one man's lifetime.

Unless, however, the rocks are of the crystalline and quartzose sorts commonly found in boulders, it seems to make little difference whether the sides of the ravine are rocky or mere incoherent drift. We could visit hundreds of localities where some little stream has cut deep through solid strata. At Watkins' Glen, in southern New York, is a very wild and interesting spot. Some of you will visit that spot. Fig. 21 is a picture which all can examine. Is it not strange that mere water could wear away the solid rocks on so vast

FIG. 22.— THE "DALLES" OF THE WISCONSIN, SHOWING RIVER EROSION. (PHOTOGRAPH.)

a scale? It is a fact, nevertheless, and all the material has gone somewhere. Let us look on the map and ascertain where. Here is Watkins in Schuyler county, at the head of Seneca Lake, and here is the tiny stream which has worn the gorge. The stuff has certainly gone into Seneca Lake, and lies spread over the bottom.

In Figure 22, is a similar example from quite another portion of the country. The Wisconsin River has cut its gorge through the ancient strata, forming a scene of beauty as well as of geological interest. A grand example of the

work of a mightier stream may be seen along the banks of the Upper Mississippi River in Wisconsin and Minnesota. Here a wide valley has been excavated through vast formations of sandstone and limestone, and the walls of rock rise on each side one or two hundred feet. Between them flows the broad Mississippi. (See Figure 23. Also Figure 51.) In the Far West is a river known as the Colorado which has worn a gorge in some places more than a mile in depth.

FIG. 23.—CLIFF ON THE UPPER MISSISSIPPI NEAR TREMPEALEAU, WIS., ILLUSTRATING RIVER EROSION, (CHAMBERLIN.)

But the rocks everywhere are wearing out. The very rain and dew tend to dissolve the cement which holds their parts together; and freezing and thawing are powerful agents in disintegrating them. You will recall what was said of kaolin as simply the result of decomposition of feldspar.   In the southern states, and in all warm countries, you may sometimes trace the encroachment of decay from the exposed surface of a bed rock downward ten or twenty feet.   All over the land the rocks are decaying, and the rains wash the powder and the grains into the streams ; and this is the source of much of the sediment which floats in the rivers and spreads over the sea bottom. It is calculated that the surface of the land is lowered a foot in six thousand years.   Of course some rocks decay faster than others. Sometimes rocks are undermined by the more rapid decay of the rocks beneath them.   Here is an interesting case in Wisconsin in the bluff of a creek.   In many cases cubic miles of rock have been eroded and removed from

FIG. 24.
MAGNESIAN LIMESTONE UNDER-
MINED BY THE DISINTEGRA-
TION OF A SANDSTONE BE-
NEATH. (CHAMBERLIN.)

the midst of the land.   All the central part of Tennessee is a vast basin sunk through the solid limestone.   All around the border the remaining limestone rises in massive walls a hundred feet high and more.   In east Tennessee is another valley formed by extensive erosion.   These are shown in the cut, Figure 25.   See, also, how the nearly vertical strata of the Unaka range have been worn down to mere stumps. Where have gone the continuations of those upturned strata ?

See the wonderful proof of vast erosions along the Appalachians. (Figure 26.) Here the actual surface is shown along A B C. Can you believe that the slight elevation at A represents truly one of the ranges of the Allegheny Mountains? And that B represents the range known as Bald Eagle Mountain? How the vast series of strata has been folded here. Notice the mountain mass represented by E, which once rose thirty-five thousand feet above the present surface, and all has been carried away by erosion. This section is in Centre county, and shows but a fraction of a full section across the Appalachian chain. But all the mountain elevations have been similarly worn down.

In other cases singular columns of the eroded rock have escaped erosion. They have been protected by a fragment of harder rock, which rests on them like a cap. In "Monument Park," Colorado, are many remarkable examples. (See Figure 27.)

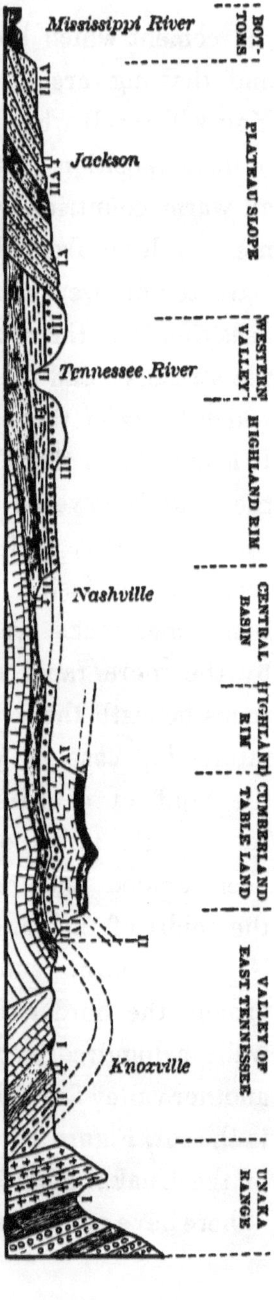

FIG. 25.—SECTION THROUGH TENNESSEE, SHOWING EROSION OF THE CENTRAL BASIN AND OF THE VALLEY OF EAST TENNESSEE. (SAFFORD.) I, Cambrian; II, Silurian; III, Devonian; IV, Lower Carboniferous; V, Upper Carboniferous; VI, Cretaceous; VII, Tertiary; VIII, Post-Tertiary (Quaternary).

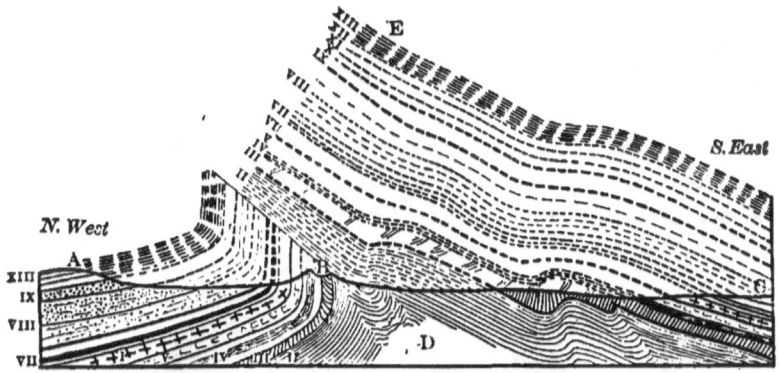

Fig. 26.—Illustrating Enormous Erosion in the Appalachian Region. A, Allegheny Mountain at Snow Shoe; B, Bald Eagle Mountain; A, B, C, present surface — all above swept away: D, probably a subterranean mountain of Eozoic rocks; II to III, Cambrian; IV to VI, Silurian; VII to IX, Devonian; X to XII, Lower Carboniferous; XIII, Coal Measures (after Lesley). Compare for explanations, Excursion XVIII.

So we learn there has been a vast destruction of the rocks during the course of many ages. They have been gradually reduced to gravel and mud, and carried off by the streams, to be laid down on the plains or spread as sediment over the bottom of the sea. Other interesting cases of erosion are shown in Figures 52, 53, 60, 61 and 73.

EXERCISES.

Can a quartzite be worn out by any means? If quartz pebbles are fragments of rocks, why are they not sharp angled? Which wears fastest, a quartzite or a limestone? If water flows through a fissure in a limestone, by what two means will the fissure be enlarged? If the fissure is underground, what will it become? Are many caverns produced in this way? Which make the steepest banks to a stream, hard rocks or soft ones? Why are not the walls of all gorges nearly perpendicular? Does weathering affect the angles of cliffs and rock fragments? What sort of climate would weather the rocks most rapidly? Would vertical cliffs be most likely to stand in a dry climate, or a changeable one? In a climate with freezing and thawing, or one with no freezing? What is the difference between erosion and weathering? Which kind of work is done by running streams? Which is done by waves? Which is done by frost? Is there any important difference between the wearing done by rains and that done by streams? Is it running water which has made the valleys in a country completely drift covered? Why have the

FIG. 27.—COLUMNS IN MONUMENT PARK, COLORADO. (HAYDEN.)

valleys such sloping banks? Has floating ice any influence on the work of running waters? Explain a possible origin of a natural bridge. Explain a possible origin of the Mammoth Cave of Kentucky. What effect has erosion on the farmer's soils? Does any of his soil go where no one can find it again? What effect has erosion on the height of the hills?

EXCURSION XVIII.—*At the Rocky Ledge.*

Strata and Systems of Strata.

You have seen the brooks and rivers at work wearing down the land. You have seen the waves corroding the beach. You have thought on the slow disintegration of all the surface rocks by rains and frosts, and have seen the waters carrying away the sediments to the sea. In thought you have followed those sediments in their distribution over the ocean's bottom. You have seen them lying and accumulating there, while dead shells and bits of coral and bones of fishes have been mingled with the growing deposit. What appearance must these sediments present in case a few acres of sea bottom could be taken out bodily and inspected? The sediments would consist of layers parallel with each other, one above another. These layers would be distinguished by different colors and by different degrees of fineness. Imbedded in the substance of the layers would be the relics of the animals which have lived in the sea. Is this a correct statement of what you would see? Think about it. The depth of the accumulated sediments would correspond to the time spent in their accumulation. You might look at them and reflect: "These layers of mud and sand were once far inland. They were once part of the soil of cornfields and gardens. Crops grew on them. The gully in the road was made by the removal of them. They came down the rivers. Some started on the slopes of distant mountains. The Missouri brought some from the gorges and summits of the Rocky Mountains.

Some came out of the deep, dim canyons of the Colorado. Some came from the storm-torn bluffs at Long Branch or Coney Island or Gay Head. Some was yielded by the slowly dissolving promontories of Nahant and Marblehead."

That is what you might think. Now suppose the layers of sediments pressed by thousands of tons of weight. They would be pressed into a solid state,— like the paper pulp which is manufactured into car-wheels. They would be a rock. The rock would be composed of *strata*. The thin layers would be called *laminæ*. The shells and corals pressed in the rock would be *fossils*. This is almost exactly what we have in the majority of the rocks underlying the country. All our limestones, sandstones and shales were once just such sea-sediments. The limestones, however, contain a very large proportion of matters contributed by the decay of shell-bearing animals.

In most of New England, however, and along the northern border of our country, the ledges of rocks which we find are hard and crystalline. From these have come most of the boulders which are scattered over the surface of all the northern states. In places where these crystalline rocks come in contact with the uncrystalline, we find the uncrystalline overlying the others. (See Figure 28.) But there are almost always some traces of stratification even in the

Fig. 28.—CRYSTALLINE AND UNCRYSTALLINE ROCKS. *a*, Granite; *b*, Gneiss; *c*, Sandstone.

crystalline rocks. You remember the gneisses and schists. Well, this is the way they lie over the granite and beneath the sandstones. They have been rendered less distinctly stratified by some action called *metamorphism*. What are the particulars of that action cannot now be explained; but you may understand that great pressure, great heat and chemical operations have had much to do with metamorphism. If, then, even the hard crystalline rocks were also once sea sediments, they must have been laid down before the sediments which formed the uncrystalline rocks. That is, *older rocks are below, and newer rocks are above.*

In the crystalline rocks it is a very extraordinary thing to find any fossils. In the uncrystalline rocks it is a common thing. So this is another particular in which they differ.

But now let me tell you something very important about the uncrystalline rocks. We do not find the same kinds of fossils in all of them. Those at the bottom contain many relics of very strange creatures, and they are all marine. There are none which lived on the land. There are none which had back-bones. That is, they were all *invertebrate*. In strata which overlie these we find the teeth and bones of fishes; but still the fossils are all marine. Still higher, we find strata with the remains of creatures which dwelt on the land; but they were sluggish, salamander-like creatures. When we come to rocks overlying these, we find in them the bones of an astonishing number of reptiles. Still higher we find bones of quadrupeds. This is all very curious; but it shows that the rocks may be classified according to the fossil remains which they contain. Let us repeat the succession: 1. Rocks almost without fossils. These are at the bottom. 2. Rocks containing only marine invertebrates. 3. Rocks containing marine vertebrates. 4. Rocks containing the lowest terrestrial vertebrates. 5. Rocks containing the remains of reptiles and birds. 6. Rocks containing the remains of mammals.

Now, the reason why the rocks containing marine invertebrates do not contain also marine vertebrates, or land animals of any kind, is because these other animals were not in existence when the lower rocks were accumulating as sediments. And so we learn that the different ranks of animals were called into existence at different times. There has been a succession and a progress in the history of life on the earth.

These are some of the most important facts in geology. Each of these series of rocks is called a *system;* and each system has received a name. It is extremely important to commit these names to memory. Here in this diagram (Fig. 29) they are all arranged in order, with the characteristic fossils indicated. All this must be well studied.

Take notice. You are learning now only the *order of superposition of strata*, and the systems in which they are *classified*. Do not think all these rocks can be found piled up in every place. You shall learn next time we meet how the various strata are distributed over the country.

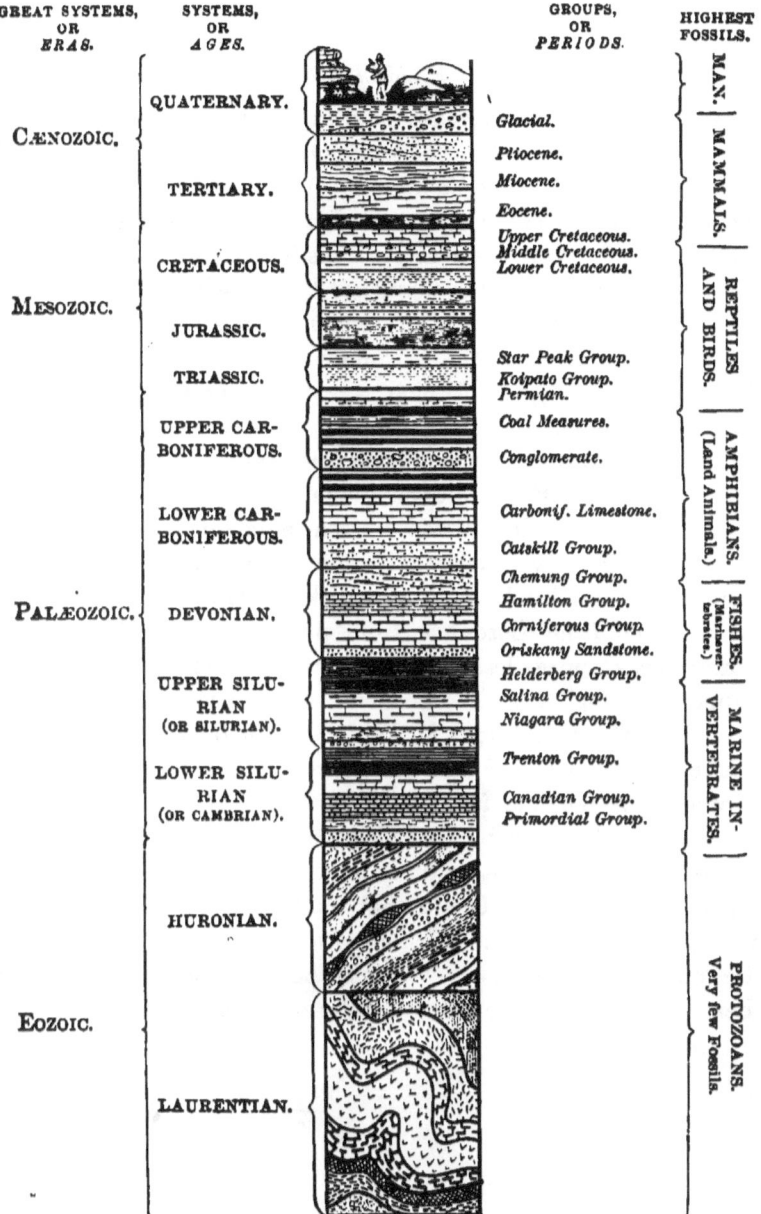

Fig. 29.—The Geological Column.

EXERCISES.

What two systems are included in the Eozoic Great System? What are included in the Palæozoic Great System? What in the Mesozoic? What in the Cænozoic? Which are the oldest strata, the Devonian or the Cretaceous? Do we find any fossil men in the Silurian? Were there any snakes in the Eozoic? Are there any snakes' remains in the Cænozoic? Are whales marine vertebrates? Are there any whales' remains in the Devonian? What do you understand by the Devonian Age? What is meant by the Cretaceous Age? Which was the longest, an Era or an Age? What are the Ages of the Palæozoic Era? Did the continent of America exist during the Palæozoic Era? Which are the hardest, Palæozoic or Cænozoic rocks? Which were hardest when first laid down as sea-sediments? What do we call that process by which the Eozoic rocks became crystalline? Mention several kinds of Eozoic rocks. Are most of our boulders derived from Eozoic or from newer rocks? Why do the Eozoic rocks appear less distinctly stratified than the Palæozoic? Suppose we find a shale in contact with mica schist, which do you think the oldest rock? Which would lie above the other? Could you expect to find a chalk under a granite? Why not? Would it be possible for mud in the bar of the Mississippi ever to become solid rock? What kind of a rock do you imagine it would make? Could it possibly become chalk? Could it possibly become granite? Could that mud be changed to limestone by any means? Was the Mississippi mud ever solid rock? Were the solid rocks ever mud? What is the use of making rocks and then wearing them into mud to make rocks of again?

EXCURSION XIX.— *To the Diagrams.*

How the Strata Enwrap the Earth.

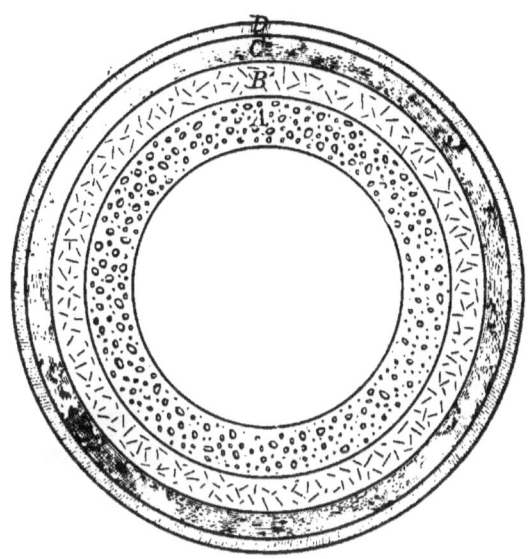

FIG. 30.—THE SYSTEMS OF STRATA NOT LIKE THIS.

If you cut an onion through the middle in such a direction that the top is on one half and the root on the other, the layers of the onion will be seen surrounding each other somewhat like the bands A, B, C, D, in this figure. But this does not represent the way the different systems of strata enwrap the earth. You have learned that all the rocks have been sea-sediments at some time. You know from this that wherever the rocks are, there has been the sea. As there is some kind of rocks — that is, some system of rocks — at every place, we may be certain that the sea has covered every place at some time. But it is not true that *all* the systems of rocks are present under every place. If they were we should have everywhere the Cænozoic rocks at the surface, and under these would be the Mesozoic, and then would follow downward the Palæozoic and the Eozoic. The fact is that any system of rocks may be at the surface. Sometimes even the Eozoic rocks are at the surface; and, in fact, we sometimes find them thousands of feet above the

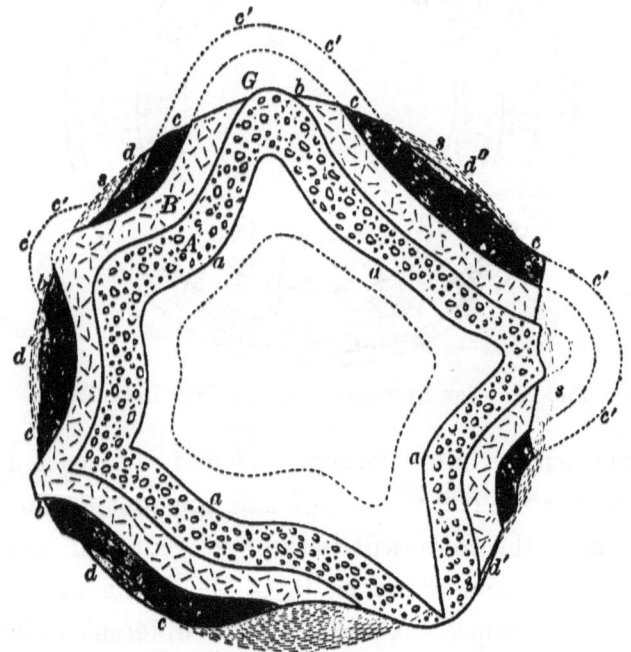

Fig. 31.—The Systems of Strata More Like This.

level of the sea. This state of things it is very important to understand.

It appears that the earth has, at various times in the past, been a little distorted in shape, as you may see in

Figure 31; though you must not think the earth has been squeezed into *such* a shape. It has not been distorted one-hundredth so much as this. Such a figure is given to make it easier for you to see the effects of distortion. In this figure we may suppose the bands A, B, C, *d* to represent the different systems of rocks as they would appear if the earth were cut through, through the middle. All these bands are near the surface. We cannot show anything in the interior of the earth, because we do not know what is there. We can guess something about it; but we must confine ourselves now to that part of the earth which is very near the surface. That part which we know to be composed of solid, rocky material is called the earth's *Crust*. In this we have the various systems marked A, B, C, *d*, the names of which you learned in the last lesson. The figure shows a section through the crust, and shows how one system of rocks *overlies* another. Where any stratum goes down under another, we say it *dips* under it. When it comes out from under another, we say it *outcrops*.

You will notice that the only system which completely surrounds the earth is the Eozoic, A. In some places the Eozoic comes quite to the surface; in others, as at *a, a, a, a*, it is *overlaid* by all the other systems. In other places, as at *b, b, b*, it is overlaid only by the Palæozoic. In still other places, as at *c, c, c, c*, it is overlaid by both Palæozoic, B, and Mesozoic, C. There are only a few places, like *d, d',* *d''*, where any Cænozoic can be seen — except Drift or other Post-Tertiary, which covers nearly all the earth's surface, and is not represented in this diagram. In some places, like d', the Tertiary (Cænozoic) rests directly upon the Palæozoic, or even the Eozoic.

If you look closely at this diagram you notice an appearance as if the Palæozoic and Mesozoic strata had at some former time extended much further than at present. For instance, the dotted line c' c' shows what may have been at some time the upper surface of the Mesozoic. If so, then the dotted line below this shows what may have been at the same time the upper surface of the Palæozoic. In fact, on all sides the arrangement of the strata looks as if they had been once wrinkled up, and then the higher places removed. That is something like the truth. But we must not suppose the Palæozoic and Mesozoic ever extended quite over all the Eozoic which is now at the surface. We cannot say precisely how far they ever covered the Eozoic. We are certain, however, that they have been eroded to a great extent. And we can understand that the sediment produced by such erosions went partly into the sea, and was made over in the patches of Tertiary which we see at d, d, d', d''.

If the dotted circle s s s represents the level of the ocean, you see that some parts of the crust rise above it and form the continents; and those parts which rise highest are mountains. You see, also, that all the systems of strata lie under the sea.

Now fix your attention on the d near the lower side of the diagram, a little to the left of the middle. The rocks there are Cænozoic; and you see a section or cut right through them and the rocks under them. This section

shows what is the surface extent of the Cænozoic area there
in one direction. Here it is, the
distance from m to n in this little cut (Figure 32). We do not
know how broad this Cænozoic
area is in the other direction;
but let us suppose it a little ob-
long; then its other diameter will
be $o\,p$, and $m\,p\,n\,o$ will be a
map of the Cænozoic area of
which a section is shown in Figure 31 at d, near the lower side
of the figure.

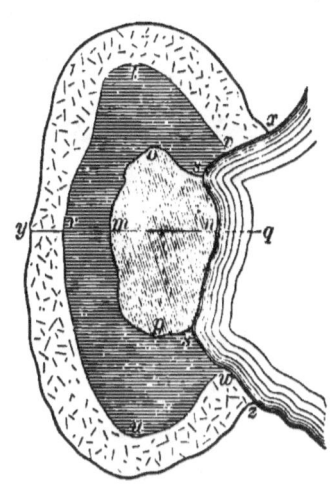

FIG. 32.—MAP OF THE REGION
AROUND $b\,d\,c$, FIG. 31.

But then, on one side of this
Cænozoic section is a section of
Mesozoic strata. Let us take the length of this Mesozoic
section and lay it off from m to r on the side of the map,
Figure 32. As the Mesozoic on the other side is covered by
the sea, we may represent the sea as bordering the Cænozoic, and may lay down as much of it as we please,— say
from n to q, on the other side of the map; and may assume
that the sea-shore leaves the Cænozoic area at s, s. Then
the distance from r across to n is the whole diameter of the
Mesozoic area, to the sea,— including the portion covered
by the Cænozoic. The breadth in the other direction is not
known; but we may assume it as extending from t to u.
The whole size of the Mesozoic area not covered by the sea
will therefore be shown by $v\,t\,r\,u\,w$. Lastly, the Palæozoic, when laid down on a map, will give a belt surrounding

the Mesozoic, as shown in $x\ y\ z$. So this is a geological map showing three systems of strata; and Figure 33 shows the appearance of a section across it.

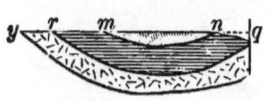

FIG. 33.—SECTION ALONG THE LINE $y\ q$, FIGURE 32.

Now, once more. Fix your attention on the point G in Figure 31. If we proceed to make a map of the region around this point, it will look something like Figure 34. Here you see the Eozoic in the middle and the newest strata around the border. Here, also, the ocean bounds the area on one side. Notice particularly the difference between this map and the other. There the strata dipped from all sides toward the centre; here they dip from the centre toward all the sides. This is shown in the section, Figure 35, where the Mesozoic c dips under the ocean on one side; the Palæozoic b dips under the Cænozoic, and

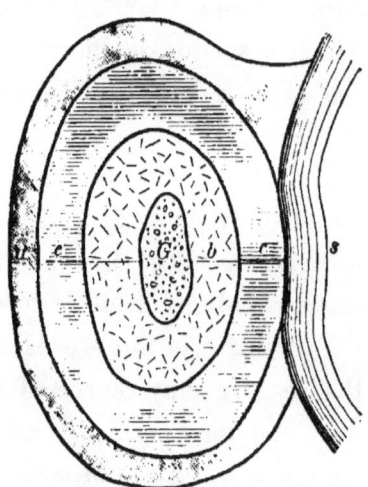

FIG. 34. — MAP OF THE REGION AROUND G, FIG. 31.

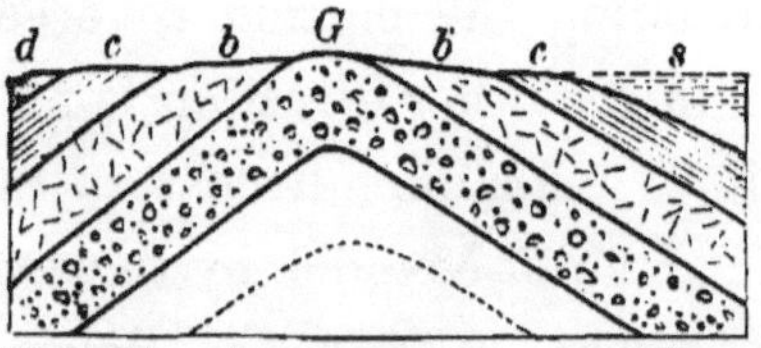

extends on one side under the ocean; and the Eozoic G dips in both directions under the Palæozoic.

Now, before we pass on to the study of the geological

FIG. 35.— SECTION ALONG THE LINE $d\ s$, FIG. 34.

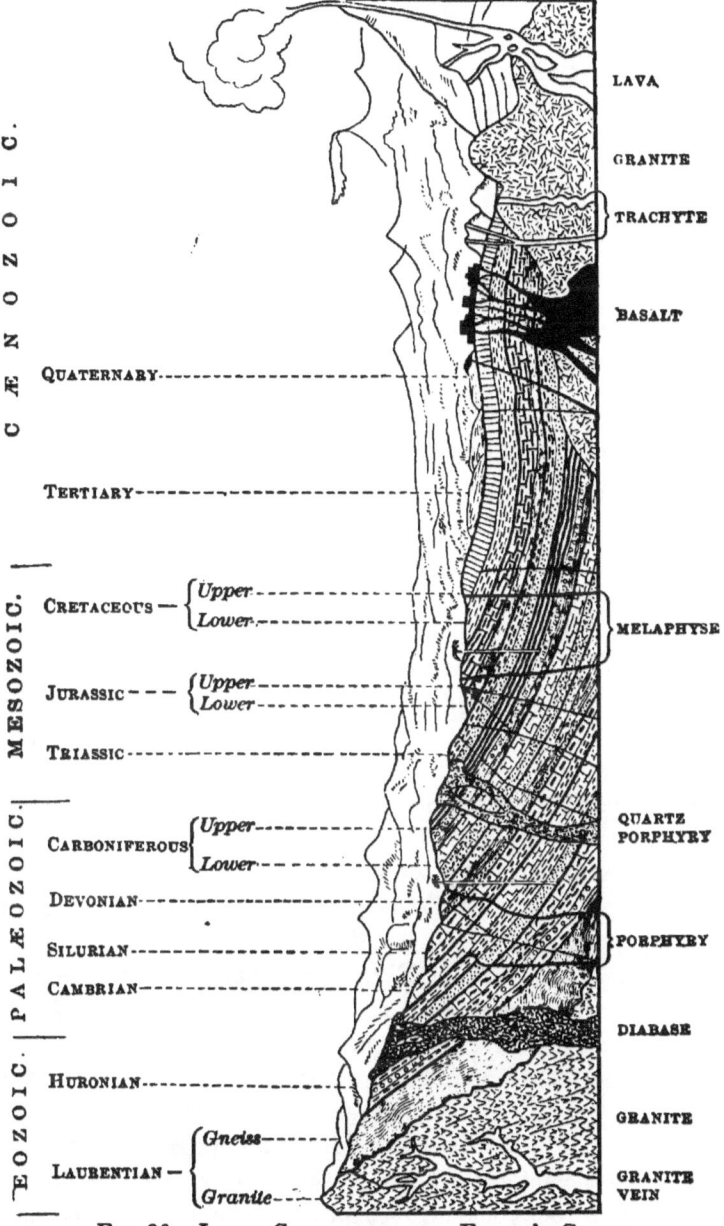

CÆNOZOIC.

MESOZOIC.

PALÆOZOIC.

EOZOIC.

QUATERNARY

TERTIARY

CRETACEOUS — { Upper
                Lower

JURASSIC — { Upper
              Lower

TRIASSIC

CARBONIFEROUS { Upper
                 Lower

DEVONIAN

SILURIAN

CAMBRIAN

HURONIAN

LAURENTIAN — { Gneiss
                Granite

LAVA

GRANITE

TRACHYTE

BASALT

MELAPHYSE

QUARTZ PORPHYRY

PORPHYRY

DIABASE

GRANITE

GRANITE VEIN

FIG. 36.—IDEAL SECTION OF THE EARTH'S CRUST.

map, look at this more extensive section through the rocks of the earth's crust. This is not intended to show what would be seen in any particular region, but would be seen in a good many different regions. The various geological phenomena which would be seen in many different regions are here all brought together. So this is not a *real* but an *ideal* section. Still everything shown is real somewhere. This section will bear a great deal of study. You cannot learn all about it now. I intend that you shall turn back to it a great many times. But you may now ask as many questions about it as you please.

EXERCISES.

In Figure 32, if we travel from the centre to the circumference, do we pass from newer to older rocks, or from older to newer? If we stand near the circumference, which way do the strata dip? Do they dip toward and under newer strata, or away from them? If we bore a deep hole at the centre of Figure 32, what systems of rocks will we pass through? If we stand near the circumference of Figure 34, which way do the rocks dip? Do they dip toward the older rocks, or away from them? Must strata always dip TOWARD NEWER rocks and AWAY FROM OLDER rocks? Suppose you bore a deep hole near the margin of Figure 34, what systems of strata would be passed through? Suppose you bore at the middle of Figure 34, what rocks will be passed through? Must a geological area necessarily be circular? Suppose the ocean should wear away two-thirds from the area mapped in Figure 34, could you then make a geological map of the region? Try it. Point out places where the Palæozoic outcrops in Figure 31. Show where the Eozoic outcrops. What system of rocks least completely enwraps the earth? How could it be that Cænozoic rocks should rest on Eozoic, with no Palæozoic or Mesozoic between them? Make a geological map of the region extending from G toward the left, through *c*, *d* and *s*, to *b*, in Figure 31.

EXCURSION XX.— *To the Geological Map.*

How to Understand a Geological Map.

I will now help you to understand a geological map of the United States. Here, in Figure 37, is such a map extended as far west as the Black Hills. This is a real map which attempts to represent things as they are. In the corner of the map is a "legend," which indicates what systems of strata are mapped. These are the same as the "Systems" in the "Geological Column," Figure 29, with three exceptions : The Laurentian and Huronian are here thrown together as Eozoic ; the Triassic and Jurassic are thrown together as Jura-Trias, and the Post Tertiary is disregarded, since this is understood to be everywhere present, covering all other formations.

First, fix your attention on the areas marked Eozoic. One large area lies north of the Great Lakes and the St. Lawrence River ; another lies along the eastern flanks of the Appalachian chain of mountains — extending from Pennsylvania through Maryland, Virginia, North and South Carolina and Georgia into Alabama. These two Eozoic masses pass *under* all the intervening strata and meet together. As the Eozoic strata are the oldest known, the strata on both sides of an Eozoic area must be newer than Eozoic, and must overlie the Eozoic. As the dips are always *away from* the older rocks, it must be that the rocks

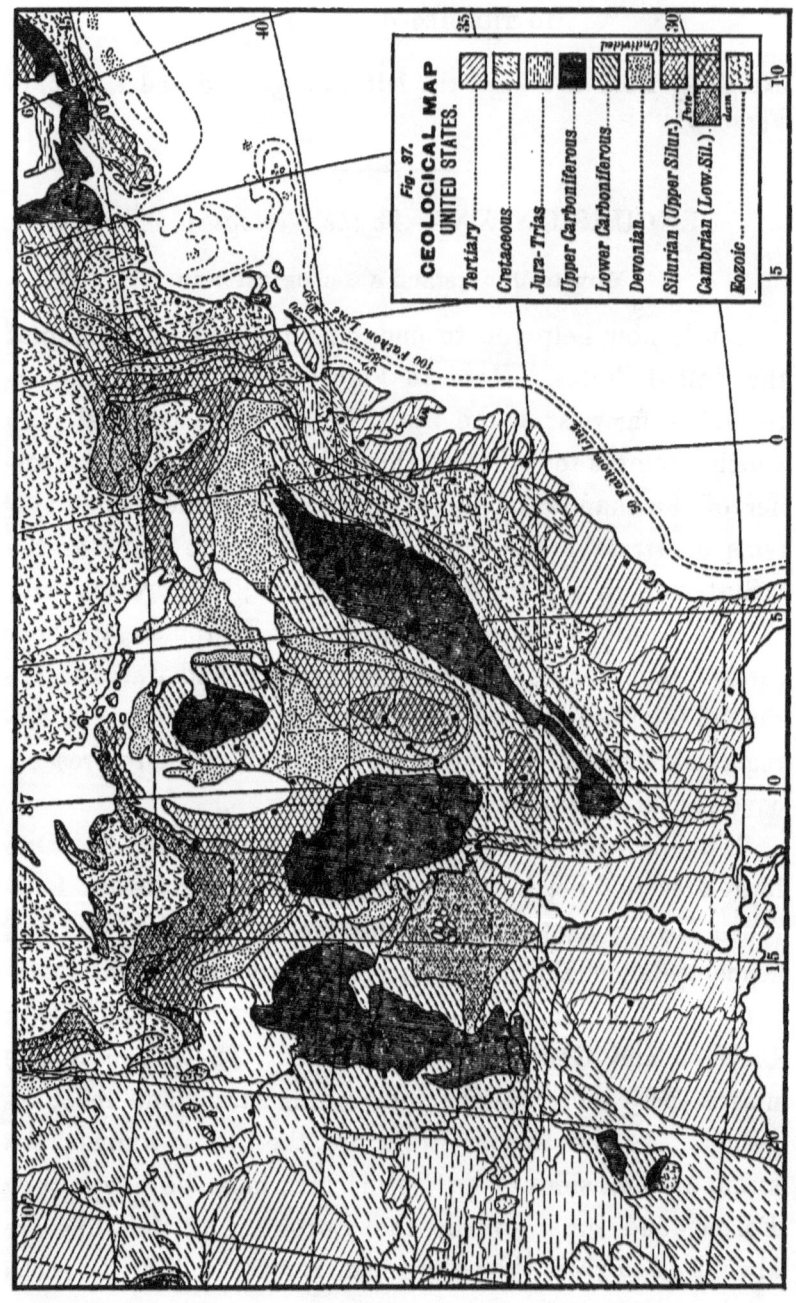

Fig. 97.

GEOLOGICAL MAP

UNITED STATES.

Tertiary

Cretaceous

Jura-Trias.

Upper Carboniferous.

Lower Carboniferous.

Devonian.

Silurian (Upper Silur.)

Cambrian (Low.Sil.),

Eozoic ...

along the eastern side of the Appalachian Eozoic dip toward the southeast, and those along the western side toward the northwest. And so the rocks along the border of the Canadian Eozoic must dip directly away from it. That is, along the valley of the St. Lawrence River, the rocks next the Eozoic must dip southeast; in the region north of Lakes Ontario and Huron, the dip must be south; in eastern Wisconsin, the dip is southeast, and in western Wisconsin, it is southwest.

Southeast from the Appalachian Eozoic we have very little except Tertiary strata. These then overlie the border of the Eozoic, and dip southeastward, extending to the Atlantic Ocean. Northwest of the Appalachian Eozoic we find strata indicated by full oblique lines in one direction and broken oblique lines in the other direction. These are explained in the "legend" to mean that the rocks are either Cambrian or Silurian (Lower Silurian or Upper Silurian, as some geologists prefer to say), but we have not yet ascertained which. These must dip northwesterly, away from the older Eozoic, and *toward* the newer Upper Carboniferous. Passing under all the Carboniferous, they come to the surface again in Tennessee, Kentucky, Ohio and Indiana, where we have learned them well enough to distinguish both Cambrian and Silurian (or, as some say, Lower and Upper Silurian). On the north, Cambrian and Silurian come up along the two shores of Lake Ontario. From this region the dip is southward all the time until we reach central Pennsylvania. In southwestern Ohio, the Cambrian which comes up from the southeast soon dips down again toward the northwest, and passing under Michigan and Lake Michigan, comes up again in eastern Wisconsin. Now try and follow the Cambrian and Silurian up and down all the way from the Appalachian Eozoic.

You must not be content to simply read these descriptions. You must, by all means, follow the systems of strata on the map. When they go under, your thoughts must follow them. When they appear in view again, your thought must see them coming from under the newer strata. You must look *under* the surface of the map and *see* the solid, thick crust of the earth with its various strata curved and overlapping, and discontinuing and beginning again, disappearing and outcropping just as I describe them. If you do this, and perform plenty of such exercises as will be given you, the study will soon be easy and delightful. If you do not, you will *never* have a good knowledge of geology.

Now let us continue the explanation of the map. On the southwestern border of the Wisconsin Eozoic, you see the Cambrian overlying it, and thence dipping southwesterly under Silurian, Devonian, Lower Carboniferous and Upper Carboniferous. We can trace it, in thought, under all these systems into Missouri and Kansas. We might reasonably expect the Eozoic to come to the surface again in the region farther southwest, but it scarcely succeeds in revealing itself. You will notice one patch in the Indian Territory, and one in southern Texas; but nearly all that region has been covered by Jura-Trias, and then most of that has been covered by Cretaceous. Even upon the top of the Cretaceous are some patches of Tertiary.

In New England you will notice considerable areas marked Eozoic; but in *some* cases we only know that the rocks are crystalline like Eozoic, while they may be in reality only later rocks hardened and crystallized by *metamorphism*. You observe, however, a patch of Upper Carboniferous in Rhode Island, and a belt of Jura-Trias running through Connecticut and Massachusetts. Farther north you will notice that the valley of the Connecticut is underlaid by Cambro-Silurian rocks — that is, rocks either Cambrian or Silurian.

In the Adirondac region of New York is an interesting Eozoic area. This connects with the Canadian Eozoic by a narrow neck across the St. Lawrence River. The strata all around this Adirondac area dip away from it. This is a case somewhat like the Eozoic area in Wisconsin. On the other hand, the centre of Michigan is an area of Upper Carboniferous, and since the surrounding strata are all older, they all dip toward the centre of Michigan.

Now let us vary the method of study. Suppose we stand on the southern side of Lake Ontario, the map shows that the dip of the rocks is south ; for at that point we have Silurian, while to the south are the (newer) Devonian and Lower and Upper Carboniferous; and, according to the rule, the dip is *toward* the newer and *away from* the older in Canada.

If we stand at Milwaukee, the dip is eastward, for Milwaukee is on the Silurian, and eastward we have the Devonian and Lower and Upper Carboniferous in Michigan. Lake Michigan must also cover a portion of the Silurian and much of the Devonian. If, on the contrary, we stand at the St. Clair River, the dip is westward on the same principle.

Again, if we stand at Sandusky, Ohio, we are on the Silurian; and if we walk straight to Cincinnati, we walk a long distance on Silurian, and then come to Cambrian. Then if we continue our travel to Nashville,. Tennessee, we pass again over Silurian, a narrow belt of Devonian, a broad belt of Lower Carboniferous, and then come to a very narrow streak of Silurian again (too narrow to show on the map at this place, though it can be seen south of the Cumberland River), and end our journey on the Cambrian. Should we continue southward to Mobile, we should pass off the Cambrian directly upon the Lower Carboniferous, which extends into Alabama. Then, in the neighborhood of Tuscaloosa, we should pass upon the Upper Carboniferous and beyond this to the overlying Cretaceous, and should find Mobile on the Tertiary.

If we should travel from Albany to Boston, we should start on Cambrian rocks and pass to Silurian rocks. Before reaching central Massachusetts we should pass to rocks which are not fully determined — perhaps Cambro-Silurian, — and perhaps also an outcrop of Eozoic. Crossing the valley of the Connecticut, would be found Jura-Trias rocks resting horizontally in a trough excavated in the older rocks. Those on the map are not extended far enough north. Beyond this valley we should find again rocks which are perhaps Cambro-Silurian. Beyond these we should have Eozoic rocks for the greater part (all Eozoic on the map) until reaching Boston. All these things and a thousand others may be studied out on the map.

EXERCISES.

If you travel in a straight line from Detroit to Milwaukee, what systems of strata will you pass over? What, if you travel from Mackinac to Cincinnati? What, between Oswego and Plattsburg? What, between Charleston and Nashville? State the dip of every system of strata passed between St. Louis and Chicago. Between Duluth and Lake Michigan. Between Saginaw and Springfield, Illinois. Between Springfield and Cincinnati. Between Cleveland and Pittsburgh. What is the dip of the strata at Cleveland? What, at Green Bay? What, at Binghamton, New York? What, at Utica, New York? Suppose you bore an artesian well at Lansing, Michigan, what systems of strata will be passed through? What, if you bore at Charleston, South Carolina? What, if you bore at Hartford, Connecticut? What, if you bore at Peoria, Illinois? What, if you bore at Galveston, Texas? What, if you bore at Montreal, Canada? Would an artesian well bored at Cincinnati pass through the Silurian? Or the Devonian? How could you travel from Albany, New York, to St. Paul without passing off the Cambro-Silurian? How from Cairo to Cape May without passing off the Tertiary? How many great patches of Upper Carboniferous (Coal Measures) are shown on the map? Into what states does the Appalachian coal area reach? Into what states, the Illinois coal area? Into what, the Kansas coal area? Into what, the Michigan? Into what, the Rhode Island? Which state has the largest area of Eozoic rocks? Which next? Which has the largest area of Tertiary? Which state contains the greatest number of different systems? Which contains the fewest different systems? What states have the largest amount of soft rocks? What ones have most Palæozoic rocks? Give the names of the cities indicated by black dots on the map, and state what system of rocks each is located on.

EXCURSION XXI.—*To the Geological Map.*

Geological Sections.

One of the most useful things for a student of geology is to take exercises on the geological map. One object of the study is to learn the geology of various parts of the country. You must not look merely upon the flat surface of the map. It is not enough even to learn the location of the different colors lying on the surface. You must think of each color or system of markings as an outcropping of something which goes down beneath the surface. You must try to follow it beneath the surface to some other region where it outcrops again. You must think which way it goes beneath the surface — that is, what is its *dip*. The rule already given determines that. So, when you look on the geological map you will learn to look *into* it, and far beneath the surface. You will then see the whole solid framework of the rocks which underlie a country.

Now we shall undertake some exercises which will give us the power of penetrating into the depths of the solid crust. With the geological map before us, we will try to construct some geological sections. That is, if we could cut straight down along the line between two points which may be selected, to the depth of some thousands of feet, and then look at the cut edges of the strata, what form and arrangement would they present to us?

To begin with a simple case, let us construct a section across the State of Michigan from Detroit to Grand Haven.

We will first draw a line G D, Figure 38, to represent the distance along the surface between the two points. We suppose ourselves facing north. We notice that Detroit stands on the Devonian. Take the

G d c b a D

FIG.38.—PREPARING FOR A GEOLOGICAL SEC-TION.

distance from Detroit to the western border of the Devonian, and lay it off from D on the line G D. This distance extends to *a*. Next, lay off from *a* the distance which corresponds to the breadth of the Lower Carboniferous in the direction from Detroit to Grand Haven. This stretches to *b*. Thirdly, lay off the distance which our route passes over the Upper Carboniferous. This takes us to *c*. Fourthly, lay off the distance to the western border of the Lower Carboniferous; this takes us to *d*. Finally, lay off the short distance to Grand Haven on the border of Lake Michigan. This takes us to G.

Next, we have to consider what is the dip of the strata at each point. On our principles, the dip is *toward* the Upper Carboniferous from both ends of the line. Draw lines down obliquely, according to the dip, from *a*, *b*, *c* and *d*, Figure 39, the boundary points between the forma-tions. Then, knowing that the Lower Carboniferous, which dips down west-

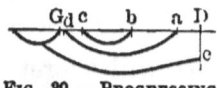

FIG. 39. — PROGRESSING WITH A GEOLOGICAL SECTION.

ward in the eastern part of the state, is the same which comes up to the surface from the eastward, in the western part of the state, we can connect the lines representing the lower and upper surfaces of this system. That is, the upper line will extend from *b* to *c*, passing down under

the Upper Carboniferous; and the lower line will extend
from a to d, passing under both Upper and Lower Carboniferous.   The dip of the strata from D must pass in the
same direction as from a and b.   But notice that Detroit
is not on the eastern limit of the Devonian.   The line from
the eastern limit — wherever it is — will pass some distance
under Detroit, as at e.   We need not know where it comes
up to the surface.   It is somewhere to the eastward, but
we may cut it off at e, as we are only required to construct
the section to Detroit.   That line, then, ending at e, shows
the bottom of the Devonian.   Passing westward it will
come up at the west side of the Devonian, wherever that is.
But the first system west of Lake Michigan is the Silurian,
and the *place* for the bottom of the Devonian is between
it and d, near Grand Haven.   The western outcrop of the
bottom of the Devonian seems to be *in the bottom of Lake
Michigan.*   This belief is confirmed by observing that on
the map, the outcrop of the Devonian strikes the south
end of Lake Michigan and seems to pass under the lake.
It comes mostly from under the lake again in the region
of Grand Traverse and Little Traverse Bays and Mackinac.
We will therefore assume that the western outcrop of the
Devonian is under the lake.   We will also draw a little
depression to represent the bed of the lake.

So far we have assumed that the surface is a dead level
from Detroit to Grand Haven; but if we happen to know
that the centre of the state swells up a little, we should
so represent it.   We ought, indeed, to know this; because
if you look on any map of Michigan you see the streams

all flowing from the interior into the surrounding lakes. If, then, we show the surface configuration, our section will be a geological *profile*. Here it is, in Figure 40, but

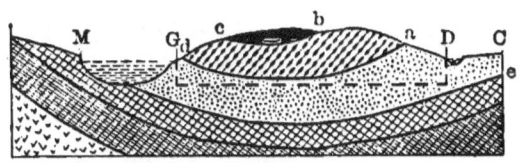

FIG. 40.—COMPLETED GEOLOGICAL SECTION BETWEEN DETROIT AND GRAND
HAVEN, MICH.

on a scale twice as large. In completing the section we may bear in mind that the Silurian which outcrops at Milwaukee passes under Lake Michigan and the state of Michigan, and we may so represent it, though a section across Michigan does not require this. It would be proper also to represent the Cambrian under the Silurian, since we see from the map that on the west of Milwaukee it passes eastward under the Silurian. And, finally, we notice that in central Wisconsin the Eozoic passes southward under the Cambrian; and we may fairly assume that it would appear beneath the Cambrian under Michigan'if we were able to make actual examination. So we fill in the lower left-hand corner of our section with the marks indicating Eozoic. Now the section is complete.

We have, in fact, extended the section farther west than was required. We might have cut it off at Grand Haven. Also, we have carried it deeper than necessary. All that is essential in a section from Detroit to Grand Haven is shown by the broken lines.

Next, let us construct a geological section from the
Eozoic north of Lake Ontario to Williamsport on the Coal
Measures of Pennsylvania; and let us suppose ourselves
facing east. Draw a line E W, Figure 41, to represent the
length of the section. Then, allowing a
little space to the right of E for the
distance to the southern margin of the
Eozoic, fix on a point *a*, for the border
of the Cambrian. The dividing line between the Cambrian and Silurian is under the lake; let us locate it under
b. The southern limit of the Silurian will be at *c*. The
southern limit of the Devonian will be at *d*; and here the
Lower Carboniferous begins. The southern limit of the
Lower Carboniferous, which is the northern limit of the
Upper Carboniferous, will be at *e*. Then the southern
extremity of our section will be at W, just over the border
of the Coal Measures.

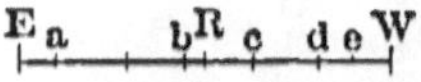

Fig. 41.—Preparing for a Geological Section.

Now, we understand that all these rocks dip southward.
So we draw lines from the points *a*, *b*,
c, *d*, *e*, Figure 42, to represent the dip,
and terminate them at such points as to
produce a neat figure showing all that
is required. Then we may fill in with
the lines and characters chosen to represent the various
systems.

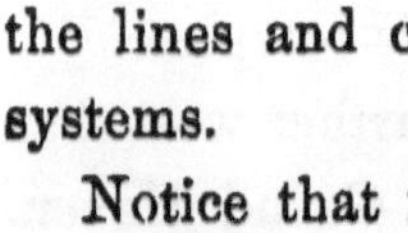

Fig. 42.—Progressing with a Geological Section.

Notice that it is customary to represent the dip somewhat greater than the reality, especially when the real dip
is but slight. Notice, also, that this makes the thicknesses
of the formations too great to be in due proportion to the

distances along the surface. All this is only for convenience.

We have constructed this section thus far on the
assumption of a dead level from end to end. But we
ought always to, represent the relative elevations of different points as well as we can. In fact, geologists often
take very great pains to ascertain the levels of different
points. If the region where E is located is somewhat elevated, we should so represent it. And if we know that a
high bluff of strata extends along the south shore of Lake
Ontario, we should so represent that. An improved section between the two points would be as shown, Figure
43. This is made on a scale four times as large as the
other, which is too small for convenience. Here we notice
a slope from north and from south toward Lake Ontario.

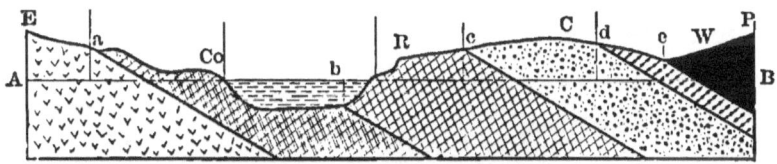

FIG. 43.—COMPLETED GEOLOGICAL SECTION.

E, Canadian Eozoic. Co, Coburg. R, Rochester. C, Corning. W, Williamsport.

Also a slope from both directions toward the Chemung
River. These things are not all shown by the map; but
if you can, in any way, obtain information about the configuration of the surface, that should be introduced into
your section. You will often have to refer to your geo-
graphical atlas to learn where places mentioned are
located. The directions in which the streams run will

also show you what regions are more elevated, and what are less elevated.

The following is the way we complete the geological profile. Having laid down the necessary points along a horizontal line A B, draw vertical lines from these points, as shown, Figure 43, and draw ˏas exactly ·as you can a line E P, to represent the surface of the earth. The points *a*, *c*, *d*, *e*, where this line intersects the vertical lines, indicate the bounds of the different formations. From these points we may draw lines to represent the dip and the thickness of each formation.

You ought to take a great deal of exercise on the Geological Map, and especially in the construction of sections. No matter if it requires two or three days to finish one Excursion.

Let us construct a section from Nashville to Savannah. Here it is (Figure 44). You will notice that the Cambrian

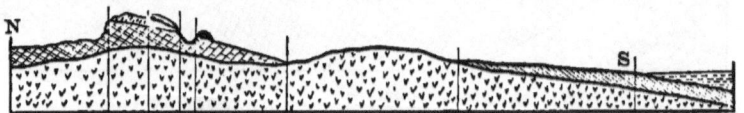

FIG. 44.—SECTION FROM NASHVILLE TO SAVANNAH AND THE ATLANTIC OCEAN.

east of Nashville is not known to be overlaid by Silurian; and when we trace it to the east of the Appalachians it is so metamorphosed that we are unable to say whether it is Cambrian or Silurian, and so it is simply put down on the map as Cambro-Silurian. After passing the dome of Eozoic we find it overlaid directly by Tertiary strata, and we must so represent. Not unlikely, however, some strata intermediate in age between Eozoic and Tertiary would be found beneath the Tertiary if we could make exploration. The Tertiary passes under the waters of the Atlantic.

EXERCISES.

Construct sections as follows: From Madison, Wis., to Chicago. From Chicago to St. Louis. From Sandusky, Ohio, to Nashville, Tenn. From Mackinac to Cincinnati. From Montreal to Albany. From New York City to Oswego. From St. Louis to Cincinnati. From Cincinnati to Newbern, N. C. From St. Paul to Chicago. From Cairo, Ill., to Cincinnati. From Kingston, Ont., to Chicago. From Detroit to Fortress Monroe. From Cleveland to Cincinnati, and thence down the Ohio to its mouth.

EXCURSION XXII.—*To the White Mountains.*

The Eozoic Rocks.

You ought now to study a little more particularly the different systems of rocks which you see indicated on the geological map of the country. We will begin with the Eozoic. Glancing at the map, you perceive that the largest region where Eozoic rocks come to the surface is north of the United States, but sending extensions southward into Wisconsin and New York.· You see also indications of the Eozoic in Maine, New Hampshire, Massachusetts and Rhode Island. There is also an extensive area along the eastern flanks of the Appalachians. There are smaller areas at New York City, in Dakota, Missouri, the Indian

Territory and Texas. In the western part of the country
are many other patches large and small ; but these are not
included in our map.

We could obtain good views of the Eozoic rocks by
visiting any of these regions. The most convenient for
most of us are the Eozoic rocks lying to the north. From
these came the boulders which overstrew all the region
south of the Eozoic down to the latitude of Cincinnati —
the boulders whose different sorts we have so much studied.
If we visit the Eozoic regions, we shall find the same kinds
of rocks as bed-rocks ; and we shall find them exposed at
the surface in very many places.

Suppose ourselves in the region of the White Mountains. We visit the Glen House on the east of Mt. Washington, and on each side of us rise the lofty rounded forms
which are characteristic of the Eozoic. In front is the
stupendous "Presidential Range," with the bald summits
of Mts. Madison, Adams, Jefferson, Clay, Washington,
Monroe, Franklin, Pleasant, Clinton and Webster rising
before us — most of them in sight together. In the rear
of the Glen House rise the similarly bald and rounded
summits of the "Carter Range." If we go to the top of
Mt. Washington and look down on the country for fifty
miles in every direction, it seems to be a dark swelling
mass of mountain tops, nearly all of like shape. This is a
good illustration of the style of *weathering* which crystalline
rocks undergo. Granitic and gneissic regions seldom present the pointed or angular features often shown by strata
belonging to some of the other systems.

Here is a view of Mt. Kearsarge, one of the White Mountains, showing the rounded forms of the summits. (Figure 45.) There are some large boulders in the foreground. In contrast with this I present you next a view of pinnacled mountains, such as exist when their summits are formed of schists turned up on edge. The summits formed

FIG. 45.—MT. KEARSARGE AMONG THE WHITE MOUNTAINS, SHOWING ROUNDED SUMMITS. BOULDERS IN THE FOREGROUND. (Photograph.)

of massive rocks like granite are evenly eroded by weathering, and result generally in smoothly rounded forms, while summits formed of schists turned on edge are eroded deepest in the spaces between the hardest strata, and this leaves the hardest strata projecting. Such summits are called "needles" in Switzerland. (See Figure 46.) Some of the

White Mountain summits present pinnacled forms for a
similar reason.   Mt. Chocorua is a pretty good example.

FIG. 46.—THE NEEDLES OF CHARMOZ AND THE MER DE GLACE.

Now let us view these massive and schistose rocks a
little more closely.   You will be amazed to see how they
have been upturned and folded.   Often the strata stand
almost vertically on their edges; and they are often crum-

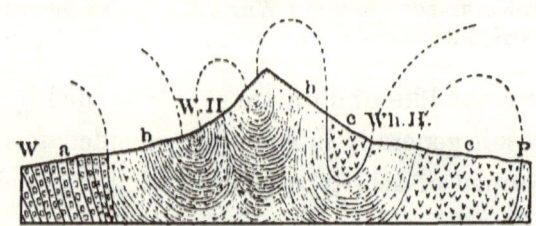

FIG. 47.—SECTION THROUGH MT. KEARSARGE, N. H.

W, Wilmot.   W H, Wilmot House.   Wh H, White House.   P, Plumbago Pt.   *a*, Porphyritic Gneiss.   *b*, Andalusite Mica Schist.   *c*, Granite.

pled like a pocket handkerchief. You see this constantly in ascending Mt. Washington. I would be glad to show you a section through this mountain, but it has not yet been thoroughly worked out by geologists. Here (Figure 47) is a section, however, through Mt. Kearsarge, the same whose summit contour you have seen. It rises in southeastern New Hampshire, and has been carefully studied by Professor C. H. Hitchcock. It shows how wonderfully the great masses of the rocks have been folded, and afterward worn down. The dotted lines indicate the supposed former extent of the strata.

Next, in Figure 48, you have a carefully investigated section through the Eozoic rocks of Canada, worked out by Sir William Logan. The first thing which impresses you is the wonderfully wrinkled condition of the strata. The dotted lines are intended to show the connections of strata. So you see also evidence of a vast amount of erosion. Notice here further the great limestone

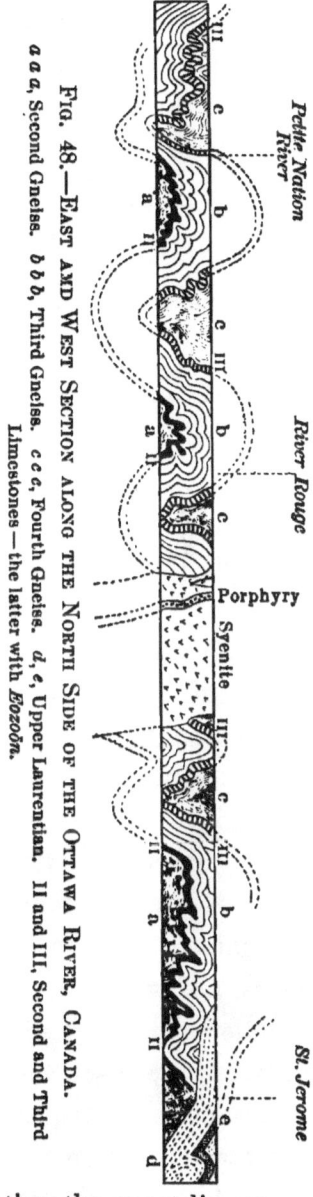

FIG. 48.—EAST AND WEST SECTION ALONG THE NORTH SIDE OF THE OTTAWA RIVER, CANADA. *a a a*, Second Gneiss. *b b b*, Third Gneiss. *c c c*, Fourth Gneiss. *d, e*, Upper Laurentian. II and III, Second and Third Limestones—the latter with *Eozoön*.

Petite Nation River

River Rouge

Porphyry

Syenite

St. Jerome

masses.   In the upper one of these are found relics of the
first animals which ever lived on our planet.

Next follows a section through the Eozoic rocks of
Wisconsin.   Here you see the two "systems" into which

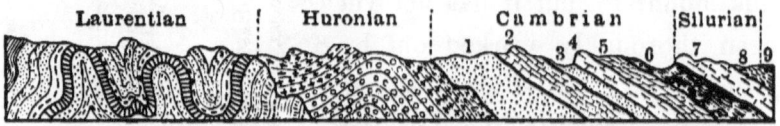

Fig. 49.—Section across the Rocks of Wisconsin. (Chamberlin.)

1. Potsdam Sandstone.   2. Lower Magnesian Limestone.   3. St. Peter's Sandstone.   4.
Trenton Limestone.   5. Galena Limestone.   6, Cincinnati Shales.   7. Niagara
Limestone.   8. Lower Helderberg Limestone.   9. Hamilton Limestone.

the Eozoic is divided — the Laurentian below and the
Huronian above.   This section extends, toward the right,
through the other rocks of Wisconsin, which we shall
speak of hereafter.   The Laurentian here and elsewhere
shown is composed of great masses of granites, gneisses
and schists, and in some regions includes great beds of
crystalline limestone, or marble.   Much of the marble
of this continent is from the Laurentian.   The Huronian
System of Rocks is composed chiefly of diorites, diabases, quartzites, slates and conglomerates.   Great beds
of iron ore are found both in the Laurentian and the
Huronian.   They occur in masses between beds of other
rocks, and generally swell out to greatest thickness in the
middle, and taper off at each extremity.   This may be
distinctly seen in the Marquette Iron Region.   At Pilot
Knob in Missouri, however, in the Penokie Range of
Wisconsin, and many other regions, the iron ore forms
thick strata, which present a structure similar to that of the

strata above and below.   Figure 50 is a section across the
eastern portion of the Penokie Range.   Here the massive
Laurentian granites, gneisses and schists, L, are *unconform-*
ably overlaid by the Huronian slates, iron-schists, quartzites and diorites, II.   These are succeeded by the "South
Range" of copper-bearing rocks (Kewenian), C, consisting
of various bedded dolerites, with alternating beds of sandstones and conglomerates.   Still farther north are the horizontal sandstones of Cambrian age.   The iron ores of
Northern New York, and of many other parts of the world,
are found in rocks belonging to the Eozoic System.

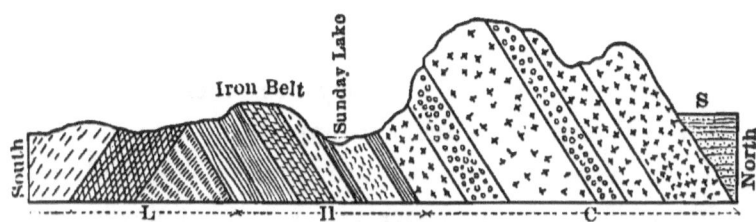

FIG. 50.—SECTION THROUGH AN IRON RANGE IN WESTERN MICHIGAN, BE-
TWEEN LAKE GOGEBIC AND MONTREAL RIVER, SHOWING POSITION OF THE
IRON ORE, AND THE RELATIONS OF FOUR SYSTEMS OF ROCKS. (Pumpelly
and Brooks.)

As these Eozoic rocks are seen everywhere to pass
under all the other rocks, they must have been formed
before the others.   The Eozoic rocks are thought to be
not less than fifty thousand feet in thickness.   And we hold
that they were originally sediments in the bottom of the
sea.   All this indicates that a vast length of time must
have been occupied in laying down sufficient sediments to
form the Eozoic and all the other rocks.   It would seem,
then, that this world has had a history, and a very long

history. We have to think, therefore, of the periods of time spent, as well as of the work done. As the whole work is divided into Systems and Great Systems of strata, so the whole time is divided into *Ages* and *Eras* of time. This is indicated in the Geological Column, Figure 29.

If the rocks which make the White Mountains were at first sediments in the bottom of the ocean, and are now five or six thousand feet above the surface of the ocean, it is plain that the old sediments must have been upraised to the extent of a mile or two. Who can imagine the power necessary to lift up the whole mass of the White Mountains? Then consider the attitudes in which the strata stand. Look again at the section of Mt. Kearsarge and trace the dotted lines. They are intended to show how the different strata seem to have been once connected together. The solid rocks have been folded and over-lapped, as if soft as molasses candy. What power could mould the substance of mountains into such shape? Look again, also, at the Canada and Wisconsin sections, and note the wonderful crumpling of the strata. These rocks are solid and massive granites, syenites, quartzites, diabases and schists. Plainly, the forces which could do such work are inconceivably vast. These things lead us to cast our thoughts backward over the world's long history. What changes have taken place since the White Mountains were soft mud in the bottom of the sea! Indeed, we are just getting glimpses of the world's grand history. It is the business of geology to study these things, and find out, as far as possible, what has been the nature of the events which have made up the history of our planet.

EXERCISES.

Is there any connection between the Eozoic of Wisconsin and the Eozoic of Missouri? Has it ever been proved that the Eozoic exists underground in regions where it does not appear at the surface? In boring to a great depth, how would we know when Eozoic rocks are reached? Do you think an artesian well likely to be found in Eozoic rocks? If not, why not? Were the first animals land or water animals? Were they fresh-water or marine animals? Would you expect them to be high or low in rank? What is the reason why the Adirondack mountains have no Cambrian strata over them? When you find Eozoic rocks exposed, can you feel certain that no strata ever covered them? Look at the Eozoic in Georgia; is there any reason to suppose the Cambro-Silurian ever extended any farther south-east? How is it possible that Cambro-Silurian rocks ever lay between the Eozoic and the Tertiary in Georgia? Could such rocks have been swept away in some age before the Tertiary were laid down? What system of rocks appears on Manhattan island? Are the artesian wells in Brooklyn bored into Eozoic rocks?

EXCURSION XXIII.—*To the Upper Mississippi.*

Cambrian (or Lower Silurian) Rocks and History.

By looking over our little geological map, you notice several regions covered by the lines which indicate Cambrian or Lower Silurian. One of the largest of these regions covers much of Wisconsin and Minnesota—on both sides of the Mississippi River, and stretches eastward through northern Michigan and the Manitoulin islands. Another stretches along the north side of Lake Ontario, and across northern New York into Vermont, New Hampshire and Massachusetts. Another region is in southern Ohio and northern Kentucky; and within this are the cities of Cincinnati, Lebanon, Madison and Richmond, Ind., and Frankfort and Lexington, Ky. Another region is in Tennessee, and this embraces Nashville, Lebanon, Columbia and Franklin. Still another extensive region stretches

FIG. 51.—BLUFFS ON THE UPPER MISSISSIPPI.   CAMBRIAN ROCKS.
(D. D. Owen.)

along the east side of the Appalachian mountains. You should trace out the boundaries of each of these Cambrian regions, and see what states and provinces they partly cover, and what cities are included in them. To do this you will have to study also the common school-atlas; but it will be very interesting and profitable.

You would be delighted to visit any of these regions and see what kind of rocks the Cambrian rocks are—how much less hard they are than the Eozoic rocks, and how much less tilted and crumpled. You would wonder also at the strange forms of the *fossils* in the rocks—that is, the shells and other remains of animals which lived in the sea when these rocks were soft sediments accumulating on the bottom. Let us first go to the Upper Mississippi. If we ascend the river by steamer to St. Paul, we shall see high rocky bluffs

FIG. 52.—" HORNETS' NEST," WIS.   EROSION OF CAMBRIAN ROCKS.
(Chamberlin.)

rising along one shore or the other, and sometimes on both shores, most of the way from Prairie du Chien. The upper portion of the bluff is generally a rusty irregular magnesian limestone, while below this lies a great sandstone formation. Figure 51 shows the appearance of these bluffs at many places. Here are evidently two ledges or formations of strata, and a great amount of earth has accumulated

at the foot of each ledge, almost burying it out of sight.
This earth has resulted largely from the disintegration of
the rocks. The lower ledge here is the great sandstone, and
the next is the magnesian limestone. In many places these
formations are less buried, and we have high vertical cliffs
of buff sandstone and limestone as shown in Figure 23.
The strata shown in Figure 22 are sandstone of the
same age.

The weathering of these rocks in Wisconsin and Minnesota has resulted in many remarkable forms. Figure 24 is
an example ; and Figure 52 is another. Here the underlying
sandstone weathers away, and leaves the more durable
magnesian limestone overhanging. In other cases, enor-

mous towers are left
standing in the midst of
a plain, showing how ex-
tensively formations have
been swept away. Fig.
53 is an example of this
kind in Dakota county,
Minn. Here the isolated
column is over 19 feet
high above the base,
which is itself 25½ feet
high, making the whole
outlier 44 feet 7 inches
above the sandy plain.

Fig. 53.—"Castle Rock," Minn. Outlier of Cambrian Rocks. (Photograph.)

As we ascend the river, these formations gradually lower.
When we reach Fort Snelling near St. Paul, we see a white

sandstone formation on the top of the magnesian limestone, and rising vertically from the water.   It may really be found at the top of the bluff most of the way from Mac Gregor. In Figure 51 is an indication of it in a third terrace.   This sandstone is *friable ;* that is, it easily crumbles to pieces.   It is called the St. Peter's Sandstone, while the lower one is the Potsdam Sandstone.

When we go back from the river to the Falls of Minne-haha near Fort Snelling, we find a limestone formation still higher in the series.   This extends to St. Paul, and makes the high limestone bluff there and at Minneapolis.   It is called the Trenton Limestone.   The Falls of St. Anthony at Minneapolis are caused by a precipice in the Trenton Lime-stone.   All these great formations together make up what is called the Cambrian or Lower Silurian.   Here are the names in regular order above the Eozoic :

CAMBRIAN SYSTEM {
    Trenton Limestone.
    St. Peter's Sandstone.
    Lower Magnesian Limestone.
    Potsdam Sandstone.

EOZOIC GREAT SYSTEM.

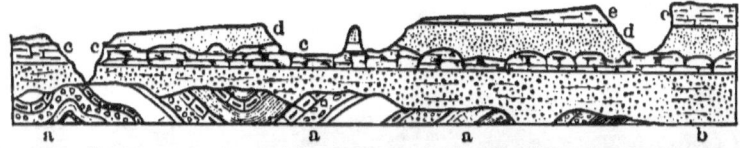

FIG. 54.—SECTION ALONG THE VALLEY OF THE UPPER MISSISSIPPI.   CAMBRIAN ROCKS.   *a.* Eozoic rocks.   *b.* Potsdam Sandstone.   *c.* Lower Magnesian Limestone.   *d.* St. Peter's Sandstone.   *e.* Trenton Limestone.

And here is a diagram or ideal section along the Upper Mississippi showing how these formations succeed each

other.   Notice the Eozoic system of rocks at the bottom.
They are much more disturbed than the Cambrian above,
and are much contorted.   A difference in the dip between
two formations, such as you see here, is called an *unconformability*.   This is illustrated also in Figures 49 and 50.
Notice also, the irregularity of the surface of the Eozoic
rocks.   It looks as if they had been extensively worn away
before the Potsdam Sandstone was deposited upon them.
This shows that a long interval of time passed after the
Eozoic rocks were formed and disturbed, before the epoch
of the Potsdam began.   Then the Potsdam sands were laid
down in nearly horizontal beds, accumulating most deeply in
the hollows of the Eozoic.   In this way the thickness of the
Potsdam Sandstone is very variable.   Figure 49, across
the rocks of Wisconsin, shows some of the same things.

Notice also, how the upper surface of the Magnesian
Limestone is worn down irregularly.   Here also, the overlying sandstone presents a very variable thickness.   So
there is a *break* also between these two formations, though
we discover no discordance in their dips.

Now I will show you another section through these rocks

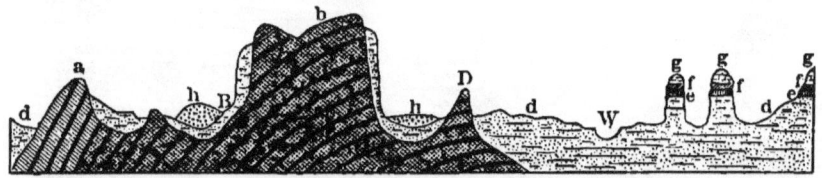

Fig. 55.—Section in Sauk Co., Wis.   (Chamberlin.)   B. Baraboo River.
D. Devil's Nose.   W. Wisconsin River, separating Sauk from Columbia
Co.   *a*. North Quartzite Range.   *b*. South Quartzite Range.   *d*. Potsdam Sandstone.   *e. f.* Upper portions of Potsdam Sandstone.   *g*. Lower Magnesian Limestone.   *h*. Drift.

—a real section, studied out by the geologists of Wisconsin. It is very remarkable. See Figure 55. The Eozoic beds here exposed are Huronian quartzite. How surprisingly irregular their upper surface! How the knobs of quartzite protrude! On this wasted knobby surface the sands were deposited which make the Potsdam formation. Toward the right (south) we cannot see the bottom of the Potsdam. In other places the Eozoic rises quite above the upper surface of the Potsdam. But the Potsdam itself has also been enormously *eroded*, or worn away, since the time when it was first completed. See how it clings to the slopes of the South Quartzite Range. These clinging masses seem to be the ends of strata which once extended a great distance. These same strata are preserved also, in the lower portions of the singular towers which appear at the right of the section. These, like the tower in Figure 53, are remnants of vast sheets of sandstone and limestone which were once unbroken and continuous over a large part of Wisconsin and Minnesota. Such outlying remnants of a formation are called *outliers*. So it appears that the present surface has been extensively eroded. How precisely it resembles those ancient surfaces at the top of the Lower Magnesian Limestone and the top of the Eozoic. How plainly these things teach us that after the close of the Eozoic there was a land surface for a long time, which wasted away quite like our present surface, and then the ocean overflowed again and deposited the sands which afterward became consolidated in the Potsdam Sandstone. And the ocean continued till the Magnesian Limestone was deposited. Then the surface of this was dry land again, and another long period of erosion followed. Then the ocean came still again and deposited the clean sand which became the St. Peter's Sandstone. And the ocean's work continued till the Trenton Limestone was laid down. Then dry land was there again, and other erosions began. The land surface seems to have continued to our times — and here we stand, beings of a day, looking on it as the outcome of almost an eternity of years. This is a little glimpse of the grand history of the world.

There are many interesting things about these Cambrian strata, both in the Upper Mississippi region and elsewhere, which must be passed over now, because I only expect you to obtain some very simple ideas in this first course of study. But you must learn something about these strata in the Cincinnati region. If you look upon the little map, you will notice that this region has coal measures upon the east and upon the west. So, according to our law of dip, the Cambrian rocks dip from the region of Cincinnati toward the east on one side, and toward the west on the other. You will notice, too, that rocks newer than Cambrian exist on the north and south also. So the Cincinnati rocks dip northward on the north, and southward on the south. You must try to picture that arrangement to your mind's eye. When you go to Cincinnati, you will see the high hills surrounding the city on three sides. From the tops of the hills the country extends somewhat level as far as you can see. When you visit the hills you will notice the out-cropping edges of limestones and shales and clay strata. From these outcrops these strata pass into the hills, under the country on all sides. If we were to construct a section across this region from east to west, it would look somewhat like this diagram, Figure 56. The Potsdam Sandstone is underneath

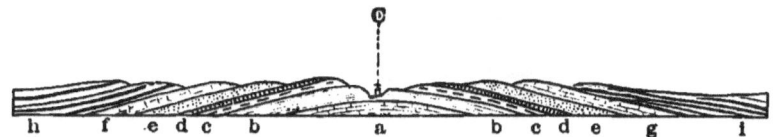

FIG. 56.—SECTION ACROSS THE CINCINNATI SWELL. C. Cincinnati. *a. b.* Cambrian. *c.* Silurian. *d.* Devonian. *e.* Waverly. *f.* Carboniferous Limestone. *g.* Equivalent of Carboniferous Limestone on the easterly side. *h.* Illinois Coal Field. *i.* Appalachian Coal Field.

the Trenton Group, which is the only Cambrian here exposed. We find nothing here called St. Peter's Sandstone, but geologists believe that the rocks immediately below the Trenton, before we come down to the Potsdam proper, correspond to the St. Peter's Sandstone and the Lower Magnesian Limestone.

The Potsdam Sandstone is not everywhere the formation which rests immediately on the Eozoic. In Nova Scotia, in eastern Massachusetts and northwestern Vermont, and in many other regions, are slaty strata older than the Potsdam and called Acadian. So in different regions are other differences in the kinds of rocks. But geologists have agreed to arrange all the Cambrian strata, in all parts of the country, in three groups; and here are their names:

CAMBRIAN SYSTEM { Trenton Group. Same as described in Wisconsin and at Cincinnati.

Canadian Group. Includes St. Peter's Sandstone and Lower Magnesian Limestone.

Primordial Group. Includes Potsdam Sandstone and Acadian Slates.

EXERCISES.

What system of rocks occupies the surface between Cincinnati and Frankfort, Ky. ?   Which way do these rocks dip at Frankfort ?   How far in that direction do they continue under newer rocks?   Where do they come to the surface again ?   What rocks are at the surface in central Tennessee ?   Which way do they dip ?   Under what rocks do they disappear in southern Tennessee ?   How far do they continue their dip to the south of Tennessee ?   Do the Cambrian strata pass under Mobile ?   What rocks are at the surface at Mobile ?   What system of rocks must be bored through at Mobile before reaching the Potsdam formation ?   Put yourself at the city of Green Bay, Wis., and walk along the outcropping edge of the formation ; in what direction do you travel ?   Which side of Green Bay will you travel to keep on the Cambrian strata ?   How far can you travel along those strata, and what places will you pass ?   Name some places in New York which are on Cambrian strata.   Mention all the Cambrian regions in the United States.

EXCURSION XXIV.—*To Niagara Falls.*

Silurian Rocks and History.

When we stand by the brink of the world-renowned Falls of Niagara, we see an enormous mass of water pouring over a precipice into a deep and fearful gorge.   The sublimity of the scene absorbs all our attention and all our interest.   Still, we must present ourselves at Niagara in a mood to study the causes of this stupendous cataract.   It is an excellent place for one who wishes to get some insight into the great facts and teachings of geology.

First, there is the great gorge a hundred and fifty feet deep down to the water; and then at least a hundred and fifty feet still deeper beneath the surface of the rushing river. Look along the walls of the gorge. There are numerous distinct beds or strata of rock divided from each

FIG. 57.—TABLE ROCK AS IT WAS.

other by joints or seams. Your eye can trace them a long distance down the stream toward the old railway suspension bridge. Notice that they all continue to rise slowly nearer the surface as they extend northward down the stream. Walk down to the bridge. You can trace these strata all the way. You see, however, that they gradually rise. You may take the railway which runs along the bank of the gorge on the American side to its termination, about five miles below. Here, if you look east or west, you see a high bluff of rocks facing north toward Lake Ontario. This great Niagara gorge looks as if it had been worn out by the river. We think it has.

If you return to the Falls, you see that the rock at the surface there is a limestone. The Falls pour over the broken edge of it. This is the Niagara Limestone. You can trace it along the upper part of the gorge all the way to Lewiston. Different strata of it keep coming to the surface and terminating. It must be much thinner, therefore, at Lewiston than it is at the Falls. Above the Falls it may be traced to the head of the "Rapids."

There is a way by which curious and adventurous people may go behind the Falls, so that the mighty cataract pours down in front of them. It is a wet and slippery place, but we can learn some geology there. Above us is the great Niagara Limestone — here we are, underneath it. We see that it rests on a thick mass of shale. This shale is a part of the series of strata, and may be traced along the gorge

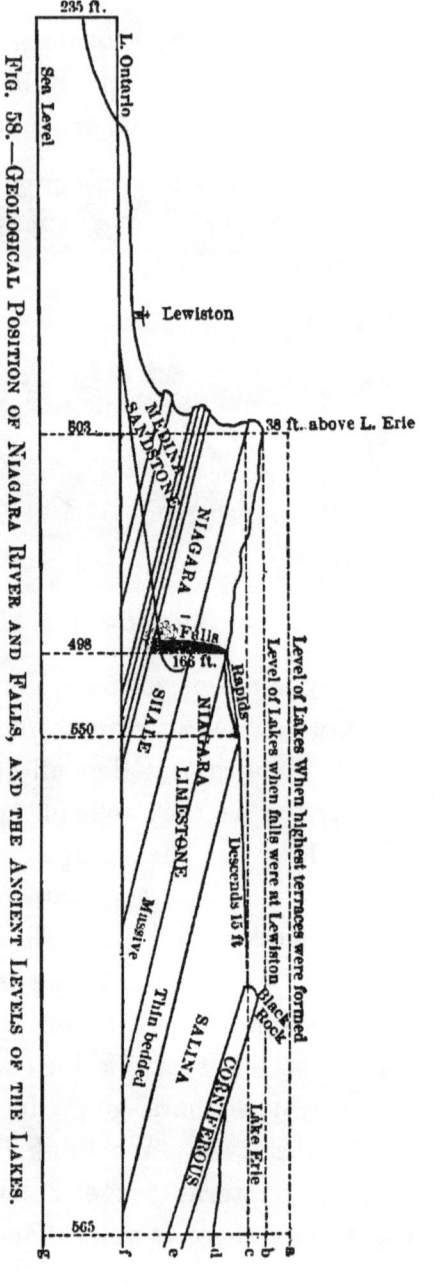

FIG. 58.—GEOLOGICAL POSITION OF NIAGARA RIVER AND FALLS, AND THE ANCIENT LEVELS OF THE LAKES.

all the way to Lewiston. It is the so-called Niagara Shale. At this place it is worn away from under the limestone, and makes the shelter where we stand. It is continually crumbling down, and making the shelter deeper. Sometimes it gets so deep that the overhanging limestone is not strong enough to bear its own weight and the weight of the water over it. Then great blocks of the limestone break off, and fall down into the abyss of foaming water. Thus the brink of the precipice is moved a little farther up stream, and the brink of the Falls is also moved. This is the "recession of the Falls." Now it may be that this shows how the whole gorge has been made all the way from Lewiston. But the extension of the gorge by such means would be slow, you say. Well, it has been shown that the Falls have receded one hundred feet in thirty-three years. That is considerable.

In Figure 57 is shown a remarkable projecting table of the Niagara Limestone on the Canadian side. This was formerly a striking feature of the spot, but it exists no more. People used to enjoy the excitement of standing upon it. But eventually "Table Rock" broke off by fragments, and fell to the bottom of the gorge. Goat Island is disappearing in a similar way. So the work of erosion goes on before our eyes.

Underneath the Niagara Shale may be traced a thin band of limestone, with a thin band of shale under it. These represent the Clinton formation, which in some regions is much more important than here, and contains beds of iron ore,—but quite different from that of the

Eozoic. Below these strata, in the lower part of the gorge, may be seen strata of red, gray and variegated sandstone. This is the Medina Sandstone, and it passes downward into the Oneida Conglomerate. The Medina Sandstone is quarried near Rochester quite extensively, for sidewalks, pavements and building purposes. All these formations together make up the so-called Niagara Group of rocks.

If you look on our little geological map, you will trace the Silurian System of rocks eastward from the Niagara River through central New York. In Onondaga and Cayuga counties we have fine opportunities to see the formation which lies next above the Niagara Group. It consists of shales, clays and impure limestones, with abundance of brine and considerable beds of gypsum. The latter is often ground into plaster to spread on farming lands, or to burn till all the water is driven off, and then employ in plastering the walls of houses. The brine oozes out of the formation, and saturates the marshes at Syracuse. In these wells are dug, and the brine is pumped out for boiling away to make salt. This is the *Salina Group*. Its outcrops extend west from Syracuse to the Niagara River above the Falls (see Figure 58), and thence through Canada to Lake Huron. You can trace it on the map. Its place is south of the middle of the Silurian belt everywhere. At Goderich, on Lake Huron, wells are bored till they reach the Salina Group, and rock salt is actually found. At Alpena, in Michigan, the same has been done. Well, if rock salt can be found in this formation in Canada and Michigan, why not in New York? So queried some New York gentlemen, encouraged by the geologist, and, by boring in western New York, they also found rock salt. And now the regions about Warsaw and Le Roy, in Wyoming and Genesee counties, are new centres of great activity in salt production. Why should they not bore south of Syracuse and find rock salt?

Now, if we try to trace the Niagara and Salina groups eastward toward the Hudson River, we find them growing thinner, and becoming lost to observation. But, on the other hand, some limestone beds above the Salina, which are thin in western and central New York, become much thicker in eastern New York, and form the basal portion of the Helderberg Mountains, which may be seen to the south of the Central railroad when traveling a few miles west of Albany. These limestones, together with some shales, form the *Helderberg Group*. This can be traced westward from Buffalo to the islands in the western end of Lake Erie, and thence south through central Ohio, covering a broad belt just off the western border of the Devonian. It is found also in Indiana, Illinois and Missouri; as also in Massachusetts, New Hampshire and Maine; and very extensively in the provinces of Quebec, New Brunswick and Nova Scotia. So the Silurian System is made up of these groups as follows:

$$
\text{SILURIAN SYSTEM} \left\{ \begin{array}{l} \text{Helderberg Group.} \\ \text{Salina Group.} \\ \text{Niagara Group.} \end{array} \right.
$$

EXERCISES.

What part of Ontario has Silurian rocks at the surface? Of what age are the cliffs along the east side of Green Bay? Of what age are those on the west side? Suppose a deep well is bored at Cincinnati, would it ever reach Silurian rocks? Explain this. Mention some other city geologically situated like Cincinnati. Name all the important cities built on Silurian rocks. Of what age is the limestone quarried near Chicago? Can you name towns near Chicago which are famous for their fine quarries? Are there any Silurian quarries in Massachusetts? The Manitoulin Islands are Cambrian on one border and Silurian on the other; which border should be Silurian? Which way do the strata dip at Madison, Wis.? Are there any Niagara Limestone quarries in the Lower Peninsula of Michigan? Could there be any limestone quarries at Milwaukee? If there are any limestone quarries at Rochester, N. Y., what is the name of the limestone? Are there any limestone quarries at Potsdam, N. Y.? Should an artesian well be bored at Chicago, what is the first sandstone formation which would be reached? Where does that sandstone come to the surface? Where do the rains go which fall on that sandstone in the region of its outcrop?

EXCURSION XXV.— *To Mackinac.*

Devonian Rocks.

In the straits connecting Lake Michigan with Lake Huron is a small island, which you can hardly find on the map, called Mackinac Island. But when you pass that way on a steamer, you see it rising 318 feet above the water, and bounded on all sides except the south by a perpendicular wall of limestone. This island is a delightful place of summer resort.

On the west, on the main land of the Upper Peninsula, and south, on the main land of the Lower Peninsula, rise high bluffs of the same kind of limestone, though not so high. One cannot help believing these bluffs were once connected with Mackinac Island. Here, in Figure 59, is a a section through the island.

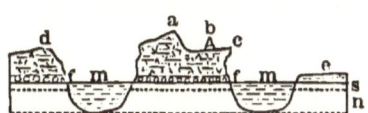

You see the same flinty conglomerate at the base of the island and at the base of Rabbit's Back on the main land. You also see the same broken limestone above the conglomerate at both places. The

FIGURE 59.—SECTION SOUTHEAST AND NORTHWEST THROUGH MACKINAC ISLAND. DEVONIAN ROCKS. *a*, Old Fort Holmes; *b*, Sugar Loaf; *c*, Robinson's Folly; *d*, Rabbit's Back on the Upper Peninsula; *e*, Round Island; *f*, Conglomeritic Stratum; *m*, Surface of the Lake.

deep valleys between the island and the main land, and between the island and Round Island, have been dug out of the solid limestone, and into the Niagara limestone, which lies below, by some agency of wonderful power. The valleys are now occupied by the water of the straits. In fact, these limestones have been dug away through the whole width of the straits, and only Mackinac Island remains near the narrowest part, to show us how high the rocks were once piled. This is another case of vast erosion, which reminds us of what can be seen at Niagara gorge. But there is no reason to think it was done by a river. And yet, let us consider a moment. The water from Lake Michigan flows through these straits and Lake Huron. Suppose the straits not yet dug through. Suppose the solid limestone stretches across from Old Mackinac, on the Lower Peninsula, to Rabbit's Back. Lake Michigan would then be dammed up. The rivers flowing into it would fill the lake till the water would be high enough to flow over the Mackinac barrier; and then a river would exist there. Perhaps a great waterfall once existed there, and dug a gorge like Niagara, and the gorge receded till the limestone barrier was cut through. Then Lake Michigan was drained to the level of Lake Huron. Now, I do not say all this has happened, but you can understand that it *may* have happened. Such reasoning as to how things have been made as they are, belongs to geological theory. I do not intend to offer you theories in connection with these Excursions, but you ought to know what we mean by theories.

The principal mass of Mackinac Island rises only about

150 feet above the lake, and forms a plain, covered by a forest growth. At one point rises a cone-shaped remnant of the higher limestone, 134 feet above this plain. The higher limestone forms a smaller or upper plateau, 294 feet feet above the lake. (See Figure 60.)

FIG. 60.—VIEW OF "SUGAR LOAF," MACKINAC ISLAND. Devonian Limestone.

On one of the sides of the island the waves have worn through the bounding cliffs, and dug under the upper strata of the limestone, leaving a real natural bridge. Both these works of geological erosion are great natural curiosities. There are also overhanging cliffs and caverns which always interest the visitor. The Indians had many romantic tales connected with these localities.

A cavern in the west escarpment is connected with traditions as thrilling and probably as mythical as those about the "Dragon's Cave" on the Drachenfels.

FIG. 61.—"ARCHED ROCK," MACKINAC ISLAND. Devonian Limestone.

The limestone of this island and vicinity is called the *Corniferous Limestone*, and it belongs to the lower part of the Devonian System. You will please turn frequently to the "Geological Column," page 99, so as to keep track of the formations about which you learn. Now, if you examine the Geological Map, you will see that the Devonian extends westward from Old Mackinac to Little Traverse Bay. As the dip of the strata is southward, you perceive that Little Traverse Bay must be excavated in the higher strata of the Devonian System. In fact, when we get to the head of Little Traverse Bay, we find a cliff of a different kind of limestone; and, as we follow around the coast toward Grand Traverse Bay, we see still other strata coming in higher up the series. They consist of limestones, shales and clays, and are packed full of fossil shells and corals. The highest formation in this series is a black shale charged with carbonaceous and bituminous matter. This series of strata forms the "*Hamilton Group.*" The high bluffs which the Hamilton Limestones form on Little Traverse Bay afford sightly and delightful situations for summer resorts.   Here, and near here, are Petoskey, Bay View and Charlevoix.

A little farther toward the centre of the Peninsula we find beds of shales and clays next in order above the Hamilton Group.   They attain a thickness of seven or eight hundred feet, and constitute the *Chemung Group*.   They contain here very few fossils.

Now, look again at the Geological Map, and trace the Devonian System eastward.   You see it passes under Lake Huron, and comes to light again on the southeast shore. Goderich stands on the Corniferous Limestone ; so do London, Ingersoll and Woodstock.   The system also passes under a large part of Lake Erie.   In New York you see Buffalo on the lower part of the system.   Near Buffalo are found many fine Hamilton fossils.   Farther east, we have Caledonia, Le Roy and the higher part of Syracuse on the Corniferous Limestone.   This limestone forms prominent ridges throughout its whole extent from Mackinac.   You see it strike east and west through central New York.   At Syracuse it rises in a lofty ridge, which is cut through by Onondaga Creek.   This runs north into Onondaga Lake. On each side of the valley of that creek are high limestone bluffs which present much fine scenery.   Here is the old settlement of Onondaga Hill on the west side.   On the east is Syracuse University.

Under the Corniferous Limestone, we find along this valley a coarse, decomposing conglomeritic sandstone containing fossils quite unlike those of the Corniferous.   This is the *Oriskany Sandstone*.   It is not a very important formation, though we find it at intervals from Missouri to the Gulf of St. Lawrence. I incline to regard the Oriskany as the base of the Devonian, though some geologists prefer to consider it the top of the Silurian.

The dip of the strata in central New York, as you will observe, is toward the south. Hence, as you travel south toward Cortland, you find the Hamilton limestones and shales coming in above the Corniferous, and, in fact, piling up the strata to a still higher level. These shales are full of fossil shells, very well preserved. If we go on from Cortland still farther south, we find the same kinds of strata occurring above the Hamilton as have been mentioned in Michigan—only they are more sandy and harder, and attain a greater thickness. These Chemung strata stretch east and west through all the southern counties of New York. They give rise to much picturesque scenery, fine examples of which may be seen at Panama, in Chautauqua county, and again at Ithaca, and in the vicinity of Cornell University. At Watkins' Glen, at the south end of Seneca Lake, the magnificent gorge before mentioned (Figure 21) occurs in this formation.

Another glance at the Geological Map will show that much of the central part of Ohio is also on the Devonian System of strata. The cities of Columbus and Delaware stand on the Corniferous Limestone. The Chemung shales stretch all the way from southern New York, along the south shore of Lake Erie, nearly to Sandusky, and thence bend southward across Ohio to the Ohio River. Their position on the map is along the east side of the Devonian belt.

Through Indiana, their place is on the west side of the Devonian belt.

So we have four groups of rocks to make up the Devonian System, and they are as follows:

DEVONIAN SYSTEM
{
Chemung Group.
Hamilton Group.
Corniferous Group.
Oriskany Sandstone.
}

EXERCISES.

Now explain why the Chemung should be along the western border of the Devonian in Indiana, but along the eastern border of it in Ohio. An artesian well was bored at Columbus, Ohio; please state what groups of strata must have been passed through. Is there any water-bearing formation underneath Columbus? Does it outcrop in any of the surrounding states? What is the nearest outcrop of the Potsdam Sandstone? What do you judge would be the prospect of getting water in an artesian boring at Columbus? Would the prospect be any better at Chicago? What is the age of the limestone at the Falls of the Ohio, at Louisville? What would be the first limestone struck in sinking a shaft at Detroit? Would there be any prospect of striking rock salt by boring at Rochester, New York? Which way do the strata dip at Lexington, Kentucky? Why are there no Cambrian, Silurian or Devonian strata over the Adirondack region? Do you think any Silurian rocks ever covered the site of Cincinnati? What reason can you give for thinking as you do?

EXCURSION XXVI.— *To Burlington, Iowa.*

The Lower Carboniferous Rocks.

We wish now to extend our survey of the rocks of our country to the formations above the Devonian. Perhaps the most favorable region for studying the Lower Carboniferous is the valley of the Mississippi River from near Davenport nearly to Cairo. Let us stop at Burlington. Here we find a bluff 175 feet high. All the upper part—beneath 25 feet of loose materials—is of limestone. The lower portion, however, is composed chiefly of beds of yellowish sandstone. These at the bottom are quite shaly, and are known to extend 65 feet beneath the surface of the river. A study of the fossils in the two beds of limestone, 7 and 8, Figure 62, shows some fossils not found anywhere else, and teaches us that those limestones ought to be reckoned as a formation quite distinct from the sandstones below. The upper formations, made of limestones 7 and 8, we call the *Carboniferous Limestone Group*. It amounts here

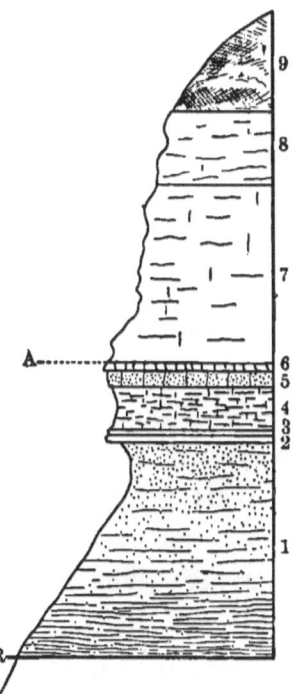

FIG. 62. — SECTION OF THE BLUFF AT BURLINGTON, IOWA. LOWER CARBONIFEROUS ROCKS. (C. A. White.)

1 to 6, "Yellow Sandstones." 7 to 8, Carboniferous Limestone. 9, Drift. R, Mean Height of River.

to seventy feet. The lower formation, made of the yellow sandstones, we designate the "Waverly Group." The limestone is full of the fragments of "stone lilies." Some beds, from two to four feet thick, are almost completely formed of the little round disc-like segments of the stems of those creatures. Many very beautiful and perfect specimens have been collected here; and this has been a favorite collecting ground for geologists for a good many years. We note some layers of limestone below these and above the sandstones which are *oölitic* — that is, they abound in little round white globules about the size of homœopathic pills. But oölitic limestones are found also in formations both older and younger. They, therefore, do not indicate any particular "group" of rocks. If we inspect the sandstones, we see that they are fine and rather soft and friable; but as to their fossils, there are no stone lilies. Instead of them we find a great abundance of bivalve shells. The oölitic limestone layers are like them in this particular, and hence belong in the same group.

This great difference in the fossils of two formations shows one means by which we are able to distinguish formations. We know, of course, without regard to the fossils, that the sandstones are older than the limestones, because they underlie the limestones. Also, if the upper surface of the sandstones were eroded and irregular, we should know that some important changes took place after the deposition of the sandstones, before the deposition of the limestones. This is what we see dividing the Eozoic from the Cambrian rocks in the section shown in Figures

54, 55, and 49. The same is seen at the top of the Lower Magnesian Limestone in Figure 54. Still further, if the lower strata should show a steeper dip than the upper, *that* would prove that the lower, after their formation, were tilted before the upper were laid down. In the same Figure 54, you see that the dip of the Cambrian strata is not conformable with the dip and crumpling of the Eozoic. Unconformability is shown also in Figure 50, between the systems L and H, and between the systems O and S. But when strata like those at Burlington are entirely conformable, without any intervening erosions, then there is no way to ascertain whether they were formed in periods quite distinct or not, except by comparing the fossils in the two. Very often such comparison shows two formations distinct when they are not only conformable and not separated by erosion, but also, are both of the same kind of rock. This, for instance, is the only means of separating the Hamilton limestones in Ohio and Michigan from the Corniferous Limestone immediately below. Even at Burlington, the oölitic limestones belong in the lower group and not in the upper.

By examining the Map you will notice that the Lower Carboniferous covers a large area west of the Mississippi River. From northwestern Indiana, also, a belt passes south to the Ohio River. Most of this is Carboniferous Limestone. At Crawfordsville, in Indiana, is another locality wonderfully rich in stone lilies. A large part of central Kentucky is underlaid by this limestone. The celebrated Mammoth Cave is formed in it. This cave was

once merely a fissure in the limestone. Water circulated
through the fissure, and by degrees made it larger. This
was done partly by wearing the rock, but chiefly by dissolving it. So, in the course of time, the fissure grew to
a cavern several miles long, with dozens of branches and
tortuous passages, and ceilings in some places a hundred
feet high, and glistening by torch-light with thousands of
crystals. This formation abounds in caves in southern
Kentucky. Wyandotte cave, in southern Indiana, is also
in it.

You must have heard of the "knobs" and the "knob
regions" of Kentucky and Tennessee. These are regions
underlaid by the Carboniferous Limestone. But the same
fissured condition of the rock which has led to its wasting
away in caverns underground has here led to similar, but
greater, wasting above ground; and so the whole surface
is gashed and gullied in every direction by running waters
—some permanent, and some merely storm waters—and
the portions unwasted by the gullies stand out as rock-
covered knobs. The unequal wasting is due partly to much
silica in portions of the limestone.

If we follow these Lower Carboniferous Limestones from
northern Alabama along the east side of the Devonian
toward northwestern and northern Pennsylvania, we find
the limestone giving out. In place of limestone are soft
red shales with some sandstones. So the upper group of
the Lower Carboniferous begins to look somewhat like the
lower, or Waverly Group in the Mississippi Valley.

In Michigan you see the Lower Carboniferous forming

a circular belt around the border of the Lower Peninsula. What answers to the Carboniferous Limestone is, of course, the inner portion of this belt. But the limestone proper is only 70 feet thick. It appears that the lower portion of this group consists of quite a different sort of rocks. They are shales, clays and gypsum, with a great amount of brine. This brine and gypsum deposit is not found in any other state. But it *is* found in New Brunswick and Nova Scotia. Now how do we know this Michigan Salt Group is really a part of the Carboniferous Limestone Group? Simply because we find in it the same species of fossils. The gypsum is extensively worked near Grand Rapids, and also, on the opposite side of the state, at Alabaster, on the north side of Saginaw Bay. The brine settles down into the sandstones of the Waverly Group and saturates them. Most of the salt wells of the Saginaw valley are supplied by borings which extend down into that sandstone.

I suppose you have seen the beautiful blue and gray freestones used for building purposes in Cleveland, Toledo, Detroit and other cities of the West. A freestone is simply a sandstone which is soft enough to be easily worked by the stone cutter. This beautiful stone is the "Waverly sandstone," and gets its name from Waverly, in southern Ohio. The best Ohio quarries, however, are at Berea, and near Cleveland. The same stone, and equally valuable, is quarried also in Michigan, in Huron county, on the shore between Saginaw Bay and Lake Huron. The place is called Grindstone City, because the world-famous "Huron grindstones" are made there. Similar grindstones are made at Berea. Now this fine stone is only an eastward continuation of the yellow sandstones which we saw at Burlington. They are, indeed, yellow and red in southern Michigan, especially in Hillsdale county. Without doubt some of the olive sandstones of northwestern Pennsylvania belong to this group, if even some similar sandstones in southwestern New York are not the same.

In eastern Pennsylvania the Waverly strata have become coarse, grayish conglomerates and sandstones, with red sandstones beneath. The red sandstones are generally thought to belong in the Devonian, and to constitute a different group, called the *Catskill Group;* but I feel doubtful about the correctness of this opinion. If the Catskill and Waverly belong to the same group, then the name which we must apply to it is Catskill, for that name was first proposed. These red Catskill sandstones extend northward, and form a large part of the Catskill Mountains.

In some parts of Pennsylvania and Virginia the lower group contains beds of coal, forming what is sometimes called *False Coal Measures.* In eastern Kentucky and Tennessee, at the top of the Lower Carboniferous, are found thick beds of shale containing valuable deposits of coal; and these are also sometimes called False Coal Measures. They are also called subconglomerate measures.

So we have in the Lower Carboniferous System two groups of strata:

LOWER CARBONIFEROUS SYSTEM { Carboniferous Limestone Group.
                            Waverly Group.

EXERCISES.

Mention places in Illinois which are on the Lower Carboniferous. Mention places in the knob region of Kentucky. Which
way is the dip of the Carboniferous Limestone at St. Louis?
Which way at Grand Rapids, Michigan? Which way on Saginaw Bay? Does the Carboniferous Limestone pass under Cincinnati? Which is next the Devonian in Ohio, the Waverly
Group or the Carboniferous Limestone Group? Which way
does the Lower Carboniferous dip in Indiana? Which way does
it dip in northern Pennsylvania? Is there any Lower Carboniferous in New York? If so, would you expect it to be a limestone
or a sandstone? If you start from Louisville to sail down the
Ohio River, do you approach newer or older rocks? If you start
from Wheeling down the Ohio, do you reach older or newer
rocks? Why is this difference on the upper and lower portions
of the Ohio? Where is the dividing line? What are the newest
rocks found in the province of Ontario? What formations does
Lake Michigan overlie? Does the axis of the lake cross the
boundaries of the formations or run parallel with them? Point
out other lakes or bays which also conform in trend to the strikes
of the formations under them and around them. Point out some
lakes or bays which trend across the boundaries of the formations. How is it with the long lakes in central New York? If
a deep artesian well is bored at Grand Haven, what formation
will be passed through? Would the Potsdam Sandstone be
reached? Would fresh water rise to the surface?

EXCURSION XXVII.—*To the Coal Mines.*

The Coal Measures.

It is immaterial what great coal-mining region we visit. We may go to Wilkesbarre, Pennsylvania, to Brazil, Indiana, to La Salle or Jonesboro, Illinois, or to any of the coal regions in Kansas, Missouri, Ohio, Kentucky, Tennessee or Alabama. We shall see huge piles of black shale rubbish lying around, and great heaps of coal ready for shipment, and great numbers of small cars running on tramways which lead through dark yawning openings into the recesses of the earth. We shall see men and mules going underground for long distances, and if we follow them, we shall find extensive passage ways excavated, like the streets of a city, sometimes aggregating several miles in length. The plan in mining is to get upon a coal bed, and then work it out in all directions. Sometimes the coal is found outcropping on a hillside, as in Figure 63, and then it is only

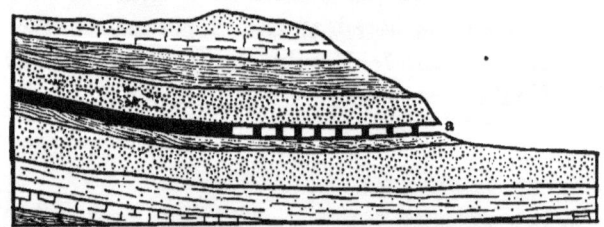

Fig. 63.—Drifting in on a Coal Bed. *a*, Mouth of the Drift.

necessary to "drift" in. There is generally water under ground, and hence the drift should enter at a place where a slight ascent will be necessary in following the bed. The water then flows toward the entrance to the mine, and escapes. Sometimes mines are opened in places where the coal beds are far beneath the surface. Then a "shaft" is sunk, as is shown in Figure 64 at S, and when a coal bed,

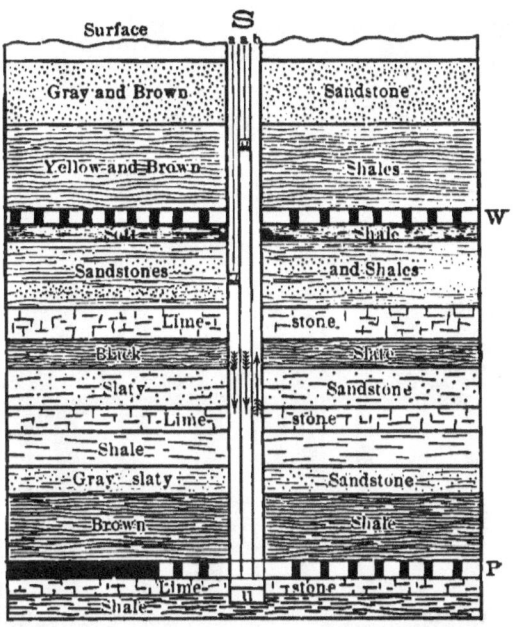

FIG. 64.—GENERAL SECTION IN THE UPPER COAL REGIONS OF PENNSYLVANIA.
W, Waynesburg Seam. P, Pittsburgh Seam. S, a Mining Shaft. a a, Down Cast.
b, Up Cast. u, Sump.

W, is reached, excavations are made on both sides. Often the same shaft is sunk to a second coal bed, P, and occasionally even to a third one. The passages or gangways are generally extended in straight lines as far as the coal continues satisfactory, and other passages are opened at right angles with these. On each side of these gangways large rooms are excavated, but with walls of coal left stand-

ing between them for the support of the roof. In the course
of time all the coal is mined out, except large columns and
walls left for support. In some mines these are also finally
removed.

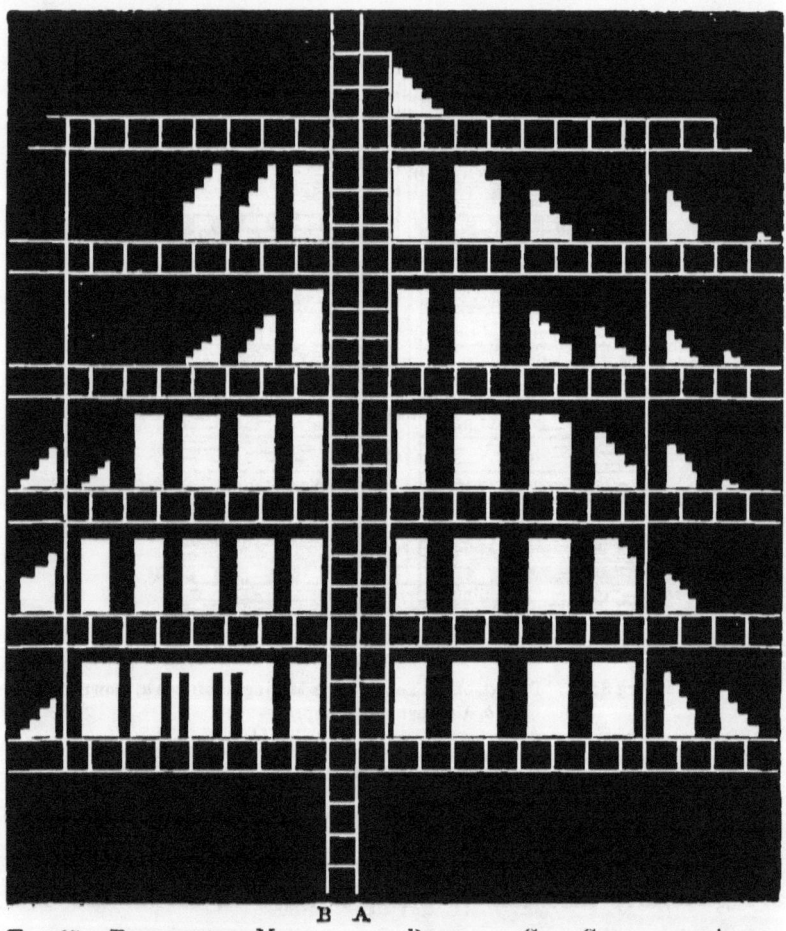

B   A
FIG. 65.—PLAN OF THE MINES OF THE BLOSSBURG COAL COMPANY AT ARNOT,
PA. Scale, 400 ft. to the inch. A, the Main Gangway. B, the Return
Air Course and Ventilating Shaft. The light portions represent the
ground worked over to 1872. (After Macfarlane.)

In Figure 65 is presented a plan of the workings in the Blossburg mines of Pennsylvania in 1872. This is a portion of a coal bed, about 1,500 feet broad and 1,900 feet long, showing where the gangways have been dug out for travel and for ventilation, and also the rooms or "breasts" from which the coal has been taken. It shows also the large amount of coal left for supporting the roof. These supports will ultimately be taken out also. In some regions the roof rock is so fragile that the gangways have to be timbered. Even then, the enormous weight sometimes crushes the supports, and occasional disasters happen in this way. The same plan of mining is pursued, whether the mine is approached by an adit, as shown in Figure 63, or by a shaft, as shown in Figure 64.

The strata which make up the so-called Coal Measures consist largely of shales and sandstones. Besides these we find beds of clay, and generally some limestones. All this is shown in Figure 64. Sometimes the whole thickness of the Coal Measures is only one or two hundred feet; and then we find but one or two beds of coal thick enough to pay for mining. In other regions the Coal Measures are several hundred feet in thickness, and then they contain, probably, three or four workable beds. Besides the workable beds, there are many too thin to pay for working. When we take a piece of the coal shales and split it open, we are apt to find the surfaces beautifully marked by the impressions of ferns. All the delicate outlines and veinings are as perfect as if pressed in a modern herbarium. In Figure 66 are shown some fern remains from Illinois.

Sometimes we find fern impressions on the coal itself. In the shales we find also the flattened stems of the trees which bore the fern fronds and other foliage. Sometimes, in the

FIG. 66.—IMPRESSIONS OF FERNS ON COAL SHALE. *Alethopteris Mazoniana,* Lesquereux,
a, Enlarged Pinnules showing the Nervation.

sandstones, the tree trunks remain unflattened, and even stand vertically in the midst of the rock. It is curious to think that these tree trunks may exist several hundred feet under ground. There they stand where they grew, and the sand has been accumulated around them. Figure 67 gives a view of one of these trees restored — that is, completed as we think it originally appeared. By the side are some portions represented on a larger scale. Figure 68 is a restoration of another sort of tree whose remains are very abundant in the Coal Measures.

In the western states the strata of the Coal Measures are

FIG. 67. — LEPIDODENDRON. A TREE OF COAL MEASURE TIMES. SEPARATE PARTS ON A LARGER SCALE. (Zittel.)

FIG. 68.—SIGILLARIA. A TREE OF COAL MEASURE TIMES. SEPARATE PARTS ON A LARGER SCALE. (Zittel.)

pretty evenly laid down. Figure 69 presents a general view of the coal-bearing strata of Illinois. You see the shales,

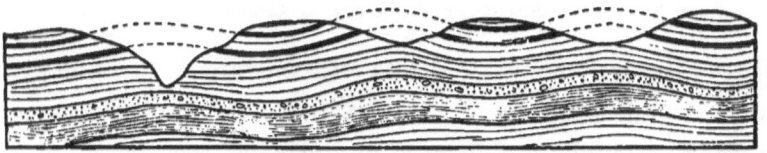

FIG. 69.—SECTION IN THE COAL MEASURES OF ILLINOIS.

sandstones and coal beds are flat and nearly horizontal, and parallel with each other. But now look at this section through the Coal Measures of Pennsylvania, shown in Figure 70. The different strata are nearly parallel with each

FIG. 70.—SECTION IN THE APPALACHIANS SIX MILES IN LENGTH, SHOWING PLICATIONS OF THE COAL MEASURES AND OLDER STRATA. (Rogers.)

other, but notice how they are all bent and broken. This is also remarkably shown in Figure 26. Sometimes at the place where a break occurs, we find the strata let down on one side below the level of the stratum on the other side of the break. This is called a *Fault*. The *downthrow* may be any distance. In some cases it amounts to twenty thousand feet, and even more. Faults occur in all formations — especially those as old as the Coal or older. Here, in Figure 71, is a series of remarkable faultings in the

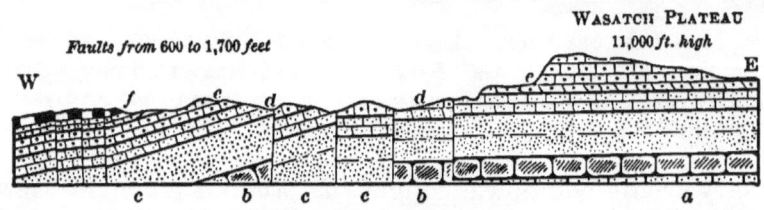

FIG. 71.—SECTION EAST AND WEST IN CENTRAL UTAH, SHOWING NUMEROUS FAULTS. (Dutton.)

a, Triassic. b, Jurassic. c, Cretaceous. d, Laramie. e, f, Tertiary.

Mesozoic and Cænozoic strata of central Utah. You will understand that a fault results from an enormous break through the whole thickness of the solid rocks. What an enormous power is required to break a pile of strata a mile or more thick!

The lowest stratum of the proper Coal Measures is almost everywhere a conglomerate or pebbly sandstone, called the *Millstone Grit.* It is often so thick as to consist of several strata. It contains a good many remains of sticks, roots and foliage. Beneath this there are generally some shales, and in Kentucky and Tennessee excellent beds of coal. The Coal Measures, when traced westward, are found to contain less coal and more limestone. But higher up, we find in our western territories, as well as in Europe, some strata which much resemble the Coal Measures. But the fossil remains are different, and these strata are set down as forming the *Permian Group.*

So the Upper Carboniferous System is composed of two groups:

UPPER CARBONIFEROUS SYSTEM { Permian Group.
Coal Measures.

EXERCISES.

Have you ever seen a coal mine? If so, what did you consider the most interesting thing about it? If not, what would you expect to be most interested in? Where does the water come from which we generally find in coal mines? In what part of the country are the strata of the Coal Measures most folded and disturbed? How would the coal beds lie in Michigan? Are there any coal beds in any New England state? Do you notice any connection between a disturbed condition of the strata and a mountainous condition of the surface? Name the states east of the Mississippi through which the mountains extend. Would you expect the coal strata to be folded in all those states? Would they be equally folded in western Pennsylvania? Is there any mineral coal in New York? If you should see any person digging for coal in that state, what would you think of his knowledge of geology? Name any other states which contain no coal. What was the coal formed from? Did those coal plants grow on land or in the water? Where was the land when they were growing? Was the Millstone Grit formed on the land? Can you think how tree trunks came to stand erect in the midst of sandstone? Where might New Orleans send to get coal by water? Which must send farthest for coal, New Orleans or Mobile? Are there any building stones in Alabama?

EXCURSION XXVIII.—*To Selma, Alabama.*

The Mesozoic Rocks.

If you cast your eyes once more on our little geological map you will notice the city of Selma located on the Alabama River in the midst of a broad belt of Cretaceous rocks stretching east and west across the state of Alabama. A little to the north are Silurian and Cambrian rocks, and, to the south of this belt, the Tertiary strata stretch to the Gulf of Mexico. At Selma the Alabama River has excavated a deep channel through a whitish chalky limestone known as the "rotten limestone." The city stands eighty feet above the river at low water. It is supplied with fresh water by a large number of artesian wells.

The "rotten limestone" is near the upper part of the Cretaceous System, and is about 300 feet thick. It dips southward beneath the Tertiary rocks. Under this limestone is a vast series of sandstones, sands and shales. These outcrop at various distances to the north of Selma—all dipping southward under the "rotten limestone." Farther west, this belt of Cretaceous rocks bends northward, and the dips are first southwest, and farther north they are west. You see this Cretaceous belt extends even to the mouth of the Ohio River. In Alabama, the lower strata outcrop at higher levels than the upper strata. The rains which fall on these lower sandy strata are carried down under Selma and all other localities on the "rotten limestone." So when a well is bored at these localities deep enough to reach the deep water-bearing strata, the water rises to the surface.

Now here is a section running south from Tuscaloosa to St. Stephens on the Tombigbee River and thence to Mobile.

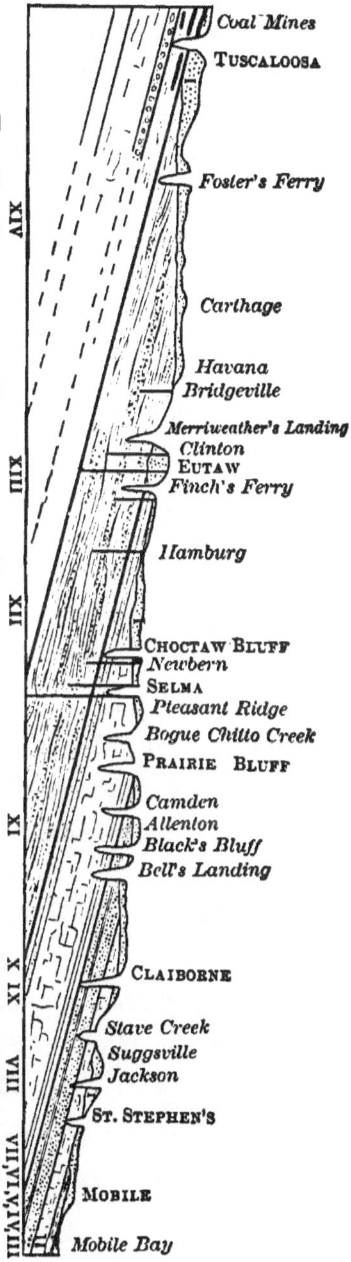

Fig. 72.—Section from Tuscaloosa to Mobile, through Cretaceous and Tertiary Strata.

I. Superficial Deposits. II–V. Eocene, with, perhaps, later Tertiary above. VI–X. Later Cretaceous. XI. Earlier Cretaceous (Eutaw Group). XII. Coal Measures. XIII. Mountain Limestone. The deep excavations show river sections, and the vertical lines, artesian wells.

Coal Mines
Tuscaloosa
Foster's Ferry
Carthage
Havana
Bridgeville
Merriweather's Landing
Clinton
Eutaw
Finch's Ferry
Hamburg
Choctaw Bluff
Newbern
Selma
Pleasant Ridge
Bogue Chitto Creek
Prairie Bluff
Camden
Allenton
Black's Bluff
Bell's Landing
Claiborne
Stave Creek
Suggsville
Jackson
St. Stephen's
Mobile
Mobile Bay

Numerous localities are named on it, but many of them do not concern us at present. You see plainly how all the strata dip southward. Here are several artesian wells indicated. Among them are two at Selma. Notice how they extend into the lower Cretaceous formations, which contain sandy strata. Here then, you have a good explanation of artesian wells. Notice the elevation of Eutaw. It is higher than the place of outcrop of any of the underlying Cretaceous rocks; therefore the water does not rise to the surface, though the well is very deep. There are hundreds of artesian wells bored through the rotten limestone in Alabama and Mississippi. In some of them the water contains much sulphur gas (hydrogen sulphide), and others yield salt water.

Now, if you glance westward on the map, you notice a vast area in Texas underlaid by Cretaceous strata. Then, farther north is a still larger area stretching through Kansas, Nebraska, Iowa, Minnesota and Dakota. All these strata, like those in Alabama, are comparatively unconsolidated. There are, indeed, some very compact sandstones, but the rocks are, throughout, very much more easily broken or crushed than the rocks of the Palæozoic formations. Many of the strata, especially the limestones, abound in fossil shells; and there are many remains of fishes and reptiles. In Europe, the Cretaceous System contains the great Chalk formation. It is probable the rotten limestone of the Southern States corresponds to the European Chalk.

The Cretaceous is the uppermost system of the Mesozoic; but you have seen from the diagram, Figure 72, as well as

from the Map, that in Alabama, no other Mesozoic formation comes between the Cretaceous and the Coal Measures,
which are Palæozoic. Probably, if we could go down and
explore the rocks under the Cretaceous, all the way to the
Gulf of Mexico, we might find the other Mesozoic Systems
actually existing. In Texas, you will see from the Geological Map, is a system called *Jura-Trias*, which covers a large
area. These strata pass *under* the Cretaceous in Texas and
Kansas. They consist mostly of shales and sandstones.
This Jura-Trias System is really composed of two systems,
the Jurassic and Triassic. In some regions, in consequence
of the absence of fossils, it is impossible to locate the
dividing line between them, or to say positively whether a
formation is really Jurassic or Triassic. That is the reason
why we say Jura-Trias. But in the far Northwest and
West, the two systems are more readily separated, and we
find that the Jurassic contains nearly five thousand feet of
shales and sandstones, and one thousand feet of limestone.
In Montana these limestones contain many bones and teeth
of monstrous extinct reptiles; but we must postpone the
study of these for a more advanced course. The Triassic
in the Far West contains over eleven thousand feet of shales
and sandstones—many of the latter being very hard and
quartzose—and about 4,500 feet of limestone.

In the valley of the Connecticut River, is a red sandstone
formation called Jura-Trias, which is extensively quarried
for building stones. At Portland, Connecticut, are quarries
from which stone is taken to New York to be built into the
so-called brown-stone fronts. On the slabs of this sandstone

may be seen many footprints of ancient reptiles. Some of these were three-toed, like birds, and walked on two feet like birds. The same sandstone extends to New Haven, and also appears on the west of the Hudson River in New Jersey. In fact, there are small patches of it at various localities in North Carolina and Virginia resting horizontally in the depressions in the old Eozoic rocks. Near Richmond is a valuable bituminous coal deposit which we have to designate Jura-Trias.

Thus, the Mesozoic Great System is made up of three Systems, as follows (see also "The Geological Column," Excursion XVIII):

MESOZOIC GREAT SYSTEM $\begin{cases} \text{Cretaceous System.} \\ \text{Jurassic System,} \\ \text{Triassic System,} \end{cases}$ $\left.\vphantom{\begin{matrix}a\\b\end{matrix}}\right\}$ Jura-Trias.

EXERCISES.

Do the Mesozoic strata of the Atlantic and Gulf regions dip toward the ocean or away from it? Explain why this is so. Do you imagine Mesozoic strata extend under the ocean? In Kansas, which way do the Cretaceous strata dip? Did they ever dip toward a large body of water? In Dakota which way do Cretaceous strata dip? On the east side of the Black Hills, which way do they dip? Suppose you bore an artesian well at the "big bend" of the Missouri River, would you ever strike Eozoic rocks? What Palæozoic rocks are exposed nearest to that point? Are they higher or lower than the surface at the "big bend"? Would your artesian well at the "big bend" bring water to the surface? Would an artesian boring succeed at Charleston, S. C.? Mention other places on the Mesozoic at which artesian wells might succeed? Are any human remains found in the Cretaceous strata? Are any reptilian remains found in the Silurian strata? Where was the seashore in Alabama

when the Cretaceous sediments were accumulating ?   Follow the
shore line through other states east and west.   Where was the
greater part of the American land at the beginning of Mesozoic
Time ?   Do you think there were rivers and lakes on that land ?
Into what water did the Ohio River then empty ?   Where was
then the mouth of the Mississippi?   Mention some rivers which
did *not* exist in Mesozoic Time

EXCURSION XXIX.—*To Claiborne, Alabama.*

The Tertiary Formations.

I took you to Alabama for a good view of Mesozoic rocks.
Now we cannot do better than remain here to examine the
Tertiary rocks.   These, in order, come next above the
Cretaceous, and we can use the same section, Figure 72, as
I gave you on the last Excursion.

Claiborne, on the Alabama River, is one of the most interesting geological localities in the country.   The town is
built on a bluff 180 feet above the river, and here is one of
those wonderful southern *chutes* for sliding cotton down to
the decks of steamboats.   The upper part of the bluff is
nearly perpendicular, and consists of chalky limestone known
as the "White Limestone."   The middle portion of the bluff
is formed of a loose, rusty-colored sand which crumbles down
and forms a slope overgrown with vegetation.   The lower
part of the bluff consists of bedded, compact, sandy clay,
containing large oyster shells, of a different species from the
modern oyster.   The sandy beds are densely packed with
fossil shells in a fine state of preservation.   They also contain the teeth and vertebræ of ancient sharks.   The white

limestone seen at the top stretches east and west across the
state.   It forms the high, white bluff at St. Stephens on the
Tombigbee River.   It contains many fossil shells, and
occasionally the bones of a whale-like dweller in the sea,
which was long and slender like the fabled sea-serpent.
Many years ago a pretty complete skeleton of this extinct
monster was dug out of the rock in Clarke county.   These
strata all belong to the Eocene, or oldest division of the
Tertiary.

   You will notice particularly three things about these Tertiary strata: 1. They are not hard rocks like those of the
Palæozoic formations.   They are not even hard as the Cretaceous strata.   2. The fossils are much more like the
remains of beings which live in human times, and they come
out of the strata in a more perfect condition.   3. The Tertiary strata lie next the seacoast.

   This last point is made clear when you understand that
the Tertiary strata extend west from Alabama through
Mississippi, Louisiana and Texas, and east through all the
Gulf and Atlantic states to New Jersey.   Look on our little
map again and see what an immense country is underlaid by
Tertiary strata in the valley of the Mississippi.   Then
toward the north notice that half of New Jersey is Tertiary.
Long Island is also thought to be underlaid by Tertiary.   It
certainly has the level and sandy appearance of a Tertiary
region.   Also the two islands, Nantucket and Martha's
Vineyard are Tertiary.   All these islands are so covered by
sand that it is almost impossible to examine the underlying
strata.   But the southwest point of Martha's Vineyard rises

high above the water, and brings plainly to view the strata which-form the body of the islands. This promontory is called Gay Head. It is a favorite excursion for the summer sojourners on Martha's Vineyard to make a steamboat trip to Gay Head. The strata here are mostly clay, and they are gaily diversified in color. Some strata are blue or white, others are red or yellow or black; and all are crumpled in fantastic fashion, and worn in almost vertical cliffs by the action of the sea and the weather. We know these are Tertiary beds because we find in them sharks' teeth and whales' vertebræ, and a few sea shells which elsewhere are found in the Miocene Tertiary.

Now notice the great Tertiary expanse shown on the western part of our map. There are, indeed, two of them. If this map embraced the whole region to the Pacific Ocean, we should see several other Tertiary areas. Now, when you remember that the Tertiary strata are the last laid down, and must, therefore, overlie all the others, you can understand that while the sediments were forming which have hardened into these patches of Tertiary strata, there must have existed seas or lakes in the interior of the continent; and you can understand that these Tertiary areas are the sites of dried up seas or lakes. Just so the Atlantic and Gulf-border Tertiary marks the site of the ancient ocean, which in this case, has not dried up, but shrunken away. The retreat of the ocean, however, has probably been caused more by an uplift of the land than by a diminution of the ocean's water; and so the interior seas were partly drained by the same elevation of the land.

When those interior seas existed, the land was populated by many species of quadrupeds which, in the earlier times, were very different from the quadrupeds which now live. In later Tertiary times, other species lived which showed a growing approach toward our modern animals. But it is not best to try to learn much about those strange extinct animals until you have advanced farther.

The sediments which accumulated in the bottoms of those seas are rocks now. They consist mostly of clays, sands and incoherent sandstones. They are made of stuff washed in from the surrounding land. Who can say how much of the land was worn out to furnish the material for the Tertiary strata? So, in every age, the work of previous ages has wasted away, and the old materials have been rebuilt in the monuments of the passing time.

But it is long since these ancient seas were thus partly filled and completely drained. The strata then new-made have in turn become the broken and decaying formations of the age now passing. The rains and the streams have ever since been doing the same kind of work upon these last formed strata, as they did in the older time to get the stuff to make these strata. These rocks are so incoherent that nature's erosive agencies have wrought vast destruction among them. In some regions immense basins have been dug out right in the midst of a Tertiary region, and the edges of the undestroyed strata expose themselves all around the border of the basin. Then the rains running down the slopes have worn them into forms resembling columns and pinnacles. These regions are generally sterile, and the first explorers of them named them "bad lands."

FIG. 73.—VIEW IN THE BAD LANDS OF NEW MEXICO. (Cope.)

Here in Figure 73 is a view of some isolated columns standing in one of the "bad lands" of New Mexico.

EXERCISES.

What states are completely covered by Tertiary? What ones
are more than half covered? What ones containing Tertiary are
less than half covered? What states afford no good quarry
stones? What are the nearest good building stones for use in
Florida? What is that singular material sometimes used for
building at St. Augustine, Florida? Would the "White Limestone" of Alabama make a good building stone? Could New
Orleans obtain granite by the Mississippi River? Where would
that city send to get granite by ocean navigation? Where does
New Orleans obtain lime? Can you think of any mineral pro-
ductions more convenient to Mobile than to Boston? What
formations were worn down to furnish Tertiary material in South
Carolina? Which way did the rivers run in South Carolina
when the Tertiary beds were forming? State what rivers along
the Atlantic coast existed in whole or in part during Tertiary
time. State what rivers along the Gulf coast did *not* exist in
Tertiary time. Trace the shore of the Gulf and Atlantic during
Tertiary time. What states did not then exist as dry land?

What states were then partly sea bottom ?   Is it supposable that
the Atlantic Tertiary border ever extended beyond New Jersey
so as to form a border to New England ?   If so, what has become
of those Tertiary deposits?   Does the Tertiary on Martha's Vineyard throw any light on this question?   Why do we find no
Tertiary in Ohio?   Should there not be Tertiary around the
border of the "Great Lakes," as well as along the Atlantic
border?   Where was the mouth of the Mississippi in Tertiary
time?   Why is it so much further south at present ?   What
rivers flow across the great Tertiary areas of the Northwest?
Did those rivers exist in Tertiary time?   Did any of them partly
exist ?   Did any water escape from the Tertiary inland seas into
the Atlantic Ocean ?   Point out the course it may have pursued.
Are there any mountains in the Tertiary regions of the United
States?   Why are Tertiary rocks less hard than Palæozoic rocks?

EXCURSION XXX.—*To the River Valley.*

Quaternary Formations.

The great Drift formation is almost everywhere present.
We began with a study of the rocks of the Drift, and now,
having learned something of the deeper-lying formations,
we come back to the Drift, to study it in a more general
way.   Most other formations began as sediments deposited
in bodies of water; the Drift generally could not have had
such an origin, though moving water undoubtedly has done
much in the arrangement of the materials.

Now look around us.   Every field is covered with a
mass of subsoil material.   In some cases we know that it
is only a few feet to hard rocks below ; but in most places
we are sure it is many feet.   All our cellars and wells are

dug in this unconsolidated subsoil deposit. In some places we find it quite clayey; in others it is sandy; in some others it is gravelly. Almost everywhere, if we dig deep, we shall find sand and gravel and clay. Almost everywhere, also, we shall sée cobble stones and larger boulders lying on the surface or buried beneath it. Fine examples are shown in the cuts, Figures 3 and 2, while the large boulder of Figure 1 may here be recalled to mind. These deposits belong to the Drift formation. The kinds of rocks and minerals to be found in the boulders we have already studied sufficiently for the present.

Suppose we travel from Canada to the Gulf of Mexico, and study the Drift all the way. We shall observe two particulars in which the northern Drift differs from the southern. 1. The northern Drift abounds in boulders; the southern Drift has none. 2. The northern Drift ends abruptly downward, and rests on a smooth hard surface of bed-rock, as a rule; the southern Drift passes by gradual transition from its sandy or gravelly condition to a decaying condition of the underlying strata. That is, in the south, the lower part of the surface deposits seems to have resulted from the decay of the underlying strata, and one can trace the stratification upward from the unaltered rock into the overlying, unconsolidated beds. These lower portions *have been formed where they lie;* only the higher, gravelly portions have been brought from some other region. The lower portions, therefore, are not properly any part of the Drift. The upper, transported sand and gravel are much less abundant than the proper Drift of the north;

but yet, in some localities are one or two hundred feet
deep.

Now look at the bottom of the Drift in the northern
states. The underlying strata are not seen partially decayed
and passing upward into the condition of soft loam. They
show a well defined upper surface. It is a hard surface.
If ever there were any decayed portions, they have been
removed. But the most striking fact is the smoothed condition of this rock surface. It looks as if it had been planed
down by some mighty power. It has not only been levelled
and smoothed; it has been scratched and grooved along
straight lines running in a general north and south direction. There is no rock so hard as to have resisted this
action. In New England and in the Canadian regions we

FIG. 74.—A STRIATED DOME OF QUARTZITE, FRAZER BAY, LAKE HURON.
(Photograph furnished by Dr. E. Andrews.)

find the most flinty rocks as perfectly smoothed and striated as the softer limestones of other regions. Dr. E. Andrews, of Chicago, has photographed an interesting example, which you see reproduced in Figure 74. A dome-like protrusion of quartzite, rising above the level of the water at Frazer Bay, north of Lake Huron, has been planed and striated by some tremendous power. The smoothed rock can be traced, extending down under the water a great distance. Such phenomena are common along the Eozoic shores of the upper lakes. Another striking example may be seen at Marquette. These facts are very impressive and very important. They seem to be connected with the history of the Drift.

In the Northern States we can everwhere notice in the Drift a distinction of another kind. Nearly all the surface portion of the Drift is partially stratified. This is shown in Figures 5 and 6. This confused stratification must have resulted from the action of water in motion. The deeper portions of the Drift are unstratified. They consist of a great mass of blue clay with imbedded boulders. The semi-stratified portion is called *Modified Drift*, and the deeper, unstratified portion is sometimes called *Till*.

All around the shores of the Great Lakes we find still another condition of the surface deposits. They are distinctly and evenly stratified, as if laid down in standing water. They consist of fine sand and clay, without cobble-stones or large boulders. These stratified deposits extend inland from the lake shore far enough to attain an elevation of one or two hundred feet above the lakes. There they

terminate, and the surface beyond consists of the usual
Modified Drift. It looks as if the water of the lakes had
once stood high enough to cover these low border deposits,
and had laid them down in the usual method of sedimentation. These beds, therefore, are not properly a part of the
Drift. The several strata descend gradually toward the
lake, and apparently pass under the lake. As their outcrops are at higher levels than any part of the surface
nearer the lake, it happens that artesian wells are sometimes attained by boring into them.

When the lakes stood at the high levels indicated by
these *lacustrine deposits*, they formed gravel beaches around
their borders. Beaches were formed at various elevations
during the progress of the lowering of the lakes. These
beaches still exist, and may be traced around nearly all the
lake borders. We call them *Lake Terraces*.

Terraces also border many of our rivers. They seem
to have been formed when the rivers flowed at higher levels
than at present. Here, in Figure 75, is a section across a

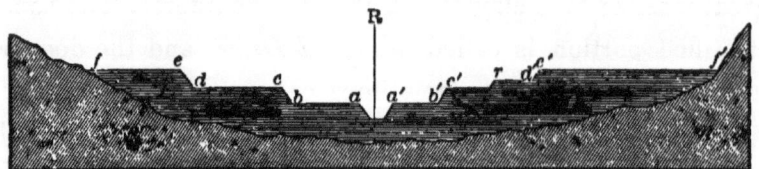

FIG. 75.—SECTION ACROSS A TERRACED RIVER VALLEY.

river valley, showing terraces at three different levels on
one side, and four different levels on the other. The main
valley is seen excavated in the underlying solid rocks.
Then, when the river flowed at the height ef and $e'f'$, it

formed the upper terrace. This may be one, two or three hundred feet above the present river level. At a later time, when the river level had subsided, it formed the lower terraces $c\ d$ and $c'\ d'$. The intermediate terrace r, on one side, has been destroyed on the other side. At the present time the river has shrunken so as only to fill the channel R, and when it overflows its banks, it throws its sediment down on the flood plains $a\ b$ and $a'\ b'$.

There must have been some powerful cause for the former high level of the lakes and rivers. The rivers could have been flooded by a former greater abundance of water. The lake-levels would have been raised also, to a limited extent, by the same cause; but to raise the Great Lakes one, two or three hundred feet, there must have been some great barrier at the outlet of the lakes, which dammed the waters. One barrier, I think, was at the termination of the Niagara gorge, as shown in Figure 58, page 142. The dotted lines there show the former level of the lakes.

If the Great Lakes have fallen as much as the high terraces indicate, it is easy to understand that small lakes may have been completely drained, or completely filled up with sediments. Figure 20 shows this filling in progress. This would take place during the same period when the terraces were forming.

Some other conditions of the surface formations exist in some regions, but these principal ones are all which we need study at present. All these modified states of the transported Drift materials have been called *Champlain*

Deposits, and the period of their formation, the *Champlain Period.*

Now let us summarize the succession of surface materials, as far as described:

QUATERNARY FORMATIONS.

Unconsolidated Surface Materials.

	Northern States.	*Southern States.*
CHAMPLAIN.	Terrace Formation, including Beds of Marl and Peat [also Löss, etc].	Terrace Formation [including Löss, Orange Sand, etc].
	Lacustrine Deposits.	
DRIFT.	Modified Drift, *with Boulders.*	Modified Drift, *without Boulders.*
	Till.	[No Till.]
	Striations on Rock-surfaces.	[No Striations on Rock-surfaces.]
	[Decaying Strata *removed.*]	Decaying Strata *in place.*
	Unaltered Rocks.	Unaltered Rocks.

EXERCISES.

How does the Drift formation differ from a Sandstone formation? Is the Drift a proper sediment? How is it unlike a sediment? What has water had to do with this formation? Was it still water, or water in motion? Did the action of this water extend over the Southern States as well as the Northern? Did the action of this water affect the whole thickness of the Drift in the Northern States? Why do you give this answer? Did the action of the water affect the whole thickness of the Drift in the Southern States? What portion of the Drift has been transported? Mention some kinds of rocks found in the Drift. •Are such rocks Mesozoic or Palæozoic? Do we have crystalline rocks in the Mesozoic or Palæozoic? Do we have them in the Eozoic? Where may we find Eozoic rocks existing as the bed-rocks? In what direction are the Eozoic rocks from the Middle States? From what direction, then, have our boulders been transported? Do the scratches on the rock surfaces under the Drift indicate transportation from the direction which you last mentioned? Is there any reason for concluding that our boulders have not all come from New England? Are there none but hard and crystalline rocks north of the Middle States? Why are there so few sandstones and limestones among the boulders? What sorts of rocks would be slowly dissolved in the soil? Would that result in a benefit or an injury to the soil? Did the Connecticut River exist before the Drift was laid down? How did it compare in size with the present Connecticut? Can you think of any evidence that the land once extended farther south at New York than it does at present? Look on the Geological Map, and notice the dotted lines off the mouth of the Hudson River, and try to think what they signify. Why are they so notched northward? If the Great Lakes ever stood 200 feet higher than at present, what are some of the cities whose sites were covered by the water? Could the lakes then have had any other outlet than the present one?

EXCURSION XXXI.— *To Switzerland.*

About Glaciers.

You have learned the main facts about the Quaternary deposits. We cannot attempt now to study very thoroughly the way in which these results have been produced. Let me only say that geologists are of the opinion that the whole country was once covered by a great glacier, as far south as the boulders extend. It is likely the surface was already deeply covered with decayed rock-material, such as still exists in the Southern States. As all glaciers move, this great glacier moved southward. It shoved along much of the loose decayed material, and, in doing so, smoothed and striated the sound rock-surface underneath. The glacier only extended south as far as the Ohio River, except in the elevated, cooler region of the Appalachians. After some ages, there was another change of climate, and the ice was melted. Great floods carried sand and gravel over the Southern States. At a later epoch, the water still flooded the rivers, and at this time the high river terraces were formed. By degrees the ice disappeared ; the lower terraces were formed ; small lakes were becoming drained; beds of marl and peat were forming, and the conditions of modern times approached. So we stand just at the outcome of great events which, in remoter times, transformed the surface of the whole country.

Geologists think a good deal of light is thrown on the origin of boulders and Drift by what may be seen in countries where glaciers still exist. A glacier is a mass of ice which has resulted from the softening and change of snows which have lain a long time. You have seen the ice on the side-walk or in the gutters, which has resulted from partially melted snow — especially when spring is approaching. Such ice is glacier-like in character and origin. The great glaciers last all summer, and continue from year to year. So they can only exist in regions with a cool climate and plenty of snow fall. The best known glaciers in our time are those which occupy the valleys of the Alps. In the cut, Figure 76, are two glaciers seen flowing along valleys which lead upward toward the summit of Mont Blanc. The one in the middle of the view is called Glacier des Bossons (Glacier of Bossons, a little village at its foot), and the one on the right is the Glacier de Taconnay. Every glacier in

its course gathers up a great amount of rock rubbish, and
deposits it in a long ridge each side.   These ridges are
called *lateral moraines.*   Another mass is deposited at the

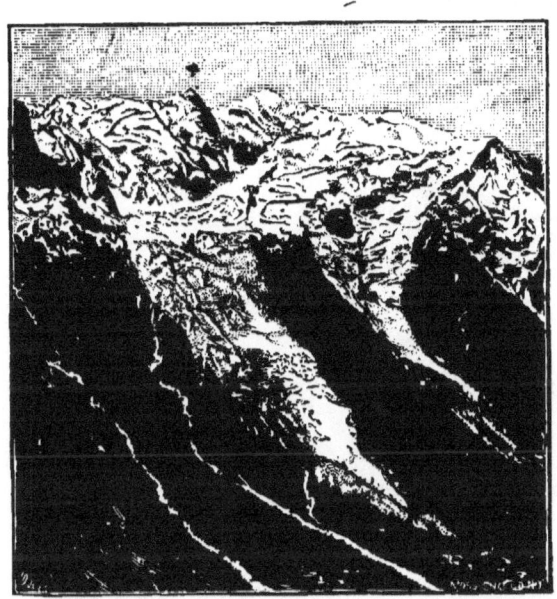

Fig. 76.—View of a Couple of Glaciers Flowing Down from Mont Blanc.

termination of the glacier.   This is the *terminal moraine.*
In this cut you can see something of the terminal moraine
about the foot of both glaciers.   It is made up of boulders
and clay.

But a more remarkable sight is shown in the cut, Figure
77, which is a vast boulder-strewn area at the foot of Glacier
des Bois, which is only the lower part of the Mer de Glace
or Sea of Ice.   (Bois is the name of a little village at its
foot.)   On the extreme right is a portion of the vast moraine
which borders the left side of the glacier, and continues

around to form part of the terminal moraine — in the same way as seen in Figure 76. Beyond this appears the white termination of the glacier, with some boulders resting on its back. The terminal face of the glacier is turned toward us, and a large arch opens at its base into a dark passage, from which a roaring, muddy stream of water rushes. There

FIG. 77.— BOULDER-STREWN AREA AT THE FOOT OF THE MER DE GLACE, VALLEY OF CHAMONIX. Compare the Boulder Field shown in Figure 3.

are in fact two streams, and these unite to form the Arveyron, which, a little further on, unites with the Arve. The glacier extends toward the right far up to the same snow-covered summit of Mont Blanc from which we see the two other glaciers proceeding in the last cut. At the very termination of this glacier, it is therefore, turned suddenly to the left. This is to avoid the enormous mass of rock which lies exactly in the main course of the glacier. This rock is shown next beyond. It is a dome of porphyry, smoothed and striated much like the quartzite dome shown in Figure

74. The glacier, some years ago, was nearly a thousand feet higher than at present, and flowed completely over this porphyry obstacle. It was the glacier which smoothed and striated its surface. This convinces us that the quartzite dome on the north shore of Lake Huron may have been smoothed and striated by a glacier. But glancing again at Figure 77, you can see beyond the porphyry mass, the great lateral moraine rising up. This continues down and connects with the vast terminal moraine shown at the left of our cut.

There are men living at that place who remember when the glacier was 984 feet higher than at present, and extended 1640 feet farther, and at that time made the great terminal moraine which still remains, and rises 80 feet high. The moraine has pushed close to the little village of Bois, which still stands close at its foot. Some of the huge boulders rolled down among the houses and the people were greatly terrified. It was in 1826 that the glacier was so much larger than at present. Since that time the glacier has retreated across the boulder-strewn area which we see, and has produced a scene which reminds us strongly of the boulder field shown in Figure 3.

If this glacier should continue to melt away until it disappears, the great moraines would remain. Now, we find in America many ridges of gravel and boulders so much like the Alpine moraines that we call them real moraines, and believe that there were once glaciers which formed them. In fact we often find them stretching across the foot of a valley which could have been once filled with glacier ice. But

there are so many which extend for long distances that the
only explanation seems to be that the whole country was
once covered by glaciers. If this theory is correct,
then we are to think of these beautiful fields and valleys,
which are now the home of a busy and happy population, as
once covered by a sheet of ice as deep, as bleak and ver-
dureless as that which in our times covers the whole of
Greenland.

EXERCISES.

Is there any part of the world where the snow does not disappear in summer? Why does it not disappear on high mountains? Is there no thawing on high mountains in summer? Does
it ever thaw in the Arctic regions? Is it conceivable there might
be so little snow in any Arctic region, as to all melt in the summer?
What is meant by the limit of perpetual snow? In what zone is
this limit highest? Why may it be higher on some mountains
than on other mountains in the same latitude? Is the climate
always too cold for farm crops in the neighborhood of Alpine
glaciers? How close to the foot of a glacier may gardens be
planted? Why is there a cold stream of air descending from the
surface of a glacier? Are all the glaciers of the Alps retreating
like the Glacier des Bois?   How much further down the valley
of the Alps may the Alpine glaciers have extended formerly?
Are there any glaciers in the United States? If so, where are
they? Is it supposable there were ever glaciers in the White
Mountains, the Green Mountains and the Alleghanies?   What
evidences of this would you expect? Was the climate any colder
then, or were the glaciers simply caused by a greater amount of
snow fall? How much of our country was covered with ice at
that time?   How far south did the ice extend? How can we tell
how far south it extended?   What was the appearance of the
country at that time?   What distinguished scientist penetrated
to the centre of Greenland in 1883?

EXCURSION XXXII.—*Through the Ages.*

About the Plants and Animals of the Past.

Let us now, finally, in imagination travel down through the Ages of the world's history, and note the appearances from time to time assumed by our planet and its populations. Everything in geology indicates that the world is very old, and has undergone many remarkable changes. It is generally believed that it once existed in the form of an intensely heated vapor, but we will say nothing about that. We are pretty certain that it was once a globe of melted mineral matter, and that after a long time, cooling caused a crust to form over the surface. At a later period, clouds of watery vapor first came into existence, and torrents of rain poured down during many ages. When the clouds were exhausted, the earth was covered by a film of water. It was a universal ocean. After many ages more, sea weeds were in existence in the ocean. Whence they came nobody knows. By and by some long ridges of sea bottom rose above the ocean level, and became the beginnings of solid land. The sea weeds floated to the beach in immense piles, and were buried beneath sediments which resulted from the wear of the land and from chemical precipitations. In course of time they were changed to plumbago—and here is some of that plumbago in the pencil with which you write.

Ages later, the first animals appeared. Their origin is another unsolved problem. They were simple gelatinous forms, with scarcely any special organs; but they existed in

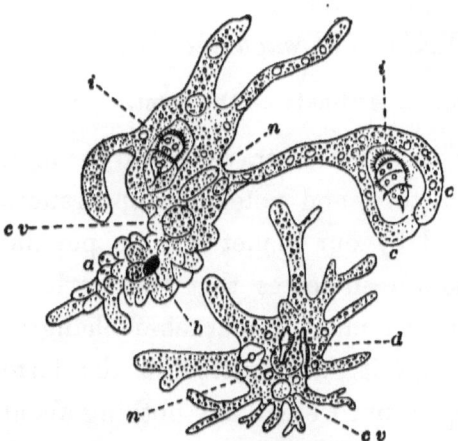

FIG. 78.—A LIVING REPRESENTATIVE OF THE OLDEST ANIMAL. *Amœba proteus* (after Leidy).

n, nucleus. *c v*, contractile vesicle. *a*, posterior portion in a contracted state. *c c*, two pseudopods closing around an infusorian (*Urocentrum*). *d*, diatoms within the animal. *b*, particle of sawdust.

Magnified 100 diameters in the upper specimen, and 125 in the lower. Found frequently in fresh waters.

immense numbers, and thousands, probably millions, of them grew in one mass, and secreted great reefs of limestone, much like coral reefs. In Figure 78 are seen modern representatives of these creatures. They are not grown together like the ancient ones, and do not secrete any coral-like substance. But their jelly-like bodies are believed to be similar to the body substance of the ancient ones. These earliest of animals lived during the Eozoic Time. When Palæozoic Time began, considerable advance had been made in sea weeds, and much more in animal life. We find in the rocks many remains of creatures related to lobsters and crabs, but very much lower in rank. We call them Trilobites. (See Figure 79.) With them were many molluscs related to the Pearly Nautilus, but most of them were straight instead of coiled. Their shells were chambered. The animal lived in the outer chamber. Some of the shells grew to a length of ten or fifteen feet. Figure 80

shows one of these straight-chambered
shells. It belongs to the genus *Orthoceras* (Orthoc′-e-ras). These rapacious beings
were the monarchs of the sea. There
were indeed other molluscs somewhat
like our modern bivalves and univalves,
but none of them was identical with
any living species. The older creatures
in all cases were simpler in their organization.

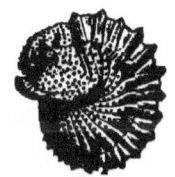

In the Devonian Age there was more
land. It supported forests of curious trees
which bore no flowers. Some of them
were much like modern Club Mosses.
We call this kind of tree *Lepidodendron*.
A view of one is presented in Figure 67.
Many coral-making animals flourished; and
the Trilobites and all the classes of mol-

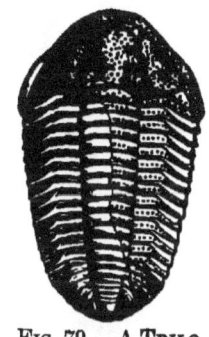

FIG. 79.—A TRILO-
BITE FROM THE
SILURIAN. The
upper figure
shows the ani-
mal rolled up.

luscs just mentioned continued to flourish. The most
important thing was the first appearance of vertebrated
animals—that is, those having a back-bone. They were
fishes. Nature always begins with the lowest forms and

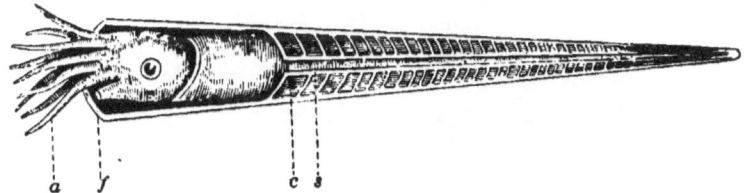

FIG. 80,—RESTORATION OF AN ORTHOCERAS—A STRAIGHT-CHAMBERED
SHELL OF PALÆOZOIC TIME.
a, arms; *f*, funnel; *c*, chamber; *s*, siphuncle.

FIG. 81. — PTERICHTHYS OR WINGED FISH (after Pander). From the Devonian of Scotland.

works upward. But they were exceedingly singular fishes, and one might almost call some of them by other names. Figure 81 shows a specimen from the Devonian rocks of Scotland, and Figure 82 a specimen from the Devonian strata of Ohio. Each of these appears to have been twenty or thirty feet in length. They were covered by stout bony plates, instead of horny scales. The Ohio fish had a head three feet long and two feet broad. The jaws were armed with terrible teeth. These fishes must have been in their time the cruel tyrants of the Devonian Ocean.

So things went on in the sea during Carboniferous times. But the straight-chambered shells dwindled away. So did the Trilobites. But coiled-chambered shells gradually took the place of the first, and higher crustaceans (like lobsters and craw-fishes) the place of the latter. The fishes were

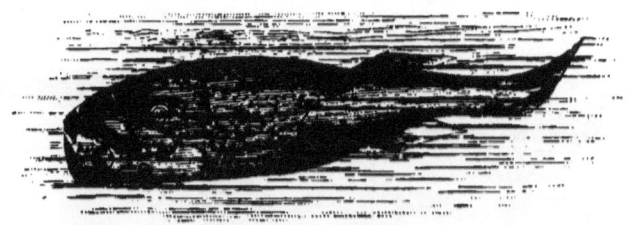

FIG. 82.—DINICHTHYS OR TERRIBLE FISH (Newberry). From the Devonian of Ohio.

much improved, but they were mostly after the fashion of the bony-scaled gar-pikes. The great characteristic of the Carboniferous age was the increase of land vegetation. But it was still flowerless, and most of it resembled vegetation which had begun to flourish in the Devonian. Views of some kinds may be seen in Figures 66, 67 and 68. It luxuriated over vast expanses which were little above sea-level, and were many times submerged by the frequent changes in the elevation of the land. The forests thus submerged did not go to decay, but were changed into the coal which we burn in our fires. There were no men to use the timber when it grew; therefore it was laid away to wait till mankind should arrive.

After the coal was laid away, the Appalachian Mountains were uplifted, and nature now introduced a great many changes. This was now the Mesozoic Time. Flowering plants now first appeared. The coiled-chambered shells became more beautiful and more complicated. Most of them belonged to the type of *Ammonites*. Here is one in Figure 83. Notice that

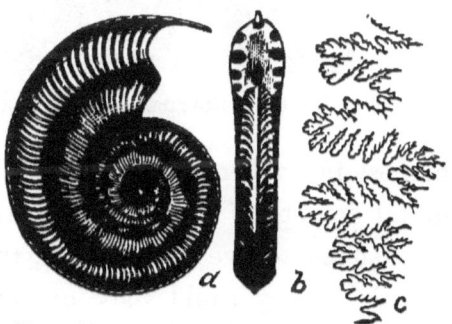

Fig. 83.—An Ammonite of Mesozoic Time. *Ammonites serpentinus*, Schl.

a, Side view. *b*, Edgewise view *c*, Plan of septa lobes.

the interior is divided into chambers by cross partitions or *septa* which are very much folded. The old kinds of bi-valves belonging to the type of lamp-shells — called *Brachi-*

opods—disappeared, and only the modern kinds remained.
Fishes with bony skeletons and horny scales came into
existence. This is the type of our common fishes. Most
important of all, air-breathing animals dwelt on the land
and in the water. They had begun to exist during Coal
Measure times, but the vertebrates were related to *Amphibians*. These vertebrates were *Reptiles*. They were the

FIG. 84.— REPTILES OF MESOZOIC TIMES.   (Hawkins.)

highest in existence on the earth. They presented a wonderful amount of diversification among themselves. They
were suited to live in the ocean, the river, on the land or in
the air. They could walk or crawl, swim or fly. Some
went on four legs, some could walk on two. In Figure 84
some of these strange types are shown. Figure 85 shows
the skeleton of a reptile which could walk like a bird on
two feet, and had also foot and ankle bones closely resembling those of birds. At the same time there were birds
which resembled reptiles in some respects. One European

bird had a long vertebrated tail like that of a lizard, but quills projected from each side. Other birds in America resembled reptiles by having teeth in their jaws. In fact, the European bird probably had teeth also. All through this time, the ocean stretched in America from the Gulf of Mexico through the centre of the continent to the Arctic Ocean.

Fig. 85.—A Bipedal Reptile of Mesozoic Time. *Hadrosaurus.* (After Hawkins.)

Next, nature introduced another great change. The central regions of the continent were uplifted. The great central ocean parted. One branch shrank to the Gulf of Mexico and the other to the Arctic Ocean. Some of those great interior seas remained, whose places are now marked by the "Bad Lands" of the Far West. This was the Tertiary Age of Cænozoic Time. But the most important changes were among the animals. Now mammals became very abundant. These are vertebrates which give milk. There had indeed been a very few mammals in Mesozoic Time; but now they swarmed. Like the fishes when they first appeared, the mammals were very peculiar, and many of them were large. We could say that they bore remote resemblances to modern mammals; but the striking peculiarity was that the same animal bore resemblances to two, three, four or five modern mammals. Such animals we call *comprehensive types*. They all had small brains, and there was a preponderance, in the earliest epoch, of five-

Fig. 86.—A Mesozoic Bird with a Reptilian Tail. *Archæopteryx.* (After Owen.)

toed quadrupeds, and many of these walked with the whole length of the foot on the ground, like the bear, the kangaroo and man. Figure 87 shows one of the earlier Tertiary

Fig. 87.—Skeleton of an Early Tertiary Mammal of America. (After Marsh.) Length, eleven feet. *Dinoceras mirabile,* Marsh.

forms. In the course of ages the comprehensive types disappeared, and new types took their place, in which the different characteristics were divided among different orders. For instance, those having gnawing teeth, like rats, no

FIG. 88.—A QUATERNARY MAMMAL OF AMERICA IMMEDIATELY BEFORE THE GREAT GLACIER. (After Riou.) *Megatherium Cuvieri*, Desmarest. Sometimes eighteen feet in length.

longer had hind teeth, like the tapir or the horse. Those having five hoofed toes no longer had canine teeth like a dog. Figure 88 shows a form closely related to the Edentates of South America. The Megatherium lived just after the close of the Tertiary. So the aspects of the animals continued to approach nearer to modern animals; and as the interior seas became filled, the face of the continent assumed the appearance it was destined to have in human times. But there was no man yet.

Next came that increase of cold which caused the wonderful glacier visitation of which you have learned. One of its effects was to renew the surface of the earth—to obliterate the old scars and gullies caused by the long continued erosions of the Tertiary Age; to supply material for a new subsoil, and make everything ready for man, who was to appear in the next act of the drama. The great glaciers were not half dissolved when man appeared in Europe. Perhaps he was in America quite as early. It is my own opinion that dark-skinned men had been in existence in the tropical regions during the whole glacial period, and perhaps much longer. But you are not to consider this settled. It is also my opinion that the first people in Europe, as well as America and Asia, were yellow-skinned, and that the white race appeared later. But, whatever may be the truth about these things, it is quite certain that the first colonists in Europe were rude, and that civilization has grown up through the long struggle of man's intelligence and better nature against the obstacles presented by his own savage disposition, and the lack of inventions to aid him in the subjugation of the earth.

After thousands of years, the white race has attained a wonderful stage of improvement; and we should feel thankful that our own lot has been cast in these later times, when we can enjoy so many opportunities for acquiring knowledge of the past and present, the distant and the near, and for attaining the highest culture of our own social and moral faculties.

Now, my dear pupils, I think it will be best to make this the end of our series of Geological Excursions. There are many things still which might be presented in a very simple way, but we must postpone them all for the present. I hope you have enjoyed these Excursions; and I hope you already feel eager to take a new start, and go with me over a more thorough course in geology.

EXERCISES.

Can you mention any animal which belongs to the class of Amphibians? In what age were Amphibians the highest type of animals? To what class of vertebrates does the salamander belong? What is the difference between a salamander and a lizard? When did flowers first appear on the earth? Was most of the coal formed from flowering plants or from flowerless plants? Mention several flowerless plants now living on the earth. Why were not trees the first plants to exist? Which are highest, marine plants or terrestrial plants? On the whole, was there an improvement of organization as the ages passed by, or was there not? What has been the best age in the history of the world for man to live in? What has been the best period since man appeared in Europe? What houses did the first European people inhabit? What implements did they use? What metals were they ignorant of? What crops did they neglect to raise? Do you think they were as comfortable as our own people? Do you think they were as happy? How have education and civilization improved the condition of mankind?

QUESTIONS ON THE TEXT.

With Additional Exercises Interspersed.

[The following questions may be used in a general review of the whole subject. They may also be employed by the teacher in connection with the daily Excursion ; but it will be better for the teacher to acquire such familiarity with the subject treated in the Excursion as to ask questions suggested by the special circumstances. In no case are the Exercises to be omitted, as these are not questions on the text, but more in the nature of applications and inferences from the facts presented in the text.]

I.

1. What objects in the garden do not grow ?　2. In what particulars do plants differ from stones ?　3. How do plants take nourishment ?　4. In what respect is an animal like a plant ? 5. In what respect does he differ from a plant ?　6. What is an organic body ?　7. What is an organ ?　8. What is a function ? 9. Name some organs of a tree.　10. What are the functions of the organs named ?　11. What objects in the garden have no organs ?　12. Can a plant or an animal perform functions without organs ?　13. Which has more organs, a bird or a plant ?　14. Which has more, an apple tree or a mushroom ?　15. What is an inorganic body ?　16. Do inorganic bodies perform any functions? 17. What is a mineral substance ?　18. Name some mineral substances.　19. Are organic bodies composed of mineral substances ?　20. If so, how do they differ from inorganic bodies ? 21. Is a dead dog organic ?　22. What is an organic product? 23. What would you call a tear?　24. Is a "living spring" organic ?　25. If not, why not ?　26. Why is it called living ?

II.

1. What is the soil in the garden composed of? 2. What is the difference between a pebble and a grain of sand? 3. What is a cobble stone? 4. How does it differ from a stone broken out of a quarry? 5. What use is sometimes made of cobble stones? 6. What use is made of pebbles and gravel? 7. How could gravel be used to purify water? 8. What is a boulder? 9. How does it differ from a pebble? 10. Are pebbles and cobble stones boulders? 11. What colors can we detect in grains of sand? 12. What are pebbles made up of? 13. What different colors can you detect in the grains of a pebble? 14. What is each different-colored portion of a pebble or cobble stone called? 15. Is a grain of sand ever composed of more than one mineral? 16. What is the indication of this? 17. What different colors of minerals may be detected in pebbles and larger boulders? 18. What colors have you yourself seen? 19. What is the shape of the separate minerals in a cobble stone? 20. Are the separate minerals quite distinct from each other, or do they blend together? 21. Are they always the same in this respect? 22. Are all loose stones boulders? 23. Mention some which are not boulders. 24. How can you tell a boulder from any other loose stone? 25. What is a ledge of rocks? 26. What parts of our country are destitute of boulders? 27. Mention some uses for boulders. 28. What is the weight of the great Gilsum boulder in N. H.? 29. Can you mention any other boulders of enormous size? 30. What parts of our country are well supplied with boulders? 31. Explain how to assort the materials in the soil. 32. What is the soil principally composed of? 33. What is mud? 34. Can you make mud out of stones? 35. If so, how would this mud differ from garden soil?

III.

1. Where can we probably find a bank or bed of gravel? 2. What uses are made of gravel? 3. What uses are made of sand? 4. Are gravel and sand mostly deep in the earth or near

the surface? 5. What different kinds of materials may we probably find in a gravel bank? 6. What is sub-soil? 7. Are the different parts of a gravel bank stratified or unstratified? 8. What is meant by stratified? 9. Are any parts of a gravel bank perfectly stratified? 10. What are laminæ? 11. When is a bed of sand said to be laminated? 12. What makes stratification visible in a sand bank? 13. What is a *talus?* 14. What is the origin of the cobble stones along the foot of a gravel bluff? 15. What is it which sometimes cements gravel stones together? 16. What is the color of the iron cement? 17. How deep do we sometimes find the Drift materials? 18. Can the bed-rock always be found at some depth? 19. Is the Drift always partially stratified throughout its entire depth? 20. Is any part of the Drift ever quite unstratified? 21. Which is uppermost, the stratified or the unstratified Drift? 22. Correct this sentence: "The well-digger came to a strata of clay." 23. How is a bed of coarse pebbles produced? 24. Mention some places where coarse pebbles abound. 25. Have these pebbles been thrown upon the beach or washed out of the bank? 26. Did you ever find a bed of pebbles cemented into a solid mass? 27. Would such a mass in the midst of the Drift be still a part of the Drift? 28. Is the Drift always composed of incoherent materials? 29. How are sandy capes formed? 30. What are sand dunes? 31. Name some regions noted for sand dunes. 32. Have you ever seen the sand drifting like snow before the wind?

IV.

1. Do any water currents exist beneath the surface of the earth? 2. What is the evidence of this? 3. What prevents the underground stream from soaking into the earth? 4. How are underground water basins formed? 5. Suppose no clay beds existed in the Drift, how deep would the water sink? 6. How deep should we then have to dig to obtain wells? 7. Where does the water of the river come from? 8. What would become of the river if there were no clay beds for it to flow over? 9.

Did you ever hear of rivers which soaked into the underlying sand and disappeared ?   10. What makes a sandy desert so dry and unproductive ?   11. In digging a well, what kind of a stratum must be reached ?   12. What kind of a stratum is water always found in ?   13. Suppose you find water above a clay stratum and then make a hole through the clay, what will become of the water ?   14. Explain how two wells very near each other may be of very different depths.   15. Explain how a well on a hill may be shallower than one at the foot of the hill.   16. What is meant by a solution of limestone ?   17. Name some substances which may be found dissolved in spring or well water ?   18. Why does spring water often deposit something ?   19. How is travertin formed ?   20. How is calcareous tufa formed ?   21. What is so-called "petrified moss" ?   22. How is marl formed ?   23. What is shell marl ?   24. What makes certain waters hard ?   25. Name some part of the country where the waters are sometimes soft.   26. What is a chalybeate spring ?   27. What substance do chalybeate waters deposit ?   28. What is its usual color ?   29. What other substance is often deposited with iron oxide ?   30. Is the deposit of iron oxide ever sufficiently abundant to have any value ?   31. What is made of it ?   32. What is yellow ochre ?   33. What is the rusty cement which sometimes holds pebbles together ?   34. Mention a locality where rusted pebbles are plentiful ?

V.

1. Of what are rocks composed?   2. Of what are minerals composed ?   3. What is a chemical element ?   4. What experiment may be performed with chalk and vinegar?   5. What other substances might be used to produce the same effect ?   6. What experiments might be performed with limewater ?   7. What is the substance which clouds the limewater?   8. What acid is in it ?   9. Where did this acid come from ?   10. What is a chemical precipitate ?   11. When the fine mud from the soil settled in our glass vessel (Figure 4) was that a chemical precipitate ?   12. What are atoms ?   13. What substances are composed of atoms ?   14.

Give an illustration to show the minuteness of atoms. 15. How
many different kinds of atoms are known? 16. What is chemical affinity? 17. What is a chemical compound? 18. Name
some substances which contain only one chemical element. 19.
Name some which contain more than one chemical element. 20.
Where may all the chemical elements be found? 21. Which is
the most abundant of the elements? 22. Which are the three
next most abundant? 23. Name the other elements which make
an important part of the earth. 24. What elements exist abundantly in the atmosphere and water? 25. Which element has an
affinity for the greatest number of other elements? 26. What is
an oxide? 27. What is a chloride? 28. Name an oxide and a
chloride. 29. What is an acid-forming oxide? 30. How is it
converted into an acid? 31. What is a basic oxide? 32. Name
some acids and bases. 33. How are acids and bases disposed
toward each other? 34. What is the termination of the name
of a strong acid? 35. What are salts? 36. When does the
name of a salt end in *ate?* 37. Can carbonic acid remain in
combination with lime when sulphuric acid is present? 38. Why
is this? 39. What appearance is presented when the carbonic
acid is driven off? 40. Where does it go? 41. After the lime-
water in the bottle is covered with a white crust, suppose we pour
on a little dilute acid, what happens to the crust? 42. If sulphuric acid was poured on, what new substance was formed? 43.
Where is it? 44. What is precipitated chalk?

VI.

1. What is the need of a hammer in studying geology? 2.
Describe a suitable style of hammer. 3. How do we determine
the hardness of minerals? 4. What is the hardest mineral
likely to be found? 5. Is it very abundant or somewhat rare?
6. What different colors may quartz present? 7. What is the
color of pure quartz? 8. What lustre has quartz? 9. What is
flint? 10. What is red jasper? 11. What causes the colors of
the different varieties of quartz? 12. What gems are nothing

but quartz? 13. Of what chemical substance is quartz composed? 14. How many elements in this substance? 15. What is the color of quartz when pure? 16. What is its crystalline form? 17. What proportion of ordinary sand is composed of quartz? 18. To what uses may ordinary sand be applied? 19. What varieties of quartz have you in your collection?

VII.

1. What can you say of the abundance of quartz? 2. How many pounds in every hundred of ordinary rocks are quartz? 3. How does the hardness of feldspar compare with that of quartz? 4. How does its lustre compare? 5. How does its crystalline form differ? 6. Can you distinguish any flat, crystalline faces in fragments of feldspar? 7. Do they look like the rough fractures of quartz? 8. What angle do they sometimes make with each other? 9. Do you mean that all the angles of feldspar are right angles? 10. Are there any right angles in a 'crystal of quartz? 11. What is the commonest color of feldspar? 12. What other color does it present? 13. Is feldspar ever glassy like quartz? 14. How does the crystalline form of a glassy feldspar differ from quartz? 15. What peculiar markings on the surface of some feldspars? 16. Is the common feldspar so striated? 17. What three substances in the composition of a feldspar? 18. What are the elements in each of these substances? 19. What is silicate of alumina composed of? 20. If silicic acid, alumina and an alkali combine, what is the chemical name of the compound? 21. What mineral does it form? 22. Mention several alkaline substances. 23. Which of these is the alkali in common feldspar? 24. What other feldspars are there? 25. What is the prevailing color of soda-feldspar? 26. What is the composition of a glassy feldspar? 27. What feldspar is most apt to be dark-colored? 28. What is the name of common feldspar? 29. What name is applied in common to all the other feldspars mentioned? 30. What causes the colors of the feldspars mentioned? 31. In 100 pounds of orthoclase, how many

pounds of silica? 32. How many pounds of each of the other constituents? 33. Of what is common clay chiefly composed? 34. What is kaolin? 35. What are some uses of feldspar? 36. In what kind of rocks do feldspars occur most abundantly? 37. What are the best states for the collection of feldspars? 38. What states do not contain rocks with crystalline feldspars? 39. Do you mean that none of these states have boulders containing feldspars? 40. Were your specimens of feldspar obtained from boulders or from rocks in place?

VIII.

1. What is the third light-colored mineral studied? 2. How does calcite compare in hardness with quartz? 3. How with feldspar? 4. Can you often find calcite in boulders? 5. Is calcite as glassy as quartz? 6. Has calcite any smooth faces like feldspar? 7. How then can you distinguish it from feldspar? 8. Do you find any right angles in calcite? 9. How do the angles of calcite differ from those of feldspar? 10. What are cleavage lines? 11. Is calcite ever transparent like quartz? 12. How, then, can you distinguish it from quartz? 13. What is the name of a common variety of calcite? 14. What is the crystalline form of dog-tooth spar? 15. What is the chemical name of calcite? 16. How does it compare in composition with chalk? 17. How many grains of carbonic acid in 100 grains of calcite? 18. How many grains of lime? 19. What is the chemical composition of carbonic acid? 20. What, of lime? 21. Represent these compounds with your chemical cards. 22. What are the different elements present in carbonate of lime? 23. If magnesia is put in place of lime, what does the mineral become? 24. If magnesia is added to the lime, what does it become? 25. What is magnesite? 26. What is dolomite? 27. Now, what are the chief means for distinguishing calcite from quartz and feldspar? 28. Which of these will effervesce with acids? 29. Which is hardest? 30. Which softest? 31. Which most pearly? 32. Which most glassy?

33. Which has right angles? 34. Which sometimes has striated faces?

IX.

1. What is the prevailing color of common mica? 2. Under what form does it exist? 3. What is mica sometimes ignorantly called? 4. Are the leaves of mica elastic or inelastic? 5. How are they in some lustreless conditions of mica? 6. What is the degree of hardness of mica? 7. What are the colors of mica? 8. Where may large plates of mica be obtained? 9. What is meant by saying that mica is the name of a family of minerals? 10. What constituents are present in all micas? 11. What are the chemical elements in each of these constituents? 12. What is the name of common mica? 13. What renders it generally dark-colored? 14. What constituent causes the dull lustre of some micas? 15. What are such micas called? 16. What other dark mineral can you name? 17. What is the color of hornblende? 18. Is this a common or a scarce mineral? 19. What is its hardness? 20. What crystalline form does it have? 21. Is this form like quartz? 22. When lamellar, how is it known from mica? 23. Can you see the crystalline form of hornblende in a rock? 24. What chemical constituents in hornblende? 25. What colors do the varieties of hornblende present? 26. What other mineral similar to hornblende? 27. What color does augite incline to? 28. What other mineral occurs in thin scales? 29. How distinguished from mica? 30. What are the prevailing colors of talc? 31. What is its composition? 32. What is the feel of talc? 33. What is soapstone? 34. What are some uses of soapstone?

X.

1. Of what are rocks generally composed? 2. Of what minerals are most of the rocks formed? 3. How can we have so many rocks formed from so few minerals? 4. Of what is quartzite composed? 5. Is it as hard as quartz? 6. What is a common

color for quartzite? 7. What is a common name for quartz
boulders? 8. What is a vitreous quartzite? 9. When is a
quartzite conglomeritic? 10. What is a jaspery quartzite? 11.
What is a quartzose conglomerate? 12. What is a granular
quartzite? 13. What is a grit? 14. What is a sandstone?
15. Name some fine sandstones used for building. 16. Have
you ever seen the New York Brownstone? 17. Where does it
come from? 18. Have you ever noticed the Ohio Freestones?
19. Where are many grindstones obtained? 20. What different colors does the Waverly Sandstone present? 21. What
impurities are sandstones likely to contain? 22. What is a
micaceous sandstone? 23. How many kinds of quartzose rocks
can you now name?

XI.

1. Why is it more convenient to study boulders than rocks
in ledges? 2. Why, otherwise, is it better to do so? 3. What
is one of Nature's methods for sticking together grains of sand?
4. How can you ascertain whether a rock contains calcium carbonate? 5. Are all rocks stuck together with calcium carbonate? 6. What mineral has great fondness for the company of
quartz? 7. What other mineral is generally found in company
with these two? 8. How can you distinguish feldspar from
calcite? 9. What is the composition of granite? 10. Is this
rock stratified or unstratified? 11. What is the coarseness of
granite? 12. Which is most valuable, a coarse granite or a fine
one? 13. What is a porphyritic granite? 14. When is any
rock called porphyritic? 15. What is the color of the quartz in
granite? 16. What, of the feldspar? 17. What, the mica?
18. What makes the reddish spots in granite? 19. How many
kinds of quartz in granite? 20. How many of feldspar? 21.
How many of mica? 22. How much mica in granite? 23. What
gives granite sometimes a dark complexion? 24. What gives it
a reddish complexion? 25. When does granite have a grayish
hue? 26. What is a granulite? 27. What is a felsite? 28.
What is a petrosilex? 29. What are the uses of granite? 30.

What is a mica schist? 31. Which contains most feldspar, gneiss or mica schist? 32. What is a hydromica schist? 33. Are schists stratified or unstratified? 34. How can you tell a mica schist from a gneiss? 35. What is greisen? 36. What must be added to greisen to make it granite? 37. What must be added to a granular felsite to make it granite? 38. What must be added to granulite to make it granite?

XII.

1. What uses are sometimes made of boulders? 2. What opportunity is furnished the geological student at the building of a boulder house? 3. What colors of rocks may be seen at a stone-cutter's yard? 4. What is the general appearance of a hornblendic rock? 5. What minerals are apt to be associated with hornblende? 6. What is syenite composed of? 7. What is the origin of the name? 8. What other rock does syenite resemble? 9. What is so called "Scotch Granite"? 10. What is "Quincy Granite"? 11. Mention some buildings constructed of syenite. 12. Where may syenite be found besides in boulders? 13. How does syenite compare with granite in durability? 14. What is a micaceous syenite? 15. What is a hornblendic granite? 16. What is a hyposyenite? 17. What is diorite? 18. How does it differ from hyposyenite? 19. What is diabase? 20. What is a plagioclase feldspar? 21. What is syenitic gneiss? 22. What is dioritic gneiss? 23. What is diabasic gneiss? 24. What is hornblende schist? 25. What is hornblende rock? 26. What feldspar is dark-colored? 27. When is a rock said to be phanerocrystalline? 28. When is it said to be cryptocrystalline? 29. Define "massive," "gneissoid" and "schistose." 30. What is protogine? 31. What is protogine gneiss? 32. What is talcose schist? 33. What is talc rock? 34. What is steatite? 35. What massive rocks contain quartz? 36. What ones contain no quartz? 37. What rocks contain hornblende? 38. What must be added to greisen to make granite? 39. What to hyposyenite to make syenite?

XIII.

1. When is a rock said to be calciferous? 2. What is a calcareous rock? 3. What degree of hardness have marbles? 4. What is the effect of acid on them? 5. What is a dolomitic marble? 6. How may it be made to effervesce? 7. Of what mineral are marbles composed? 8. Are the separate crystals visible? 9. What is saccharoidal marble? 10. What is statuary marble? 11. Mention different varieties of marbles. 12. What causes reddish colors in marbles? 13. What blackish colors? 14. What bluish colors? 15. What is a pudding-stone marble? 16. What is a shell marble? 17. State where different kinds of marbles are quarried. 18. What is common limestone? 19. How does its composition compare with that of marble? 20. How does its stratification compare with that of marble? 21. In what three ways may limestones be distinguished from most other rocks? 22. What is oölitic limestone? 23. How are the following words used: silicious, argillaceous, arenaceous, ferruginous, carbonaceous, bituminous, petroliferous? 24. What distinction may be made between argillaceous and aluminous? 25. How does chalk differ from common limestone? 26. Where does marl originate? 27. What is it? 28. What is travertin? 29. What is calcareous tufa? 30. What is a stalactite? 31. What is stalagmite? 32. How does it compare with travertin? 33. Which is the most durable material, marble or granite?

XIV.

1. What is graphic slate? 2. How does the hardness of slate compare with that of quartzite? 3. Why does slate not effervesce with acid? 4. What does slate become when pulverized and moistened? 5. Of what are bricks made? 6. Is there any fine sand in clay? 7. How may it be separated? 8. What is the characteristic substance in clay? 9. When is a substance said to be aluminous? 10. What is the difference between slate and shale? 11. What is argillite? 12. How does it compare in hardness with shale and slate? 13. Of what is argillite com-

posed? 14. What is kaolin? 15. From what is kaolin formed? 16. What has become of the alkali in the feldspar? 17. What is the use of kaolin? 18. What effect has remaining alkali upon the porcelain? 19. What is sometimes used in porcelain-making besides kaolin? 20. What is the cause of the red color of bricks? 21. What are the groups of fragmental rocks? 22. What are the four conditions in which fragmental rocks exist? 23. Name some indurated silicious rocks. 24. Name some indurated calcareous rocks. 25. Name an incoherent calcareous rock. 26. Name a crystalline calcareous rock. 27. Which is the commonest class of bed rocks? 28. What class of rocks furnishes the greatest number of species and varieties? 29. In what parts of our country are the bed rocks mostly fragmental? 30. Where are they mostly crystalline? 31. What is a micaceous slate? 32. What is a calcareous sandstone?

XV.

1. What are the two principal divisions of crystalline rocks? 2. What are the two divisions of phanero-crystalline rocks? 3. Which division embraces the greatest number of species? 4. What is the only phanero-crystalline rock which effervesces with acids? 5. If a rock is composed wholly of quartz, what is its name? 6. What, if of quartz and feldspar in crystalline grains? 7. What, if composed of quartz and mica? 8. What, if of quartz, feldspar and mica? 9. What rock is made from the union of hydromica and quartz? 10. Hornblende and quartz? 11. Hornblende and orthoclase? 12. Hornblende and plagioclase? 13. Augite and quartz? 14. Augite and plagioclase? 15. Talc and quartz? 16. Talc, quartz and orthoclase? 17. Talc alone? 18. Hornblende alone? 19. Augite alone? 20. What are some cryptocrystalline rocks? 21. What is felsite? 22. What is aphanite? 23. What is hyposyenite? 24. What is diorite? 25. How does diorite differ from diabase? 26. How does felsite differ from granulite?

XVI.

1. How does water assort the materials which it moves? 2. Would any assortment take place if all the water continued to have the same motion? 3. When a torrent flows down a slope, where are the coarser materials deposited? 4. Where are the finer deposited? 5. What is alluvium? 6. What is the origin of the shells found in some alluvium? 7. In what kind of water do flags and rushes grow? 8. On which side of a pond may we find them? 9. What is the origin of peat? 10. What caused the marsh and meadow flat upon the border of the pond? 11. Is there any danger that the pond may become completely filled? 12. What would be in its place after that? 13. Why does the peat form on one side of the pond, and not on all sides? 14. What is the prevailing direction of the wind in our region? 15. Then on which side of the pond should the peat marsh be? 16. What is contributed to the pond from the surrounding hill slopes? 17. How is the matter transferred to the pond? 18. Where are the coarse portions of it deposited? 19. Have you ever seen a spot where there was once a lakelet which has been filled? 20. What are bivalves and univalves? 21. Where do they get the material for their shells? 22. What becomes of the shells when the animals die? 23. What is the origin of marl? 24. Where does the mud in the stream come from? 25. Where is it going? 26. How does the sediment get in the sea? 27. How does the Mississippi become so muddy? 28. What does it do with its mud? 29. What is the bar of the Mississippi? 30. Do other rivers also have bars? 31. What is a river delta? 32. What becomes of the sediment carried far beyond the mouth of a river? 33. What is river sediment forming in the bottom of the ocean? 34. What effects do ocean waves produce upon the shores? 35. What becomes of the material of the crumbling shore?

XVII.

1. What is the source of the sediment in the roadside stream?
2. What is erosion? 3. How has the ravine been produced? 4. Why is the bed of the brook so stony? 5. Where have the sand and loam gone? 6. By what means does the stream widen its valley? 7. How do we know its valley was once narrower? 8. Mention a fine example of a rock-worn gorge. 9. Where has the sediment gone from Watkins' Glen? 10. Mention a fine case of river erosion in Wisconsin. 11. What great river has performed a vast amount of erosion? 12. In what states may examples of it be seen? 13. What river in the Far West has worn very deep gorges? 14. Where, besides in the river gorges, are the rocks wearing away? 15. By what means are the rocks everywhere destroyed? 16. Where may be seen a great thickness of decayed rocks? 17. What is the evidence that the rocks are decayed? 18. Have the rocks decayed similarly in the Northern States? 19. What has become of the decayed material? 20. How may a natural bridge be caused? 21. What grand examples of erosion may be seen in Tennessee? 22. What is the basin of middle Tennessee? 23. What is the valley of east Tennessee? 24. What enormous example of erosion may be mentioned in Pennsylvania? 25. How high a mountain has been worn down? 26. In what part of Pennsylvania may this result be seen? 27. How do we know such a mountain was ever there? 28. How do rock columns come into existence? 29. Where may rock columns be seen?

XVIII.

1. How would the sea sediments appear if we could bring up an acre and inspect them? 2. How would the different layers be distinguished? 3. What relics would they contain? 4. On what would the depth of the sediments depend? 5. Where could you say the sediments came from? 6. How might the sea sediments be converted to rock? 7. What would make the rock a stratified one? 8. What would be the laminæ in the rock? 9.

What would make fossils in the rock? 10. Are there really any rocks such as these sea sediments would be under the circumstances stated? 11. What rocks are they? 12. What besides sediments do limestones contain? 13. In what parts of the country are the rocks mostly crystalline? 14. In what parts are they mostly uncrystalline? 15. Which kind contain most fossils? 16. From which kind are most of the boulders derived? 17. Which kind are uppermost? 18. How is their age indicated by their relative position? 19. What is metamorphism? 20. What three kinds of action had much to do with metamorphism? 21. What is the position of the older rocks? 22. How do the fossils differ among the uncrystalline rocks. 23. Which existed first, marine animals, or terrestrial? 24. State the order of appearance of different types of animals. 25. What are said to be some of the most important facts in geology? 26. Give the names of the Great Systems in their order. 27. Give the names of the Systems in their order. 28. Now recite them in the opposite order. 29. What Systems belong to the Mesozoic? 30. What to the Palæozoic? 31. What to the Eozoic?

XIX.

1. How can you illustrate the systems of strata with an onion? 2. Is this a good illustration? 3. In what respect is it incorrect? 4. Are Cænozoic rocks everywhere at the surface? 5. Are Mesozoic rocks always the next under Cænozoic? 6. What system of rocks may be found at the surface? 7. Is the earth's surface completely undistorted? 8. What does Figure 31 represent? 9. In what respect is this figure incorrect? 10. Why is nothing represented in the interior? 11. What is the earth's crust? 12. When is one formation said to overlie another? 13. What is the dip of a formation? 14. When is a rock said to outcrop? 15. What system of rocks completely surrounds the earth? 16. Is this system everywhere covered by later formations? 17. Is it anywhere covered by all the later formations? 18. Which system of rocks has least extent on the

earth's surface? 19. Why do not Mesozoic and Palæozoic strata cover all the earth? 20. Why do they not have as great an extent as formerly? 21. Is it to be supposed they ever covered the whole earth like the Eozoic? 22. What were the Cænozoic rocks formed from? 23. How is it that some portions of the Eozoic rocks are now above sea level? 24. How are they higher than some Mesozoic and Cænozoic strata? 25. Explain how to make a little map of the region about d near the lower side of Figure 31. 26. Please make a map of the region about G, Figure 31. 27. What is the difference in the dip of the strata in these two maps? 28. Which way do rocks always dip in respect to newer and older strata?

XX.

1. What is shown by a geological map? 2. In what part of the United States are the newer rocks? 3. In what part are the older rocks? 4. What are the principal Eozoic areas shown on our geological map? 5. What system of strata is generally seen next to Eozoic rocks? 6. What is the law of the dip of strata? 7. If Devonian rocks pass under Coal Measures, may the same Devonian rise anywhere to a greater height than the Coal Measures? 8. Explain how this can be. 9. Draw a diagram illustrating it. 10. What systems belong between the Cambrian and the Lower Carboniferous? 11. Now look at the Cambrian region in Tennessee along its eastern border; what system of rocks joins it? 12. Why are there no Silurian and Devonian? 13. Can you find any Jura-Trias in Connecticut? 14. What system of rocks does it rest on? 15. What systems are wanting between the two? 16. Why are they not there? 17. Where is the most elevated region in Wisconsin? 18. On the line from that region to Chicago, which way do the rocks dip? 19. If there is a sandstone at the bottom of the Cambrian, would that be found under Chicago? 20. Would the outcrop of that sandstone in Wisconsin be higher or lower than the surface at Chicago? 21. If rain should fall on that elevated Wisconsin outcrop, how far would it flow through the sandstone? 22. Do

you imagine it would ever get as far as under Chicago? 23. Then if you should bore down at Chicago, into that sandstone, what would rise out from the hole? 24. Would this be an artesian well? 25. Now please make a drawing explaining it all.

XXI.

1. What is a geological map? 2. Does a geological map teach anything more than what appears on the surface of the earth? 3. What must we attempt to do in studying such a map? 4. What is a geological section? 5. In constructing a section from Detroit to Grand Haven, what is the first thing to do? 6. Is it necessary to lay off precisely the distances shown on the map? 7. Will the section be correct if we take any multiple of the map distances? 8. What is a multiple? 9. How do we know in what direction to draw the lines of dip from the points determined? 10. Why do we not draw lines of dip down from Detroit and from Grand Haven? 11. Where, on the west, is the boundary between the Devonian and Silurian? 12. What is a geological profile? 13. How, from the study of a common map, can we get an idea of the surface configuration of a region? 14. How is it shown that the centre of Michigan is somewhat elevated? 15. What right have we to represent Cambrian and Eozoic in a section from Detroit to Grand Haven? 16. Explain how to construct a section from Canada to the Coal region of Pennsylvania. 17. What may we infer about the surface configuration along this line? 18. Why do we generally represent dips steeper than they really are? 19. What effect has this on the apparent thickness of the formations? 20. In representing the elevations and depressions of the surface, can we conveniently use the same scale as in the distances along the surface? 21. Explain how to complete the section when the surface features are to be shown. 22. Construct a profile section from St. Louis, Missouri, to Columbus, Ohio.

XXII.

1. Name all the states in which any Eozoic rocks appear. 2. Name all in which none appear. 3. What state has the greatest area of Eozoic rocks? 4. What areas in the United States are connected with the Canadian Eozoic? 5. By what means may we easily become acquainted with the kinds of rocks in the Eozoic? 6. What New England mountains are mostly composed of Eozoic rocks? 7. Mention some separate mountain summits of the White Mountain chain. 8. What forms does weathering most commonly produce in granitic and gneissic rocks? 9. How are pinnacled mountains produced? 10. In what mountains are such summits common? 11. What is the arrangement of the strata in Mt. Kearsarge? 12. What evidences are shown of extensive weathering? 13. What is the appearance of a section through the Canadian Eozoic? 14. Where have been found the remains of the oldest animals that ever lived on the earth? 15. What is the appearance of a section through the Wisconsin Eozoic? 16. Into what two systems is the Eozoic divided? 17. What kinds of rocks occur in the Laurentian? 18. What occur in the Huronian? 19. What is the geological position of the oldest iron ores? 20. Does the Huronian produce iron? 21. Where? 22. How does the iron occur in some cases, as, for instance, at Marquette? 23. How does it occur at Pilot Knob? 24. How in the Penokie Iron Range? 25. Point out some locality where the Laurentian and Huronian are uncomformable. 26. What overlies the Huronian in the Penokie Range? 27. What useful metal is afforded by the Kewenian rocks? 28. How do we know the Eozoic rocks to be older than any others? 29. What is the thickness of the Eozoic rocks? 30. What indications have we of the vast age of the world? 31. What do Ages and Eras correspond to? 32. What evidences of the exertion of immense forces are revealed in the Eozoic rocks? 33. What is the aim of the science of geology?

XXIII.

1. What northwestern states contain Cambrian rocks? 2.
What parts of Canada contain them? 3. What interior states
contain them? 4. What sea-board states? 5. What large
cities are located on Cambrian strata? 6. In what respect
do Cambrian strata differ from Eozoic? 7. How are the bluffs
of the upper Mississippi formed? 8. What has caused the burial
of the bases of those bluffs? 9. Explain how the "Hornet's
Nest" has been formed. 10. How has "Castle Rock," in Minnesota, been formed? 11. What is meant by an outlier? 12.
What is the name of the lowest sandstone? 13. What is the
formation next above? 14. What is the St. Peter's Sandstone?
15. On what formation does the city of St. Paul stand? 16.
What produces the "Falls of St. Anthony"? 17. State the four
formations which make up the Cambrian system in Wisconsin
and Minnesota. 18. State why the St. Peter's Sandstone is at
the river level at Fort Snelling, and not so at McGregor. 19.
Describe the condition of the upper surface of the Eozoic in
Wisconsin. 20. Is extensive erosion shown by any other mem-
ber of the Cambrian system? 21. What do these eroded surfaces
indicate? 22. What great changes took place while these formations were accumulating? 23. Why is the Potsdam Sandstone
in Minnesota of such varying thickness? 24. Describe the section in Sauk county, Wisconsin. 25. Explain how the columns
shown have been caused. 26. What are the indications of a
break between the Eozoic and Cambrian? 27. Describe the
Cambrian strata in the Cincinnati region. 28. Describe the dips
about Cincinnati. 29. How do the rocks here differ from the
Wisconsin Cambrian? 30. What three groups, in general, constitute the Cambrian?

XXIV.

1. What is the depth of the gorge at Niagara Falls? 2.
Which way do the formations dip along the Niagara River? 3.
Where does the gorge of Niagara terminate on the north? 4.

What is the upper formation of the Falls? 5. In which direction does the Niagara Limestone grow thinner? 6. What forms the rapids above Niagara Falls? 7. What may be seen under the Falls? 8. How is space made there for standing? 9. What causes the recession of the Falls? 10. How rapidly do they recede? 11. What was Table Rock? 12. What formations may be traced below the Niagara Shale? 13. What ore is found in the Clinton Group? 14. Where is the Medina Sandstone? 15. What is its appearance? 16. What are its uses? 17. What group next above the Niagara Group? 18. Where may the Silurian rocks be studied? 19. Of what do they consist? 20. What valuable products are found in the Salina? 21. How is brine obtained at Syracuse? 22. Is any rock salt found in the Salina Group? 23. At what places? 24. What new salt district has recently been developed? 25. Is there any prospect of getting brine by boring at any other points in New York? 26. What change do the Niagara and Salina groups undergo when traced eastward? 27. What group above the Salina? 28. Where is it extensively developed? 29. In what western states is the Helderberg known? 30. In what eastern states? 31. In what British Provinces? 32. Name now the groups which make up the Silurian system. 33. Name the groups of the Cambrian and Silurian from below upward. 34. Name them from above downward.

XXV.

1. What is the elevation of Mackinac Island? 2. Of what rocks composed? 3. How do they compare with the rocks on the main land? 4. Through what formations have the Straits been excavated? 5. By what agency does the excavation seem to have been made? 6. Describe " Sugar Loaf " at Mackinac. 7. Describe " Arched Rock." 8. What is the name of this limestone. 9. To what region westward may the Devonian be traced? 10. What is the age of the rocks at Little Traverse Bay? 11. In what direction from Little Traverse Bay are Chemung rocks to be found? 12. What is their character in Michigan? 13. To

what regions may the Devonian rocks be traced eastward? 14. What Canadian cities are located on the Corniferous Limestone? 15. What New York cities are on the Devonian? 16. What is the geological position of Syracuse? 17. In what formation is the valley of Onondaga Creek excavated? 18. What is the Oriskany Sandstone? 19. From Syracuse, which way must we travel to find newer rocks? 20. What group of rocks overlies the Corniferous? 21. What overlies the Hamilton? 22. Mention localities of the Chemung. 23. What Ohio cities are on the Devonian? 24. In what part of Ohio are the Chemung strata? 25. Recite the names of the groups of Devonian strata. 26. Enumerate all the groups from the top of the Devonian to the bottom of the Cambrian.

XXVI.

1. What is the height of the bluff at Burlington, Iowa? 2. What kind of rocks at the top of the bluff? 3. What kind of rocks at the bottom? 4. How many different groups are found here? 5. What is the name of the upper group? 6. What the name of the lower group? 7. How do we know it is proper to divide these rocks into two groups? 8. What interesting fossils in the upper group? 9. What kind of limestone at the top of the lower group? 10. How do we know it belongs to the lower group rather than the upper? 11. By what other means than the fossils may two groups be distinguished? 12. Mention a case where an eroded surface separates two groups. 13. Mention a case where difference of dip separates two groups. 14. May two groups be truly distinct without any appearance of unconformability or intervening erosion? 15. How then, can we know they are distinct? 16. Suppose there are no fossils, can we then prove them distinct? 17. Point out regions covered by Lower Carboniferous. 18. In what formation is Mammoth Cave? 19. How was the cave produced? 20. What is the knob region? 21. How are its features caused? 22. What change takes place as we follow the Carboniferous Limestone into Pennsylvania? 23. How is the Lower Carboniferous located in Michigan? 24.

What is the character of the lower part of the Carboniferous Limestone Group in Michigan? 25. How do we know the gypsum formation is a part of that group? 26. What other region has a salt-and-gypsum deposit in the Lower Carboniferous? 27. How is brine obtained along the Saginaw Valley? 28. Does this brine come from the same formation as the brine at Syracuse and Warsaw, N. Y.? 29. What uses are made of the Waverly Sandstone? 30. Mention localities where it is quarried. 31. What is the character of the Waverly in eastern Pennsylvania? 32. What underlies the Waverly? 33. If the Catskill Sandstones should prove to belong to the Waverly Group, what name must we apply to the Group? 34. What is the position of the False Coal Measures?

XXVII.

1. Name some towns where coal-mining is carried on. 2. What is the method of mining when the coal bed outcrops? 3. What is the method when the coal bed is deep beneath the surface? 4. Define the terms *drift* and *shaft*. 5. How is the work in a coal mine laid out? 6. Why are two drifts or two shafts necessary? 7. Of what kinds of rocks are the Coal Measures composed? 8. What is the thickness of the Coal Measures? 9. How many beds of coal may there be? 10. What fossils are found in coal mines? 11. How do the strata of the western Coal Measures differ from those of Pennsylvania? 12. What is the cause of the difference? 13. What is a *fault* in geology? 14. What is a *downthrow?* 15. How extensive are faults in some cases? 16. What is the cause of faults? 17. What is the lowest stratum of the Coal Measures?' 18. What is sometimes found beneath the Millstone Grit? 19. What formation in some regions rests on the Coal Measures? 20. What are the two groups of the Upper Carboniferous? 21. Enumerate now all the groups of the Carboniferous.

XXVIII.

1. What is the geological position of Selma, Alabama? 2. What systems of strata north and south of Selma? 3. What is the "rotten limestone"? 4. Trace the Cretaceous belt westward from Selma. 5. Explain the numerous artesian wells of Alabama. 6. Explain the section, Figure 72. 7. What is the source of the water in the artesian wells? 8. Why would not artesian water rise to the surface at Eutaw? 9. Name the states which are partly underlaid by Cretaceous strata. 10. What is the character of the Cretaceous rocks? 11. How do they compare with Palæozoic rocks? 12. What formations in Alabama between the Cretaceous and the Coal Measures? 13. Explain this absence of formations. 14. What is meant by Jura-Trias? 15. Where do we find the Jurassic System distinctly exposed? 16. What System underneath the Jurassic? 17. Where is it in America, and how thick are the rocks? 18. What formation in the valley of the Connecticut River? 19. What footprints on the layers of the stone? 20. What use is made of this sandstone? 21. Mention other states in which the same sandstone occurs. 22. Now give the names of the three systems embraced in the Mesozoic Great System. 23. Enumerate all the systems of the Palæozoic Great System. 24. Enumerate all the groups of the Palæozoic Great System.

XXIX.

1. In what part of Alabama are the Tertiary rocks? 2. What of geological interest may be seen at Claiborne? 3. Of what is the Claiborne bluff composed? 4. Where else may the "White Limestone" be seen? 5. What interesting fossil remains have been found in it? 6. In what three particulars do the Tertiary rocks differ from the Palæozoic? 7. To what regions does the Tertiary extend? 8. What islands on the northern Atlantic border are probably underlaid by Tertiary? 9. What sort of rocks is to be seen at Gay Head? 10. What fossils have been found there? 11. What great Tertiary areas

west of the Mississippi River?   12.   In what territories do they lie?   13.   How do we know that great lakes or seas once rested there?   14.   Why have those lakes or seas disappeared?   15. Why has the Atlantic retreated from the eastern border Tertiary? 16.   How did the earlier and later Tertiary quadrupeds differ from each other?   17.   What was formed from the sediments which accumulated in the interior lakes?   18.   Where did the sediments come from?   19.   What has since happened to the rocks made from those sediments?   20.   What is the nature of our western "Bad Lands"?   21.   How have their columnar forms come into existence?

XXX.

1.   Where may the Drift be found?   2.   Why could not this formation have originated in a marine sediment?   3.   Of what sorts of materials is the Drift composed?   4.   In what two particulars does southern Drift differ from northern?   5.   What is the nature of the lower portion of the surface materials in the Southern States?   6.   In which region is the true transported Drift most abundant?   7.   What is the character of the rock surface under the northern Drift?   8.   In which region do we find decayed strata still remaining in place?   9.   In what direction do the grooves and scratches of the northern Drift extend?   10. Mention localities where they may be seen.   11.   Have you ever seen any smoothed or striated rock surfaces?   12.   Do you think they exist in the neighborhood of your home?   13.   Explain what is meant by "Modified Drift."   14.   What is "Till"?   15. What is the condition of the Drift around the shores of the Great Lakes?   16.   What is a lacustrine deposit?   17.   What are lake terraces?   18.   How have several river terraces been produced along one river?   19.   What is the proof of former higher water in our lakes and rivers?   20.   How may the water of our lakes have been dammed up?   21.   What are Champlain deposits? 22.   Enumerate now, in regular order, the surface materials of the Northern States.   23.   Enumerate the surface materials of the Southern States.   24.   What Quaternary phenomena exist at

the North and not at the South? 25. What exist at the South, but not at the North?

XXXI.

1. What is the theory of geologists about a former great glacier in America? 2. What became of the decayed rock material which once covered the surface? 3. How could the rock-smoothing and striation have been produced? 4. What could have caused the continental glacier to disappear? 5. From what source may we obtain light on these questions? 6. What is a glacier? 7. Does a glacier imply constant, extreme cold? 8. Would a glacier exist in a region where no thawing ever took place? 9. Would a glacier exist where but very little snow fell? 10. What would you say is requisite that a glacier may come into existence? 11. Where are the best known glaciers of modern times? 12. What is a lateral moraine? 13. What is a terminal moraine? 14. Of what are moraines composed? 15. What striking scene is displayed at the foot of the Glacier des Bois? 16. What is the source of the stream issuing from the foot of a glacier? 17. Has the Glacier des Bois been increasing or decreasing? 18. What are the evidences of this? 19. How much has it lowered? 20. How much has it retreated? 21. What records of its former action may be seen? 22. When was the glacier close to the village of Bois? 23. How have the boulders been strewn over the area at present intervening? 24. What do we find in America to remind us of this moraine? 25. How is it supposed the gravel ridges of America were produced? 26. How extensive must have been the American glacier? 27. What country presents a real picture of glaciated America?

XXXII.

1. What does geology intimate respecting the age of the world? 2. What is thought to have been the earth's primitive condition? 3. How did the ocean originate? 4. What was the beginning of solid land? 5. What were the first living things? 6. What is the origin of plumbago? 7. Give some description

of the first kind of animals?　8. In what time did they begin to
live?　9. What animals appeared in Palæozoic Time?　10. What
is a straight-chambered shell?　11. What changes were introduced with the Devonian Age?　12. What can you say about
Lepidodendron?　13. What can you say about *Pterichthys?*
14. What about *Dinichthys?*　15. What animal types dwindled
away in the Carboniferous Age?　16. What was the character of
the vegetation in the Carboniferous Age?　17. How were beds
of coal produced?　18. When were the Appalachian Mountains
uplifted?　19. What can you say about *Ammonites?*　20. How
did the Devonian fishes differ from modern fishes?　21. When
did the modern types of fishes first become abundant?　22.
What were the first air-breathing vertebrates?　23. What were
the highest vertebrates during Mesozoic Time?　24. Mention
some of the different kinds of reptiles.　25. Which of these
kinds no longer live on the earth?　26. In what respect were
some Mesozoic birds reptilian?　27. What part of North America
was under water during the Mesozoic?　28. How is this shown
on the geological map?　29. What change took place in the
land at the end of the Mesozoic?　30. What were the highest
animals during the Tertiary?　31. What is meant by *comprehensive types?*　32. What peculiarities about the brains of the
oldest mammals?　33. What about their feet?　34. What was
the use of the continental glacier to man?　35. What was the
condition of the people who first inhabited Europe?　36. How
have European people become so greatly improved?　37. How
can knowledge make people happier?

INDEX.

This index serves also as a glossary. The *star* denotes subjects illustrated by cuts.

www.ingramcontent.com/pod-product-compliance
Lightning Source LLC
Chambersburg PA
CBHW020108030726
47498CB00006B/2001